Glynis Peters lives in the sea [...] 4, she was shortlisted for the [...]nt Award.

When Glynis is not writing, she enjoys making greetings cards, Cross Stitch, fishing and looking after her gorgeous grandchildren.

Her debut novel, *The Secret Orphan*, was an international bestseller.

www.glynispetersauthor.co.uk

𝕏 x.com/_GlynisPeters_
⧉ facebook.com/glynispetersauthor
⧉ instagram.com/glynispetersauthor
BB bookbub.com/authors/glynis-peters

Also by Glynis Peters

THE ORPHAN'S HOMECOMING

GLYNIS PETERS

One More Chapter
a division of HarperCollins*Publishers* Ltd
1 London Bridge Street
London SE1 9GF
www.harpercollins.co.uk
HarperCollins*Publishers*
Macken House, 39/40 Mayor Street Upper,
Dublin 1, D01 C9W8, Ireland

This paperback edition 2024

First published in Great Britain in ebook format
by HarperCollins*Publishers* 2023
Copyright © Glynis Peters 2023
Glynis Peters asserts the moral right to
be identified as the author of this work

A catalogue record of this book is available from the British Library

ISBN: 978-0-00-866694-1

Printed and bound in the United States

24 25 26 27 28 LBC 5 4 3 2 1

Dedicated to my mother.
Joan Honeycombe, nee Avenell.
1937 – 2022

Chapter One

September 1944

A blackbird tugged at a worm on damp ground beneath the park bench opposite and Kitty Pattison watched him pull, wholeheartedly relating to his frustration. He stomped his feet to gain better ground and eventually succeeded in his task.

'If only my tug-of-war situation was as easy,' she muttered to herself as she watched the bird fly away with its prize. She also felt sorry for the worm and understood the feeling of being tugged and pulled, although in her case it was mentally rather than physically.

Life was so very different now from the one she had lived in Parkeston. Long gone were the innocent days of playing in the narrow street between the small, terraced houses, or roaming along the Essex seafront and enjoying the English coastline. There was no more helping at the local holiday camp given over to the evacuated Kindertransport children.

Childhood memories of her dead parents were like faded words on a page.

Even the loving arms of her aunt no longer wrapped themselves around her, and Kitty reflected upon the many dramatic changes every man, woman and child were faced with the day war between Great Britain and Germany was announced that September in 1939.

A year later, in September 1940, her life had suddenly become a series of never-ending challenges, when she decided to answer the government's call for young women to help with the war effort. Her aunt and uncle had bravely let her go to do her bit for the greater good. The loving couple, who had brought her up and doted on her from the age of four following the death of her parents and sibling in a boating accident, let her leave the safety of their home even after having already suffered the pain of losing their son in a battle against the enemy.

Kitty's innocent observations of life changed dramatically when she moved to train as a Red Cross nurse in Birmingham and met three young women who would become important influences: Joanne Norfolk, Trixie Dunn and Annabelle Farnsworth. Each one brought their unique outlook on the world to intersect with hers and, along with it, friendships and friction. They had influenced her in more ways than just how to wear lipstick or do her hair; they were by her side as she grew from a protected, small-community girl into a woman who faced the horrors of war. Joanne – or Jo, as she preferred – was a practical person not fond of frills and lace, whereas Annabelle – otherwise known as Belle – adored life's fripperies and had expensive tastes. Trixie had a quieter nature, and like Kitty, preferred practical but feminine fashion.

All three taught her different levels of tolerance, kindness and of what other people's lives were like before they were forced into dramatic situations thanks to Hitler and those intent on holding the world hostage.

In her new world of survival, everything changed for Kitty the day she met a doctor, a Canadian working in Great Britain who eventually joined the British Army as a medic.

The night Michael McCarthy found her lost in a snowstorm with a twisted ankle and helped her back to the hospital was the night she fell in love with him.

At times, their relationship had the dips and dives of the waves at sea – some days stormy, and others calm and soothing – but distance couldn't pull their love apart, even when they were sent on different postings, and their bond was tight.

That was ... until her dreams of becoming Mrs McCarthy, wife of Dr Michael McCarthy, were dashed. Michael's return to England from France with severe head injuries had resulted in a transfer back to Canada to undergo experimental medical treatment. She missed his soft accent, his wide smile and reassuring ways. She missed his lips upon hers and the way he held her tight. Kitty held onto his image through a photograph, but longed with an aching heart to hear his voice once again, for him to tell her he loved her, for them to have an opportunity to sit and talk about what life could be like after the war – marriage, a family, where in the world they would honeymoon and live. Not being able to bury her head into his neck and inhale his unique masculine scent felt like a punishment for something she had not done.

Despite putting on a brave face, when away from her friends, Kitty often sat and reflected upon her life without

Michael. Today, unfortunately, the Cornish coastline no longer brought her the comfort she sought. Unlike the blackbird, Kitty could not fly away with a prize, or flee from her obligations. She could only adapt to those sent her way.

The war still raged in 1944, and Kitty's newspaper declared that although Allied forces were making great advancements, Germany was not prepared to give up its fight for world supremacy. Attacks by the enemy along the South East Coast of Great Britain proved that fact, and the devastation caused once again brought fear that this war would be never-ending, which in turn increased determined vows of defiance.

Kitty was sure that, if drawn on a graph, the peaks and troughs of the emotions belonging to the British people would show that hope and courage overruled despair on many an occasion.

Kitty had seen Jo through the loss of her family members in Bristol as a result of a bomb attack, giving the same love and support Jo had given her during her most miserable times. And though most days were thick with the fog of daily struggles to see the end of the ruthless war with Germany, both friends tried their hardest to cling onto happier memories of the past in order to battle through the heavy-hearted moments. They accepted invitations to dances and the cinema far more than they had in previous years and threw themselves into anything that took their minds off the dark days.

Earlier that day, Kitty had received news of a new placement within the Red Cross, one which excited her, and yet saddened her at the same time. She was to nurse orphaned children injured in the blitzed city of Liverpool, in a private home funded by a wealthy family. Her reputation for orphan support work within the private home of her friend, Stanley

Walker-Fell, and his late wife, Jenny, at Fell Hall, Brancepeth, had been brought to the attention of the allocation officer by Kitty's original recruitment contact. With no hesitation, Kitty jumped at the opportunity to be working with children once again. Shrugging off the dull mood of melancholy, Kitty stretched her legs and readied herself to head back to The Stargazy Inn. She reflected upon the time she had first walked into the place, made new friends, and discovered new things about an old colleague that had horrified her.

The small, sleepy Cornish village was now busy with important wartime work, thanks to the American forces moving in to support Great Britain in defending against Hitler's advances. Kitty gave a sigh. Wherever she went, there were always reminders that the past four years had brought so many tragedies into her life. Her head was filled with confessions of dying men, and of the cries of women and children faced with heartbreak.

Looking at her watch, she saw it was time for her to do something practical and take her mind off the tough times of the past few years. Kitty stretched her arms above her head and took a deep breath.

With Michael out of the picture, it would be so easy to let herself get carried away with some other soldier, falling into a hasty marriage. However, Kitty was not one for taking the easy road out of anywhere. Besides, she was not prepared to give up on Michael. She loved the man with every bone in her body and would wait as long as it took for him to return and hold her once again.

Kitty thought through the telephone conversation she needed to have with her uncle later that day. He had struggled with his wife's death but slowly built a new relationship with his widowed neighbour, and Kitty had given him her blessing. She knew her aunt would just want him to be happy, the same way Kitty did. She wanted to speak to him and tell him about her new posting, rather than just writing. There had been so many moves for Kitty in the past few years and as she had endured some horrendous outcomes when Hitler dropped his bombs, she knew her uncle fretted and it would be easier to assuage his fears over the telephone.

Kitty had always reassured her aunt and uncle that she was strong enough to handle whatever came her way, but given that Michael was incapacitated in Canada and she was alone in the war, aside from those whom she worked alongside, Kitty knew her uncle would worry even more than usual. Kitty was particularly concerned as his heart had endured more than enough stress recently.

Moving onto a new position in a new city no longer fazed Kitty having worked in Birmingham, Scotland, Consett, Brancepeth, Cornwall and Southampton, with the addition of a horrendous experience spending forty-eight hours belly-crawling across a bloodied Normandy beach. Her new kitbag – a gift for her birthday from her uncle – and his old one, from the Great War, which he had given her the day she left home, were packed and waiting for her to pick up when she had finished in the gardens.

Kitty's heart was heavy and saddened by so many losses, and she wanted to make her final wishes of good luck and safe passage for those still fighting for her right to freedom. Most of all, she wanted to honour and pay respect to those who had already died on French shores for Great Britain. Rising to her feet, she stood tall and gave a salute, which she followed with a kiss blown towards the sea. Nothing she could do would bring them home, but inside her heart she had a knot, one which would not be untied until she had taken a moment to set her mind in order and ensure she lived a life showing respect for the reason they lost theirs.

Her friends, Wenna and Pots, were busy in The Stargazy Inn, where she had stayed for a week after enjoying a surprise birthday visit from her other friends Trix, Smithy, Meryn, and baby Kedrick, who had come down from Yorkshire. The sight of Trixie's tiny body supporting her already rotund pregnant belly made them all smile, and as they teased her about delivering before Christmas, Kitty felt a kind of peace settle on her shoulders. It was a welcome change from her usual worries.

Several villages in Cornwall were experiencing the departure of the American troops, so chaos was all around them, but Kitty never failed to love the place, especially when her friends were around her. Her greatest dream was to enjoy time there with Michael once again, but she was wise enough to know it was simply a dream for now, given that his return from Canada – and even his survival – was not guaranteed. The pain in Kitty's heart would never leave, and she hoped the burden of guilt she had felt waving her fiancé goodbye would eventually ease. Her time as his personal nurse was over and she had to step back into her working role. Kitty needed to be focused upon others in need.

'It's Kitty, Uncle. How are you keeping?'

Kitty listened to the muffled cough and tinny echo down the telephone line as her uncle organised himself. She could see him now, laying down his pipe on the ashtray, standing awkwardly whilst getting the earpiece to his ear, then shuffling himself into a comfortable standing position. She remembered with fondness her aunt reprimanding him for wasting Kitty's precious time with his ritual.

'I'm well. How are you? How is Michael, any news?' he replied.

Kitty smiled to herself as she held the handset a few inches away from her ear. No matter how many times she told him he didn't have to shout, he always did – again, her late aunt's voice rang in her ears, telling her uncle they didn't need a telephone, he just needed to bellow his message to Kitty from the back garden.

'I'm ticking along fine, thanks. Listen, I haven't got long, my telephonist friend here has turned her back for just a moment so I can let you know that I am on the move again – to Liverpool, this time.'

Kitty tried to ignore the scathing remarks about inconsiderate co-ordinators and leaders, that were flowing down the telephone line.

'I worry about you, Kitty, that's all. All this moving around the country and the danger you are in on those rescue missions, it's not right.' He spoke like the true father figure he was, and Kitty heard his concern as he stressed his words heavily down the line.

'I used to mind, but now I understand the need. It's fine, Uncle. You don't have to worry about me as I am going to care for orphans in a home, something I have plenty of experience with. I wanted to let you know that I've only got a forty-eight-hour turnaround though, so can't get home yet. Sorry.'

She heard the gentle sigh and the draw of him puffing on his pipe. In the past, she had often felt guilty about not being able to visit home more often, but today she had to focus on getting ready and not allow the wall of protection she had built around herself to crumble.

'I will get home as soon as I can, but in the meantime, the children need my help. From what I gather, it's a private home, just like Fell Hall where I loved working. As soon as I'm settled, I'll write and let you know how I am getting along. I love you, Uncle.'

Another moment of silence came between them before she heard a gentle cough.

'Yes, well. I, um … you take care of yourself and come home soon, you hear me. Stay safe, girl.'

Kitty smiled. Her uncle was never one for expressing affection verbally.

'I hear, Uncle. Take care and I'll write as soon as I can.'

'Well, goodbye and good luck, then.'

Kitty heard the click of the handset and smiled. Her uncle was not a man of many words but the concern in his voice spoke volumes.

'Goodbye, Uncle,' she said as she went to set down the handset, and then before doing so swiftly added, 'See you soon,' for fear of jinxing their goodbye.

Chapter Two

When Kitty arrived in Liverpool along with Jo, who was driving a new Red Cross entertainment van to the now Blitz-devastated Liverpool Docks, she was ready to accept another new challenge in life.

Jo was to meet her colleagues later in the afternoon, which meant she could help transport Kitty to the city and spend some time with her. Both were thrilled with the news they were moving to Liverpool at the same time and would be living close to one another for the first time since they had trained together in Birmingham.

Being an orphan herself, Kitty hoped the staff at the orphanage understood the needs of newly created orphans and those suffering trauma from either before the war or at the start of it. Sometimes she had noticed people never bothered to find the time to talk to orphaned children, they simply focused on getting them a new home. It frustrated Kitty as she knew from personal experience that a kind word could help a child find a way out of a nightmare corner.

'Here we are then, your new home,' Jo said, standing back to look at the large Georgian townhouse.

Kitty pulled her belongings from the back of Jo's van and joined her.

'Not quite as grand as Fell Hall,' Kitty said softly, 'but it is somewhere new for me to explore as I help the little ones come to terms with being orphans. This war is becoming tiresome, Jo.'

'You should get out of this side of the Red Cross then. Come drive for the American entertainment crews; it's worthwhile and just as important,' Jo said as she closed the van doors.

'I'm not old enough. Besides, I need time to think about what it is I really want to do. I'm torn between medical nursing and caring for children – specifically orphans,' Kitty replied.

'Yes, but you are getting closer to recruitment age, so think about it,' Jo said as she walked towards the front gate of the house. 'Come on, let's get you settled in before I have to leave again.'

Being four years older than Kitty, Jo had recently become a permanent *Donut Doll*, driving a doughnut van. It was perfect for Jo as she loved driving and had no regrets about giving up her nursing post, but Kitty was still extremely keen to continue in her own callings – the two fields of medical nursing and assisting orphans through trauma.

'Right, here goes, another city and more new people to meet,' Kitty said in an upbeat voice as she rang on the doorbell.

Inside the orphanage, the bustling matron of the house apologised, saying she could not give Kitty a tour just then as she was on her way to collect another batch of orphans from

London at the rail station. She refused Kitty's offer of help, insisting she rested after her journey and pressed a note into Kitty's hand.

'Take it to Cook, introduce yourself and enjoy a meal with your friend – goodness knows it will be the last quiet one you will have,' the spritely, middle-aged woman said with a hearty laugh. 'Take the rest of the day to rest and explore. We'll meet again in the morning at seven o'clock sharp. Now, forgive me as I am already running behind schedule. It is a pleasure to meet you, Kitty – you, too, my dear,' she said, turning to Jo. 'And thank you for the doughnuts. What a gift to receive! I will enjoy one with Cook when I return.' Matron addressed both of them with a genuine smile and gave Jo's hand a firm shake.

Jo's gifts of doughnuts were always welcome wherever she went, and whenever she visited Kitty, she brought a treat or two. As a friend, Jo was not always as demonstrative in her emotional displays as Kitty was, but today she presented Kitty with a small plant for her bedroom, taken from the grounds of Fell Hall when Jo's team had paid a visit to Brancepeth. Kitty's expression and gasps of thanks were all Jo needed, but Kitty showered her with warm hugs as always.

The matron was friendly, and Kitty had no concerns she would be unapproachable, as had been the case with some she had worked with in the past. Both Kitty and Jo agreed this would be the ideal place for Kitty to refocus her mind. The house had been given over to the orphans and stood proud behind high brick walls, with a sprawling lawned garden surrounding it. It was not set in the countryside, as Fell Hall had been, but closer to the city centre.

After getting Kitty settled in her room, they inspected most of the rooms in the house, ate their meal and walked into the city, following instructions drawn by the cook, taking in the destroyed buildings around them and the heaped rubble mountains. Liverpool had taken a hit, much like the rest of the other cities Kitty had been sent to, and as she walked past elegant homes reduced to nothing, her mood altered.

Jo chatted on about her new friends and work colleagues and gave comparisons between the British and Americans. Kitty listened with little interest. She said yes and no in the right places but all the while she took in her surroundings wondering how on earth Britain would ever be able to recover from such devastation. Displaced residents wandered amongst the crushed memories of what were once their homes in the vain attempt at finding something to treasure in whatever new home they would be allocated. Kitty's heart went out to them. The bombings had happened three to four years previous, in 1940 and '41, but many were still searching through the wreckage, never having given up hope. By the time they arrived back at her new residence, Kitty was upset by the destruction they had seen, and it triggered memories of the Blitz rescue missions she had undertaken in the past.

Back in Kitty's room at the orphanage, both women agreed it was a good size, airy, and came with the added bonus of privacy as it appeared she was not expected to share with anyone. The room was sparsely furnished with a single bed with a highly polished headboard, a wardrobe, chair and dressing table – each in varying types and shades of wood. A rag rug and dark green curtains were the only colour in the room as the bedspread was a beige cotton and the linen, white. A wooden cross hung above the bed and a small black Bible sat on the dresser. It was a room with no personality. Even when she put her own items on the dressing table it still looked bland.

'It is much better than the cupboard I lived in at Drymen military base. I am lucky, considering,' Kitty said and slumped onto the bed. Jo sat on the dressing table chair and grimaced at the hard seating beneath her.

'Don't be such a drama queen, you never lived in a cupboard. It will soon feel like home,' she said to Kitty and gave a grin. 'Mind you, I don't think you'll linger too long putting your makeup on; this chair is like a rock beneath my cheeks.'

Kitty giggled then pulled a serious face. 'You are right, and I should be grateful. I am not sharing, and I have a roof over my head. Many people are not so fortunate,' she said.

'Listen, don't let yourself get into that low mood of yours. Bring out the happy Kitty again. Michael would be furious if he saw you upset each day,' Jo said.

Kitty gave a nod.

'Some days I am afraid my legs tremble as I step outside, and it takes every ounce of courage for me to open my eyes and face the devastation in front of me. Other days are spent embracing the fact I am still alive to do these things. Then there are the days when I think about Michael – and only him. I carry a heavy load of mixed emotions and have no control over them, Jo. I am done with one man dictating to the world what he wants – I am fed up with the political mess dumped on our doorstep, and I am angry that they've made me angry…'

On her last words, Kitty flung herself across her bed onto her back and gave a loud, dramatic sigh.

'Finished?' asked Jo, now sitting on the windowsill with her legs outstretched.

With a laugh, Kitty threw her pillow at her friend.

'No. Not by a long way. I am so angry right now,' she replied. 'When we see those newsreels in the cinema, I want to scream. How can one man become so powerful, and others allow him to destroy so much? What does he promise them?'

Jo raised her eyebrows and gave a nasal huff.

'Power. It is always the promise of power – and money – with those kinds of men,' she said and joined Kitty on the edge of the bed. 'Don't become bitter, Kitty. Michael would not want you to become bitter. He was proud to fi—'

'IS,' Kitty shouted. '*Is* proud to fight. Just because he's shellshocked does not mean he is dead – he is still alive, and I am convinced he will re-join the medics. He's a strong man.'

Everyone she spoke to knew Kitty refused to believe otherwise. A visiting Red Cross nurse from Michael's rehabilitation home had written her a letter, mentioning him smiling at a postcard of Dovercourt Bay which Kitty had sent him. The joy of the news had given Kitty a bolt of hope that Michael was simply buried deep inside himself and the memory of them walking the prom together in her hometown was just waiting to be retrieved, triggering his recovery and his return to normal life.

Jo launched herself to her feet and raised her hands in the air.

'Truce. Time for me to leave. Got everything?' She looked around the room at Kitty's few belongings still in their bags. 'Need me to help you unpack?'

Kitty stood upright and shook her head.

'No, thanks. I'll be fine. Thanks for the lift and for the cinema treat. I can't believe you won't be far away. I'll let you know how I get on here. It is so quiet. I bet tomorrow will be different when the new children arrive,' she said.

'Good luck with that,' Jo said with a laugh and gave Kitty a hug. 'Be kind to yourself. I think they've done the right thing by sending you here but don't go putting yourself in danger of not coping. The minute you feel on edge, head for a beach somewhere; you know the water always calms you.' Jo pulled Kitty in for a hug, which was something she had only recently taken to doing, and Kitty drew comfort from her friend. 'Right. I'm off. See you soon. I love that I can say it and I actually will for a change!'

Kitty listened for the engine of Jo's truck starting up and driving away, then watched from the window of the bedroom she was to call home. When Jo was no longer in view, Kitty set her few belongings out and settled down to read what was expected of her in her new position. An involuntary sigh escaped her lips as Kitty picked up her paperwork. A sudden lethargy overcame her, along with the realisation that she was tired of the nomadic life and hankered for a settled home, much like Trixie's. Unsettled, she took another tour of her workplace and tried to find reasons to remain positive, talking to herself the whole time.

'The children. You are doing this for the orphans. They need you,' she told herself as she headed back to her room. 'Once you are settled, this feeling will go away. Michael would be happy you are helping other orphans again. It will be fine, Kitty. Keep going.'

Chapter Three

October 1944

A month later, the cook, known as Mrs C, handed Kitty four letters wrapped in twine as she settled in the kitchen for her breakfast.

'Morning. It looks as if someone in this room is popular this week,' Mrs C said. 'Oh, and if you are going out today, best take a brolly. It looks like rain. Tea's mashed and ready. Sort yourself, I've gorra busy day. Read your werds and I'll get her ladyship's messages done. She wants me to find a decent pair of scissors today,' she said, flicking her thumb towards the door to the matron's office.

'Given that all things metal are off the shelves and melting in the factories, it will be a task longer than five minutes, I tell you!'

Kitty gave a giggle. She loved Mrs C's accent with its exaggerated nasal r and throaty k sounds. The friendly manner of the Liverpudlians towards her had been overwhelming when she first arrived – even Matron couldn't hide her softer side – and whenever Kitty walked through the city, the Liverpudlians she came across shared all they could with no expectations in return.

'But we all know you will find a pair, Mrs C,' Kitty said with a warm smile. The woman had friends in many places and often came home triumphant from even the most difficult of shopping missions.

Kitty selected toast from the toast rack in the centre of the table, spread a scraping of butter and homemade damson jam on it, and took a bite. She looked around the kitchen and wondered how Mrs C managed to make it look as if rationing was not an issue. Her pantry was filled with items salted, stored in isinglass or in vinegar. Fresh – albeit a bit grey in colour – bread sat in rows of six by six on long cooling racks. Enough to feed the two children's homes Mrs C catered for in the area. Kitty found the kitchen to be the cosiest place in the large house. Although it was a comfortable home, there was little personality to it and the children were made to keep quiet and move around in total silence. There was no happiness around her aside from the comfort of Mrs C's cooking.

If asked, Kitty would say her month of work in Liverpool had been an easy one, but, in her private moments she couldn't help but acknowledge that she experienced an unsettled sensation from morning until night. As much as she hated to admit it to herself, Kitty did not feel fulfilled in her job.

Walking the children to and from their school, taking them out for recreation time, attending to their scraped knees and wiping away their tears, were not jobs which challenged her enough. Not anymore. She wanted to nurse and nurture, but could not always find peace with her posting in Liverpool.

And being told the work she did for the orphans and war effort was valuable was not enough.

Kitty had lost the passion she once had – it had been slowly watered down and the fire in her belly at the beginning of her service to the Red Cross was now a minor flicker. Matron was a woman of many talents and loved to control everything. Even when Kitty volunteered to help ease her workload, the woman refused, stating that Kitty's role was the one she needed to focus upon. For days Kitty sat wondering what to do with the vast amount of spare time she had on her hands. She felt guilty when others out in the wider world were juggling work with home life and the inconveniences and upsets of the war, many without the support of another. Kitty's job was far too easy. It saddened her to think she felt that way, and it was something she needed to address. She had not seen Jo for a while as their schedules never seemed to work together, and so her days off were spent wandering alone around the battered streets. She knew Liverpool had more to offer, but her current mood did not allow her to seek out what that might be.

At the start of the war the situation might have been acceptable, but the trials and turbulence of what she had seen and been through had altered Kitty's view on what kind of work she found fulfilling. She had pondered whether to change her path and find something new to do to support her country, but her loyalty to the Red Cross was still strong, which meant it would take something special for her to leave. Orphans needed the support of anyone who could give it in peacetime, but even more so during war time. Kitty told herself to stop being selfish with her personal needs and look at the wider picture.

She and Michael were orphans, she cared for orphans, she

had nurtured orphans, but now, sometimes she felt at a loss as to what to say to them. She had run dry of the right words to use and knew some of her struggles stemmed from the loss of her aunt.

Her death triggered the childhood emotions Kitty had carried with her since her parents had died. It was a stark reminder that if something happened to her uncle, with them having adopted her after her parents' accident, she would become an orphan once again and it was not something she wanted to face.

Turning her attention to the letters, Kitty carefully untied the string, wound it into a ball and popped it into her apron pocket. She laid them out on the table and stared wide-eyed and open-mouthed at the letter in her hand, which was stamped with an address for a building she hoped she would never see the inside of – Holloway Prison. The letter had been posted and delivered by the central Red Cross postal service.

'Bad news?' Mrs C asked as she bustled back into the kitchen from the pantry.

Kitty shook her head. 'I am not really sure why I've received this one, but I do have a good idea from the handwriting of who sent it. I am not sure want to read it, if I'm honest,' she replied.

The cook gave a harrumph of a cough and continued about her business.

Kitty rotated the letter in her hand several times as she decided what to do with it. She was tempted to return it to sender unopened, but eventually chose to read it, despite it being sent by Annabelle Farnsworth who, from the moment they first met, had been an annoyance in Kitty's life. When she dishonoured crown and country, Kitty had reported her as a

German spy. From that moment on, Kitty had assumed she would never hear from Belle again.

Now Belle's words stared back at her, and Kitty fought two emotions: anger and pity. Anger for what Belle had become and pity because of a life wasted on an enemy intent on total world control. Resigned to the fact that she was too curious not to read the contents of the envelope, she slid the letter opener across the top and pulled out two pages of neat handwriting on cheap, off-white paper. Not something she would associate with the Belle of the past, as before her incarceration she would have used a top-quality brand of stationery and ink. The blotches on the paper in Kitty's hand suggested a leaking ink pen from the cheapest range possible.

Kitty,

Before you tear this letter into shreds, please know I don't blame you for what you did, it was the right thing. Reporting me to the authorities was brave on your part.

I was such a fool! A naïve idiot.

Where do I start? This is the only letter I am allowed to write and as my parents are no longer alive and I have no remaining family, my thoughts turned to you. Why, you might ask? Well, the truth is, prison is a humbling place, and you would no longer recognise me. There is also the fact that I long to be more Kitty than Belle right now.

My parents drew me into something I thought was to be explored and the side of me which used to seek excitement, fell foul. I have apologies to make to Meryn and Pots, and ask you make them on my behalf. My solicitor will be in touch, but the long and the short of it is that you are a beneficiary of my will. The law has dealt with what is part of the investigation, but the inn is no longer of interest and my personal contents are yours, should you accept. I will not be around to know what your decision will be as I join my parents in twelve days. I wish you and Michael well. Remember me to Jo and Trix, not that they'll be bothered either way.

The Stargazy Inn has been bequeathed to you, with a percentage of the takings to go to Pots, Wenna and Meryn. I'll leave you to explain the situation to them as my solicitor will not release the letters until my final hearing. My confinement in prison has given me endless days to think and time to form regrets, and one of those is not seeing what a friend I could have had in you. The night at Mrs Smith's, the first time we met, I acted ungraciously and moved around as if the world owed me a favour. I apologise and if ever you meet with that patient landlady again, please tell her I no longer dress for dinner! I was a useless nurse and a dreadful person.

I admire you, Kitty. You never walk away from those in need.

Keep doing your duty as the kind-hearted, gentle soul you are, and I hope life is good to you. You and Michael are meant for one another, and I truly hope you are still a couple in love.

It was my hope we would meet again someday so I could say these words to your face, but alas it is not meant to be. Be brave. Be strong. May God protect you.

My regards and deepest respect,

Belle (Annabelle Farnsworth)

Belle's letter pained Kitty, not for Belle but for her friend, Mrs Smith, who had lost her life in an air aid and never learned of Belle's second career as a spy for German intelligence. Had she done so, Ma Smith would have had a few choice words to express about her 'hoity toity' resident. Out of the two, Kitty would far rather be reading one of Ma Smith's letters, full of her reports on the comings and goings of her tenants in Birmingham.

The thought of the fine clothes and trinkets Belle had mentioned, no doubt some of great value, served only as a reminder of Belle's position as an aide to the enemy. She would explain the situation to Pots and tell the solicitor she did not want to take on the items Belle had bequeathed to her.

Chapter Four

After spending a half hour wandering the building pondering Belle's letter, Kitty decided to walk the surrounding streets, browse a few shops, and purchase a magazine and more writing paper. Anything to alter the pattern of her mind. Once she had finished her browsing, she chose her stationery and selected a local newspaper instead of a magazine. As she turned the corner at the end of the road she bumped into a woman with short black hair and round spectacles.

'I am so sorry. Clumsy of me,' Kitty said, but the woman just looked down at the newspaper Kitty had dropped in front of her as if it was an obstacle preventing her from moving forward. Kitty bent to pick it up, looked at the woman again and gave another apology, but the woman swiftly turned her head, ignoring her, and rearranged the large collar on her coat, which hid her face. Kitty noticed the red weal of a scar above the tip of the collar and looked at the paper now in her hand.

'Again, sorry,' she said and stepped to one side, allowing

the woman to walk away. Kitty's heart pounded and she refrained from looking over her shoulder as she walked across the road and turned into another street. Once she was well away from the area she stopped and leaned against a wall. Despite knowing it wasn't her, the woman had reminded Kitty in some way of Belle. Especially when Kitty noticed the twist of lips before she bent to retrieve the newspaper, a habit Belle had when something annoyed her.

Kitty tried to convince herself she could not have just seen Belle, but when she recalled the woman's walk as she hurried away, she realised it too had had a similarity to that of Annabelle Farnsworth. If it was Belle, how did she escape from prison? At first, Kitty thought to tell Jo and see if they should report it to the police, but she suspected Jo would only laugh and suggest Kitty was fatigued and seeing things.

Too curious to let it go, Kitty retraced her steps until she spotted the woman who now appeared slightly shorter than Kitty recalled Belle to be, but Belle was fond of shoes with heels, so it was hard to tell properly. The woman was with a man staring into a shop window, both constantly looking around and over their shoulders. Kitty froze. Had she stumbled across something? Was Belle free and back to spying?

'Kitty Pattison, you stop it right now. Belle was captured and there is no reason to be so paranoid!' Kitty whispered to herself. As she went to turn away a black car pulled close to the kerb and the couple climbed inside, and Kitty realised they had simply been looking around for their driver as they waited.

Kitty cursed herself for having an overactive imagination, and headed for home, telling herself that she was simply overtired and the letter from Belle had triggered unwelcome memories and suspicions, nothing more. She dismissed the incident as fanciful.

Back in her room Kitty read through Belle's letter two or three times before putting it away, annoyed at herself for wasting time on someone who did not deserve her attention.

She settled down to write a response to one of the other letters she had received, this one from Lewis Porter, a man Kitty classed as her newest but much thought of friend.

Lewis was a soldier in the American Army who had been sent to support Britain. They met when Michael was still in England and had first had his accident. Lewis, also on sick leave, took control of a difficult situation and she and her friends drew him into their friendship circle. She lifted out her letters and reread his. Lewis reported he was still convalescing and was now in Yorkshire, which gave Kitty a twang of envy as he said he had written to her friends Trixie and Smithy, who insisted he visit them at the Pinchinthorpe surgery whenever he was free. He said Smithy declared Lewis had helped two of his dearest friends remain connected and the least he and Trix could do was to give him home comforts on his days off. Lewis signed off by encouraging her to join them as soon as she was able.

Kitty snatched up her writing pad and penned a letter back stating she would most certainly make Pinchinthorpe a visit in the near future but had to visit her uncle back home first. Guilt tugged at Kitty when she acknowledged that she would prefer visiting her friends over her uncle at present. It wasn't that she didn't love her uncle, it was just that Lewis, Jo, Trixie and Smithy brought a different level of energy into her life. Her uncle had a new life with his new companion, and although Kitty was happy for them, she missed her aunt – her mother figure – so much when she visited that it was often too emotional to handle. So, she focused on her friends.

Whenever they could, the group of friends would meet up and Kitty loved the vibrant personality of Lewis, which always lifted her spirits. He insisted on her attending dances and had introduced her to many of his own friends. The Americans were warm and friendly, and despite being in uniform, the soldiers made it feel as if the war was not hammering the world apart outside of whatever dance hall they attended. They had a way of lifting her morale even after a bad day, as their style of dancing and music filled the rooms with so much joy it overrode the memories of pain and loss. Whenever she went to a dance, Kitty's chest would pound with excitement, and she embraced the opportunity to let off steam. Her only regret was she could not share those moments with her darling fiancé. She had once drafted a letter to him about one of the dances but felt a lot of guilt as she wrote of fun times and, as she still didn't know enough about his medical situation to be sure, Kitty wondered if it might upset him and his recovery to hear about her having a good time. So, she tore the letter up and from then on only wrote more generally about her life and work.

Autumnal weather brought with it crisp frosts and the coal shortage made the large house bitterly cold first thing in the morning. Kitty hoped the war would end and life would return to normal before the severe winter weather set in, as she feared many would lose their lives to illnesses relating to cold rather than the enemy bombs. For some time now the bombings had not been as fierce as in the past and Kitty, like many others, listened intently to the radio for news of the German Army surrendering.

With France liberated during August and news of an air attack supporting Holland, Kitty clung onto the snippets of news filtering through that, along with the British Army, the Canadian and American forces, and other allies of Great Britain from around the world, were making headway. She was not naïve though and knew the cost of such successes and attempts would mean thousands of lives lost. Heroes who sacrificed everything to restore peace.

Each day she shared a few thoughts to the ether and hoped her words of thanks and encouragement to remain strong would reach the service men and women fighting on her behalf. Kitty never failed to whisper out to those who had given their lives so she could live hers and vowed to their spirits that she would remember them and ensure others always did the same.

Noises on the stairs shook Kitty from her thoughts and she strolled out into the hallway. Eight children aged between nine and twelve bounded down the stairs and were chattering amongst themselves.

'Morning. A little quieter please,' she called out to them and glanced towards the matron's door, reminding them she may be in her office.

'Shoes on. Coats, scarves, hats and mittens today. And please bring them home!' she implored as she put on her own coat and stood with the front door open allowing leaves and a chill wind into the house.

As they walked in a crocodile line towards the schoolhouse, Kitty let out a sigh. She was bored. The children filled the void with their questions and need to know what, why and wherefore, but this wasn't what she was used to, and the frustration mounted. As she encouraged the children along, she spotted movement ahead.

A man lighting a cigarette stood watching them, greeting the children at the front with a friendly 'good morning'.

As she got closer, he tipped his hat, blew out a puff of smoke and walked away. Kitty frowned. He looked familiar, but she couldn't place him in any situation she had been in. She shivered.

'Move along, it is far too cold to dally this morning,' she called out in encouragement to those dawdling ahead.

Once the children were chaperoned inside the school gates, Kitty headed for the local newspaper seller to collect Matron's daily read. She gave her coin and glanced over the front page. Printed in various boxes were glimpses of victory in some areas of France, especially for the British and Canadian forces. The Americans had also fought hard and held off the enemy in other areas of Europe. As always when it wasn't raining, Kitty took the opportunity to linger at the newsstand, quickly scanning the paper for other titbits of news. As she turned a page she glanced around to check she was not central to the pavement, and as she did so she saw a familiar male and female walking arm in arm. It was the couple she had seen previously. She also noticed not far behind them, but obviously keeping his distance, was the same man who had greeted her and the children earlier.

Then came the laugh. The woman might be dressed in non-descript clothing, with her hair covered by a headscarf and tortoiseshell spectacles obscuring most of her face, but that laugh could only belong to Annabelle Farnsworth. The woman knew it too, because she glanced around swiftly and moved closer to the man she was with, whispering with a sense of urgency. Out of the corner of her eye, Kitty watched the man from earlier watching Belle and the other man and not wanting to be caught staring, Kitty pretended to read the newspaper, her mind too filled with questions to take in anything she was reading.

What was Belle doing in Liverpool?

Kitty slowly folded the newspaper into a neat state, with the intention of walking in the opposite direction of Belle. But that would mean crossing paths with the man who greeted the children earlier. With a slight hesitation, Kitty decided he was the lesser of two evils and opted to walk towards him, continuing into a side road she knew led back to the house.

Alarmed by what she had seen, she went to her room after dropping the newspaper onto the hallway table and made notes with the dates and locations she had seen the woman she thought was Belle, and the man following her. After a brief chat with Matron about a couple of the children and their behaviour during the walk to school, Kitty made her excuses and ventured into the city. She hovered for a short while outside the police station before eventually making her decision and taking a step towards the entrance.

Chapter Five

'Don't go inside. She wants to speak to you. Come with me, don't be frightened,' whispered a voice close to Kitty's right ear. Surprised, she turned quickly to the speaker and saw it was the man she had seen following the couple that morning. Before she could say anything, he took her by the elbow with a firm grip and guided her away from the building.

'Get off of me!' Kitty said loudly and shrugged the man's arm away.

'Shhh, it's not what you think,' the man said.

'How do you know what I think?' Kitty hissed and again attempted to tug her arm away. 'I suggest you let go or I will scream the place down and considering where we are…' Kitty said, her voice several octaves higher than usual.

The man released her arm and quickly spun round to face her properly. Kitty saw a kind face staring back at her.

'Believe me when I say I am sorry, but we had to make sure it was you, Miss Pattison; Kitty.'

Kitty shivered.

'You know my name?'

'We know a lot about you. Speak with my colleague, listen to what she has to say. Believe me, it is to your advantage,' the man said. 'My name is Robert Mann, and I am as British as they come. I suspect you were about to report seeing the woman you know as Belle, but I assure you, whatever information you file inside that building will get lost and ignored, and every move you make will be watched going forward.'

Kitty pulled herself to her full height and pushed the paper she had written her facts on down into her pocket. She kept her hand there and gripped her handbag with the other to stop them trembling.

'Is that a threat, Mr Mann?' she asked indignantly and with a large amount of frostiness to her voice. She was nervous but angry that Belle had caught her up in something which might cause her a security problem and ruin her career.

'No. No, Miss Pattison. Just some well-meaning advice. Please, speak to my colleague. I promise you will come to no harm if you do, and maybe a bit of light on the situation might help you rest easy. Do you have time to do this now? Again, I promise you will be free to go home after you have listened to my colleague,' Robert Mann reassured her.

Kitty glanced towards two policemen who were entering the station and then back at the man offering a reassuring smile. Fear and curiosity got the better of her and Kitty gave a slight nod.

'Well done. If you come with me, we will walk to a house nearby as if we are a visiting couple. This is just a safety measure, Kitty. Do not be afraid. I am not the enemy, far from it, in fact. Do you trust me?' he asked.

Kitty shook her head from side to side, her heart hammering inside her chest. 'No, but if I don't do this I won't rest. I warn you, I've reported her before and, for the sake of Great Britain, I will do it again,' she said with a boldness she did not feel inside.

Robert Mann said nothing, just turned back in the direction Kitty had walked from. 'It's not far,' he said over his shoulder and Kitty quickstepped to catch up with him. Neither one of them spoke until Robert gave a random laugh, and hissed from the side of his mouth, 'Please put your arm in mine.' He angled his right arm and Kitty linked hers through.

'This is madness,' she said.

'I agree, but war creates mad situations. In two minutes, you will learn a little more and hopefully have all your questions answered,' Robert said.

They approached a long, narrow street and moved towards a small building standing alone surrounded by mounds of rubble.

'It was an old shop. We've converted it to an advice centre – the government, I mean.'

'Advice for?' Kitty asked.

'Anyone. Homeless, injured. Anyone who needs help. It is the flat above that we'll be visiting.' He nodded his head upwards to a windowed apartment above the advice centre. 'Round here, we'll go in the back way. A couple – newlyweds – live there.'

Kitty hesitated. The alleyway was not an inviting walkway and she weighed up whether speaking with Belle was worth the risk she was about to take, if in fact she was going to come face to face with her.

'I've changed my mind. I'll go home and I promise I won't

say a word to anyone. This doesn't look safe to me,' she said, unlinking her arm and backing away from Robert Mann. He stood patiently waiting for her to either walk away or take her chances with him. Kitty couldn't see anything threatening about the man in his mid-thirties, he looked official in his raincoat and trilby, but she still tried to reason this was a dream she had stepped into and not actually happening.

'Again, I promise you no one will harm you, Miss Pattison, but you do need to be aware of what you have stumbled across, and we need assurances from you, too,' Robert said, his voice slightly firmer than before and Kitty sensed he too was nervous.

'No locked doors and I am free to leave at any time?' Kitty asked.

'Absolutely. I promise we are no threat. Hear us out,' Robert Mann said.

Kitty stepped forward and they climbed the stairs leading up to the flat. Robert gave a sharp knock on the door at the top, and Kitty saw what she assumed was the kitchen window curtains twitch. The door opened and Robert encouraged Kitty inside by placing his hand into the small of her back.

'Quickly,' he said and followed her.

As her eyes adjusted to the dim room, Kitty took in two figures standing a short distance away.

'You said it would be you and Belle,' Kitty said, turning to Robert.

She'd walked into a trap.

'Sorry about this, Kitty,' a woman's voice cut through the air as she joined them. 'This is Frank, who is currently acting as my fake husband.'

Kitty's body trembled with shock and fear. The woman

standing before her was a version of Belle, but her appearance belonged more to the lower-class end of society than the old money Kitty knew she came from.

'I know this must be a lot to take in, and I am sorry about all of this, but we do need to talk, Kitty. Please, sit down,' Belle said, pointing to a dining table and chairs. 'I will make us tea, then put you in the picture.'

The thought of Belle making a cup of tea was absurd, and out of everything that was happening around her, Kitty found the thought that Annabelle Farnsworth waiting on other people was the most farcical. She couldn't help but give a grunt of a laugh.

'Well, that will be a first,' she said with heavy sarcasm.

'Strong with sugar, I think,' said Belle, ignoring the snipe at past behaviour as she walked into a small kitchen area. Kitty sat in silence, then heard the pop of gas and the tinny sound of the kettle being set into place.

Robert approached the man Belle said was her husband – Frank – and they muttered between themselves and lit cigarettes. Robert offered her one, but Kitty shook her head. The men then moved to the other side of the room and lingered near another door, leaving the front door accessible, as Robert had promised.

The whistle of the kettle and the rattling of teacups filled the air and eventually, Belle walked through with a tray. She placed it down on a table, poured the tea and pushed forward a cup for Kitty.

The men joined them and, as all three sat, Kitty looked at her cup unsure of what to do. Suddenly it became too much, and she jumped to her feet.

'This is ridiculous, Belle. What is going on? I receive a letter from you telling me you are to die for your acts against Great Britain, I am then followed and watched, and now I am made to sit and drink tea with an enemy agent who should be dead. For what? For bumping into you outside of a newsagent? This is ridiculous. Let me out. I'll not say a word,' she said, her voice rising the longer she spoke.

Robert rose to his feet and Kitty edged away from her chair.

'Don't be nervous, Kitty. We are not the enemy. Lizzie, or Belle as you know her, will explain. Trust us, please,' he encouraged and pointed to her chair.

Unsure whether she would be able to get out of the door fast enough, Kitty resigned herself to listening to the reason she was in their company.

She stared at the woman Robert had called 'Lizzie' and tried to erase Belle as she knew her from her mind. The woman touched the scar on her face. It was an act of self-consciousness; Kitty chose to ignore it rather than ask about how it had come about – the answer would probably be a lie anyway, so it was best left for her to use her imagination. For Belle to have such a scar it must be a dreadful blow because, in Kitty's eyes, vanity was one of Belle's most unsavoury traits.

'Kitty, I know this is a shock. What I am about to tell you is highly confidential, but as you recognised me – who knew we would end up in the same city? – we have little choice but to enlighten you on the situation. I had you followed to see what you would do. Kitty, I work for the British government. Always have. The Belle you know doesn't exist,' Lizzie said.

Kitty shook her head. 'I don't understand,' she said. 'And I feel bullied into coming here, what sort of dangerous game are you playing?'

Lizzie took a deep breath. 'Hear me out,' she said and took

a mouthful of tea. She replaced the cup carefully on the saucer and nodded to the cup in Kitty's hand. 'Drink up before it gets cold, I promise it's perfectly safe,' she said, smiling. Lifting her cup to her lips, Kitty hesitated but then took a sip of the hot tea and allowed the contents to warm her insides. Her hand shook so she laid her bag in her lap and held the cup in both hands.

'Don't be scared, Kitty. Robert and Frank are no danger to you,' Lizzie said.

Kitty looked up at the man named Frank. He didn't look like her uncle Frank, but he did have kind eyes. She smiled and he gave her a brief one in return.

'When you gathered information on me in Cornwall, you did the right thing. It wasn't convenient at the time from our point of view, but you proved loyal to crown and country. I'd had my suspicions you were aware of my movements but could do nothing about it as we had to keep the wheels turning. My role at that time was to entice the men, the enemy spies, into relaxed situations in the Stargazy Inn basement – I found a few brandies and food after a boat journey always worked. I then had to move them on into safe houses where other agents extracted information for our protection. Understand?' Lizzie said.

Kitty sat stunned, unable to nod or shake her head in response to the question. She believed the part about Belle enticing men but could not comprehend that not only was she now called Lizzie, but she was also a British agent. Eventually, she found her voice.

'This is ludicrous. Totally unbelievable. Belle was sent to Holloway. You wrote to me to tell me you were going to die for being an enemy supporter, that your parents were already dead. You left the inn and so much to us, those who knew

Annabelle Farnsworth, and now here you are telling me you are a British agent with the name Lizzie. Elizabeth who? A fake name no doubt. I'm leaving before you try to fill my head with other stuff and nonsense.'

Kitty rose to her feet catching the table with her knees in her haste and the teacups rattled.

Robert and Frank stubbed out their cigarettes and moved to her side.

'Don't be scared,' Lizzie said. 'I know it must be hard to process as it is hard to explain. I have cut all ties with my past, hence my leaving you and Pots my worldly goods. They are of no use to me anymore. I am heading across the channel soon and the outcome of that mission is, well … let's just say my return is in no way guaranteed. I was encouraged to wrap up my affairs so I sent you that letter. When I knew you had recognised me, I had to act as I cannot afford to be held at a police station until the powers that be can get me released. Time is valuable. I appreciate you coming here and talking with me today. You are brave.'

'Gullible is the word I would use,' muttered Kitty, walking backwards towards the door.

'No. You *are* brave. I know about your mission and, Michael, poor Michael. I have friends in the right places, and I will do all I can when I can, to try and get him home when he is fit enough,' Lizzie said. 'But in the meantime, I need you to forget you ever saw me, met Robert or Frank and came here. It is much safer that way. I am pleading with you, Kitty. Please believe us and give us a chance to carry out our orders to keep the enemy from invading.'

'This is a joke. You are not serious, government orders, preventing the enemy from invading, who do you think I am,

Belle … Lizzie … whatever your name might be. I am not stupid!' Kitty shouted.

'Shhh, please don't draw attention to us. I am serious, Kitty. I will find a way of proving it to you, but in the meantime we need you to go about your business as usual, tell no one of what has been discussed here today, and know that one of our senior colleagues will reach out to you should they think there is a need. I know it must be difficult for you to trust me, but please, for the sake of so many of our British forces, trust me this one time.'

Kitty heard the pleading in Lizzie's voice. She heard the crack of nervous tension in her throat. She knew that tension. She'd faced enemy fire. She also knew if Germany had special agents, so would Britain. It also occurred to Kitty that Lizzie need not reason with her like this, that she could ensure Kitty was not able to report them by using force.

'I am confused, scared and not sure who I trust anymore, but as you say, having been on a mission to save our soldiers, I know the urgency and importance of orders. I trust and hope you are telling the truth because I am going to keep your secret. Now, I have children to collect from school. Am I safe to do this, and will Robert be watching me?'

Lizzie shook her head.

'You are safe. He only watched you to see what you would do once we realised you had recognised me the other day. The children are safe,' Lizzie said and glanced at the clock ticking on the wall across the room. 'Go and collect them. You won't be followed, I promise. And Kitty, have a good life. The words in my letter still stand. I admire you and am glad I met you,' Lizzie said and held out her hand to Kitty.

Kitty could think of nothing but leaving and walked hastily

to the doorway. She turned to look back at the three figures in the room. 'You can trust me to be quiet; I don't think anyone would believe me anyway. Good luck, to all of you,' she said.

Once outside and clear of the building, Kitty found a bench and bent her head to her knees. She felt sick. Had she let enemy agents leave or had she done the right thing? One thing she knew for sure was that Belle no longer existed and if Lizzie was telling the truth, she had just been in the company of three extremely brave people.

Chapter Six

For two weeks Kitty tussled with her conscience but finally turned her mind to herself, to her unhappy state. Liverpool was not working out for her, and the complications of recent events added to the need to get away.

She went through phases of guilt, courage and fear. Matron even commented on her distracted mind and melancholy mood.

When she and Jo met at last, it was for an evening at the cinema, so the opportunity to talk with Jo in private about anything was not an option, but throughout the evening she sensed a tension from Jo and needed to find out what was going on in her friend's life. At the end of the showing, they stepped outside into the cold air and Kitty shivered. As always since her encounter with Lizzie, Robert and Frank, she glanced around to reassure herself she was not being watched. All she saw were lovers cuddling close, and groups of friends laughing and cajoling one another. She sighed.

'Something bothering you?' Jo asked as she linked her arm through Kitty's.

'You are. You're in a strange mood, I can tell,' replied Kitty with a playful tug of Jo's arm.

Jo gave a dismissive sniff. 'Strange mood?'

'I've known you long enough to sense you have something to tell me, and don't deny it,' Kitty said and stopped walking. She focused on Jo in the dark, leaning forwards to stare her out.

Jo threw her arms upwards.

'Yes, there is something. Let's meet at the government restaurant, the Falkner Street one, tomorrow at one o'clock. We'll have a cheap lunch and I'll share my news then. It is nothing important, but I don't think standing chatting in the dark is a good idea, besides, I need to get back to camp,' Jo said.

Kitty quickly ran through her plans for the next day in her mind and answered, 'I am free from mid-day tomorrow, so that works for me. I'll see you then. Mind how you go home,' Kitty pulled her friend in for a hug before walking home down the darkened main road.

The following morning Kitty went through the same routine with the children, and it reiterated the fact she needed to find something more to do with her spare time. Matron was rarely around and when the children returned home there was little for Kitty to do. She felt her nursing skills wasted yet again and she decided to put in an application for an appointment with the head of the local Red Cross to find out if there was more help she could offer the city. After dropping the children off at school she walked into town. Once inside the Red Cross headquarters, she waited in a queue where several young women were waiting for their interviews. Kitty's mind went back to the days she had spent pondering her choices back home before eventually arriving in Birmingham for her training. Would she do the same again, was a question she often pondered. Yes, because it was through her work with the Red Cross that she had met Michael.

'Can I help you?' a voice interrupted Kitty's thoughts.

She smiled at the tall, thin woman looking back at her.

'I hope so. I've written out an application to see if I can help in the city or elsewhere. You will see I have a vast experience in nursing around Great Britain and am presently supporting orphans locally. That said, my days are more or less my own and I have a feeling I'm wasting time when I could be making myself useful,' Kitty said in a rush.

The woman opened the envelope Kitty handed her and smiled, then frowned, then smiled again.

'My goodness, you certainly have seen the war on both sides of the water. What a brave young woman you are. We are lucky to have you, Kitty. I see why you feel wasted, but I encourage you to look on it as a restful period, a time where you can regroup and gather your thoughts,' the woman said. She smoothed out Kitty's application form and tilted her head from side to side.

'Ever been to Yorkshire?' she asked.

Kitty's heart performed an excited skip. 'Yorkshire? I visit whenever I can as I am friends with a nurse I met during training and her husband is a GP there. So yes, I have, why do you ask?' she said.

The woman walked towards a filing cabinet and pulled out a buff-coloured file. 'Come with me, into my office. I have an idea which might appeal to you,' she said, holding open a door for Kitty. The room was neat and tidy, with files piled high on a desk.

'My workload increases daily, Kitty. I envy your free time but at the same time, I know better than most that keeping busy helps. Now, about my idea…'

After her meeting, Kitty gathered up the papers the woman she now knew as Miss Wright had given her. She looked at her watch. There was another hour to go before she was due to meet with Jo, so she took herself back home. In her room she composed her words of resignation for Matron and pulled out her kitbag and suitcase. She placed a few items she would not use over the next four days inside, and smiled to herself. She couldn't wait to share her news with Trixie, but first she had to break it to Jo that she was moving on.

Jo was early and stood outside the restaurant waiting in the queue. The government restaurants drew in the crowds as they were somewhere for people to get a decent meal for a few coins, no ration book necessary. The Women's Voluntary Service had taken up the task of running them initially and they were still rising to the challenge three years down the line.

Kitty waved, and as the smell of freshly cooked food drifted down the road towards her, she increased her speed. She hadn't realised how hungry she was and remembered she had skipped breakfast.

'Well, someone looks happy. Have you had news of Michael?' Jo asked when Kitty joined her in the queue.

Kitty ignored the moaning from the woman behind them about queue jumping and gave Jo a grin.

'Lots to tell when we sit down. Sadly though, no more news of Michael,' she said, getting her coins ready to hand over at the till. She and Jo both chose the vegetable soup, with a roast beef main course and a jam pudding with custard and a cup of tea. They found two seats at the end of a long table and settled down to eat. The room was noisy with chatter and clatter, but where they'd chosen to sit allowed them to ease their seats into a corner away from the crowd to enjoy their cups of tea and talk at a normal level.

'As we are here for you to tell me your news, you go first,' Kitty said, lifting her teacup to her lips.

Jo shifted in her chair. 'Wait for it…' She took a deep breath. 'I'm leaving town,' she said bluntly.

With care, Kitty placed her cup on its saucer.

'And where are you leaving for?' she asked.

'France. We're relieving the girls who went out in June,' Jo replied, her voice flat and void of emotion. 'I'm also going to use my Red Cross nursing skills out there, so they are not wasted after all.'

With Jo mentioning France, it was on the tip of Kitty's tongue to mention the Belle – Lizzie situation, but she opted not to say anything about the affair. The fewer people who knew, the safer it was.

'Oh my, that's a tough call,' Kitty said. 'How do you feel about it?'

'Driving through enemy gunfire and over craters? I am ecstatic, Kitty. Seriously, I am nervous but also feel this is what I've been waiting to do. Drive, serve and save – where possible, of course. I've been restless just dishing out the doughnuts. The other two girls I work with have had the same thoughts; we need to utilise skills we had before dishing out the coffee and tea,' Jo replied.

'When do you go?' Kitty asked, not really wanting to hear the answer.

'Friday, in two days' time,' Jo said. 'Anyway, why were you looking so chipper earlier on?'

Kitty cleared her throat. 'Well, I am not going to France, but I am leaving Liverpool,' she said.

Jo spluttered out the mouthful of tea she'd sipped.

'So soon. Where have they allocated you this time? You must be furious,' she said.

With a quick shake of her head, Kitty spoke. 'No, this is my choice. I feel my skills are wasted around here as I am nothing but a glorified babysitter. The orphans all support each other, Matron deals with any issues and so I simply walk them to and from school. I don't actually get to care for them in the sense I had expected. I'm bored, Jo,' Kitty said with a discontented sigh. 'I went into HQ here in the city earlier and there's an opening for a nurse at a Prisoner of War camp in Yorkshire. The Italians have left, and the camp houses German prisoners now. After a lot of discussion of what would be expected of me, I accepted the offer of transfer. I leave on Saturday for Harrogate. I pick up transport from there to a place called Malton, then onto Camp 250 – Eden Camp. Miss Wright at headquarters said she came from York and knows the area and when I asked how far from Trixie's home I would be, she said it was under two hours.'

Jo leaned back in her seat and laughed. 'I'm thinking you're lucky with the cushy posting you have here, but now you are looking to take on tougher things. German POWs eh? Should be a challenging job, but better than playing Pied Piper, I agree. Good on you, Kitty!'

With a wide smile for her friend, Kitty followed it with a frown. 'I'll worry about you, though. Be safe, Jo. No heroics. Promise,' she said.

'Oh, so no belly crawling on the beaches to rescue soldiers like you did, you mean. Seriously, Kitty, don't fret. We'll get through this war and sit back in our dotage reminiscing about our time in the Red Cross. Trixie will be moaning about the endless trials and tribulations her twenty kids bring to her door, and all will be well in the world.'

Kitty gave a laugh. 'Jo Norfolk, I think you are right! My hardest task will be telling my uncle. Last time we spoke he moaned about having to purchase a new address book just for me as mine is constantly changing.'

Chapter Seven

November 1944

Seeing Jo off a few days later was a painful affair and although Kitty tried her best to be bright and cheery, all she could envisage were the terrors she had encountered on the French beaches back in June and she wouldn't wish the same nightmares on her worst enemy, let alone her closest friend.

Jo, in her usual bullish manner, had dismissed Kitty's tears as unnecessary, but it was not missed by Kitty that Jo also wiped away a tear or two.

'Give Trixie a hug from me when you see her again, and hopefully I'll be back for some of her fabulous baking by Christmas. Tell Smithy his old schoolfriend wishes him well and to be a better father than we both had to cope with,' Jo said, and waved to someone in the distance. 'I have to go now, old thing, but I'll happily take a hug with me.'

Once they'd hugged and parted, Kitty watched Jo walk

away, her back straight with determination. Cold chills of fear ran through Kitty's veins as she waited until Jo turned for a final wave. Was this the last time she would see her friend? A sense of fear and loneliness overwhelmed her, and she rushed from the quayside.

Back at the home her mood lifted slightly when the children called her into the room they used as a common room, and she saw their beaming smiles directed at her. Each child had written her a good luck card and she received a gift from the house in general of three prettily embroidered handkerchiefs. Matron said a few kind words and then it was back to normal. On the table near Matron's office Kitty spotted a letter for her and took it to her room to read in private. It was from the Gaskin brothers and their adopted brother Eric, updating her on their lives on the farm near Brancepeth.

The boys were now nine and eleven years old and, according to the letter, Peter was showing signs of a moustache already. Their hilarious tales of tormenting their younger sister and adoptive parents brought a lightness to Kitty's heart. The first of her orphans were thriving and she reflected on her time with Stanley Walker and his wife Jenny, without whom the children would never have survived the torment of losing their parents in the enemy bomb attacks.

She missed Stanley's banter and Jenny's gentle ways. Stanley was busy in the RAF and when Jenny passed away, he threw himself into projects to cover the pain of her loss. In his correspondence with Kitty, he had urged her many times to continue her care of orphans, but she knew he would understand her decision when she wrote back to tell him that she wanted to support the injured once more.

During the final days at the home, she wrote to Trixie,

Lewis, Sarah, Pots and Wenna, Tom and Maude, informing them of her new adventure, in the hope that their replies would arrive at her destination and she would feel as though her friends were supporting her in her first few days there. She asked them to post via their local Red Cross recruiting offices who would forward mail on to her as her address was confidential.

Kitty clambered down from the truck and waved her goodbyes. She was exhausted from her journey and was thankful for a lift from Malton rail station.

She walked down the pathway noting the silhouettes of endless buildings and huts in rows ahead of her. Male voices and laughter travelled on the wind, and someone played a lively tune on a mouth organ. It was not what she had expected from a prisoner of war camp – the bleakness of her surroundings maybe, but the sound of normal life, definitely not.

She tramped her way up the potholed driveway and was immediately saluted and greeted by two guards who stepped out from the guardhouses, one on either side, and saluted when she showed her identity card and permit papers. Kitty glanced around and saw several prisoners within her eyeline.

'I'm used to orphaned children, let's hope this new post brings about a welcome change,' she said with a jolliness to her voice in an attempt to be friendly.

'Much the same but on a larger scale, really. Some are lost and lonely, some are young and grateful they are being treated with respect,' the taller of the guards said. He nodded at her papers and stepped to one side to allow her through. 'Welcome to Malton, nurse. The name's Rankin, Jimmy. If you need anything, ma'am, just ask any one of us.' The soldier pointed down the pathway ahead of them. 'You'll want to go straight ahead and report in at the last hut on your right. I believe you are expected. See you around,' Private Rankin said, and Kitty gave a grateful wave before continuing on her way.

She walked past the huts, some with the glow of a fire or oil lamps, others dark and uninviting. All around were men talking in groups and some acknowledged her walking past with a nod and a greeting, which she assumed was 'good evening' in German. She simply nodded her reply, not sure of what was expected of her considering their status.

She rapped on the hut door and entered when beckoned inside. The room was warmer than she'd anticipated given the biting cold wind outside.

A well-built woman rose to her feet when Kitty entered and promptly held out her hand.

'I've read your Red Cross record and would like to shake the hand of one of our silent heroines. I am extremely proud of our nurses and what you had to overcome on that special mission was quite something. Now sit, have you eaten?' the woman said without introducing herself.

Kitty stood with her back rod-straight and offered a smile before sitting on the chair beside her.

'Thank you. Yes, I ate before catching my last train. A cup of tea would be welcome though,' she said.

'As luck would have it, I had just mashed a pot for myself,' the woman said and went to a coal stove in the corner of the room, where she poured Kitty a tin mug of tea.

'I see you have also qualified as a registered nurse with the backing of your local Red Cross. It is good to see girls taking their careers from volunteer to a more secure footing. As I understand it, your uncle funded you and you are an orphan. It's good to have family support, I thrive on it myself. I also realise I forgot to introduce myself.'

By the time Kitty had finished in the company of Senior Sister Vera Craven, she had a brain filled with knowledge that would not settle into place. Another nurse, Louisa Barker, escorted her to their quarters and reassured Kitty she would find her feet much quicker when she started working with the prisoners, than trying to decipher the instructions of their superior, who was a woman renowned for confusing even the most organised of the staff. She was also well-liked though and had a reputation of being fair and kind.

Kitty settled into her bunk, something she had not experienced before, but was grateful she was on the bottom of an empty one. The hut housed eight to ten, but Kitty learned there was only her and Louisa living in the building at present, so it was also doubling up as a medical store.

With gratitude and tired feet, Kitty washed, tugged out a fresh uniform, placed it on a coat hanger for the creases to drop overnight, and then wriggled under the blankets, choosing to unpack fully the following day.

Sleep came easily and, by the time morning reveille was called and the regimental trumpeter signed off with his last note, Kitty was wide awake and alert. Louisa greeted her and they walked to the canteen together.

'Call me Lou, everyone does. Grab a tray and we'll sit over there,' she said, pointing to a long table filled with a mix of males and females. 'The non-POWs tend to stick together at breakfast so that we can plan our day. Today, we've the joys of a visiting dentist as the German prisoner who usually deals with the inmates is helping at another camp and, as I am not a fan of teeth, maybe you can assist and I'll tidy,' she said with a beaming smile. Kitty could not imagine disliking such a friendly girl as Louisa, but she also felt cornered into a job she had no stomach for either.

'Hmm, not my favourite inspection day, either. Who on earth would want to be a dentist? Not me for sure, I'll toss you for it,' Kitty said, laughing.

'No, this is the new girl event. I've done my duty in the past, it is your turn this afternoon,' Louisa said, patting Kitty on the shoulder and laughing loudly.

Kitty shook her head in a friendly manner. 'I lost that one, but be warned Louisa, I won't fall for another task for the new girl challenge.' Both laughed and finished eating. Once they had cleared away their plates and trays, they headed towards the camp reception station – or as Louisa called it, the sick bay.

The morning was slow with splinter removals and a sprained wrist, and as Kitty watched Louisa deal with the prisoners with polite professionalism, she was surprised by the easy, relaxed manner the men had. She was convinced if held captive by the enemy she would not be laughing and practicing the language, but the men she encountered during her first day did just that, and all said they were happy enough to be free from the horrors of fighting, and that the British company they found themselves in treated them with friendship, not disdain or distrust. Kitty was also surprised to find the men were counted out into the surrounding farms to help and then counted back in and all returned back to camp with no pressure or aggression. By the end of her first shift, Kitty felt she had stepped into a strange world connected to the war, but separated by a band of trust and, surprisingly, goodwill.

Kitty's days rolled into weeks, and she found herself relaxed and happy in her work. She watched over a sick patient after his appendix was removed and gained great satisfaction when he was finally discharged back to his hut. Although not as frantic as in the past, Kitty no longer felt her nursing skills were going to waste. Each day she removed endless splinters as the men were carving wooden toys for Christmas to give to local children. Those who could communicate well told her of their lives and families in Germany. She heard the pain in their voices of being separated from them and of their hope to return to their homeland. Some of the younger men told her of their desire to remain in Great Britain, often because they had set their sights on a local village girl as a future wife and their families did not object to the idea. The whole situation fascinated Kitty. Prisoners were invited to homes for tea and their requests were granted. The advances of Britain and her allies made the end of war seem much closer and rules with regards to the prisoners appeared more relaxed than she had imagined.

Louisa was good company and, with her family living about an hour away from the camp, took Kitty on the bus one day to meet her parents and shop for essentials, pointing out villages and towns along the way as all signposts had been removed.

Before the war, Louisa's father was a travelling salesman and claimed to know Yorkshire and the surrounding areas 'like the back of his hand'. He spent time talking to them about his journeys to and from Harrogate using the cross-country shortcuts in the dark at the start of the war before he suffered a collapsed lung after his unit was attacked in France. They laughed when he said that one evening he took a wrong turn and ended up in a field surrounded by large animals, and was too scared to move. When dawn came, he saw the animals were in fact discarded theatre scenes propped against a dilapidated barn wall.

On their return to the camp, Kitty drafted a letter to her uncle. Listening to Louisa's father made her miss him and she realised she hadn't written to him in a while. She expressed how much happier she was in her new posting.

As she was writing she became aware of a strange sound outside the hut window near her bed. Kitty listened hard to interpret the noise and established it was sobbing. She heard muffled words muttered and then more sobbing. After a while of listening to the heart-breaking sound, she decided enough time had been given for the person in distress to suffer alone and Kitty grabbed her cape. Stepping outside into the cool early evening air, she walked towards the crouched figure on the floor.

'Hello. Can I help?' she asked.

The tear-streaked face of a young male stared up at her, then he dropped his head forward to his knees again. Kitty saw he wore the uniform of a prisoner and took a moment to consider her next move. He was not supposed to be outside of his hut during the evening, and calling for a guard would only bring more trouble to a young man in distress. She didn't want to be the cause of more upset for him.

'*Bist du verletzt?*' she asked, using the first German words she had learned when she had arrived at the camp. The young man remained crouched and sobbing.

'Are you injured?' she repeated in English, just in case she hadn't quite got the question right in German. '*Kann ich Ihnen helfen?*'

'Nay, you canna help him lass,' a voice whispered from behind her, and Kitty swung around, fully aware the weeping young man had leapt to his feet. She held out her hand to signal he should stay where he was. She faced the tall, well-built redheaded guard with his gun tight in his hands.

'I think he is hurt or sick,' she said quickly, not knowing if either statement was true, but she was not prepared to hand the young man over to the Scottish guard who she already knew from camp gossip had a reputation for working in a firm manner – some told her fierce – without taking time to discover what had caused the prisoner's distress in the first place.

'Naw, he's a wimp, lass. He needs toughening up, so he does,' the soldier said with a deeper gruffness to his voice.

Kitty drew herself to her full height.

'I am not your lass, so show a bit of respect for my rank, private,' she said firmly, fully aware she outranked him enough to have him reprimanded for disrespecting his senior.

'Apologies, ma'am,' the soldier said and saluted her, but Kitty sensed there was a touch of sarcasm to his voice, such was his usual brash manner around the camp.

'Accepted. Now, help me get my patient to sick bay,' she said and returned her attention to the now quiet prisoner. She noted the fear on his face and guessed he'd experienced torment from the Scot in the past.

'Gently does it,' she said in a calming voice and placed her arm underneath his elbow. 'Come with me.'

The soldier moved to the other arm of the prisoner and Kitty could feel the tension between the two men, one angry for being put in his place because of the one he considered weak.

The young man looked into her face. '*Danke*,' he said, and Kitty gave him a wide-eyed, encouraging stare, speaking with her eyes to try and reassure him she was going to help him, not report him. She let go of his arm and bent down to tap his leg. '*Schmerzen*?' she asked. 'Pain?' she repeated and, in the hope she would be seen, gave the prisoner a quick wink for him to agree.

'*Ja. Ja*,' he said and lifted his right leg from the ground. Kitty silently thanked his sensibility and understanding. Again, she offered her arm as support.

'Kind. *Danke*,' he said and accepted the offer of her arm.

'Lean on me,' the gruff voice of the soldier cut in, and he took the weight of the slim young man, allowing Kitty to step behind them as they walked towards the medical hut. She was taking a risk by allowing the prisoner to fake his injury, but she was not prepared to hand him over until she was satisfied that he was not a victim of bullying.

The prisoners in the camp had shown her nothing but respect and although they were classified as the enemy, she could not bring herself to hate. Too much hatred and greed had caused the war and Eden Camp was a place where cautious understanding of both sides could be learned in the hope another war could be prevented in the future. Word was out that Great Britain and her allies were the stronger force, and the end of the war was in sight, but the country was fully aware that there were still raging battles needed to completely defeat Hitler's army and individual healings to be made.

'Who do you have there, Kitty?' Louisa asked as Kitty, the soldier and prisoner entered the sick bay.

'Someone to keep you company for your night shift,' Kitty said and gave a brief nod towards the young man with his foot raised off the floor.

'Broken or sprained?' Louisa asked, looking down at the limb.

'Simple sprain but painful enough to make him cry out,' Kitty said as she turned to the guard. 'Thank you for your help, you may go now.' She used a dismissive tone as she wanted rid of him as soon as possible.

'Ma'am,' the soldier said and saluted both nurses before leaving the hut.

'Right, let's look at the leg,' Louisa said and pointed to the nearest seat. The prisoner hopped over and sat down. He looked nervous.

'Was he trying to escape?' Louisa whispered to Kitty as they walked over to an examination trolley for bandages.

'No, at least I don't think so. He was sobbing his heart out beneath our window, and I went out to him, but the soldier was either following or chasing him there because he arrived very quickly behind me and wasn't best pleased to see me. I had to pull rank on him and I'm not sure if he'll report the boy for not being in his quarters this late, but he seemed to accept my story of his injury,' Kitty said, knowing she was taking a risk telling Louisa she had lied, but suspecting Louisa would have done the same thing to protect someone so upset and obviously frightened.

'Sprain it is then,' Louisa said and snatched up a bandage.

'A bad one, I'd say, wouldn't you?' She winked at Kitty. 'It must have happened when he was helping us move things around in here earlier,' she said and launched into a full conversation in German with the young man.

It was Louisa who had taught Kitty when she arrived the basic words for those who did not speak or understand English. She told Kitty that, from the moment war was announced, she had decided to learn the language in case of invasion so that it might help her and her family survive. The medics and prisoners had helped her polish her basic knowledge and now she was able to hold a conversation quite handily.

'I've told him to say he twisted it earlier, before they were due back to quarters, and he couldn't manage to walk on it. He became upset for fear of being in trouble. As it is, it appears he received a Dear John – or Josef in his case – letter. He's only nineteen, bless him.'

Kitty gave the young man a sympathetic tap on his shoulder. He looked up at her through red eyes and she saw his pain. A relationship which had given him hope whilst so far from home was over, and he had no way of reaching out to his girl verbally. His sadness was probably much like Kitty's own when she thought of Michael and their separation.

'Let's write him up as in pain with swelling and keep him here tonight as there are no other patients. He'll probably sleep and hopefully be able to start afresh tomorrow. I am happy to swap shifts if you are uncomfortable with that,' Kitty said.

Louisa tapped the young man's leg, said something to him and he rolled up his trouser leg to take off his boot and sock. She smiled at him as she bandaged his foot and spoke in a soft voice to which he responded with a smile at both her and Kitty.

'*Danke. Danke,*' he said softly, and a large teardrop fell from his chin, staining the leather of his boot in his hand.

'He'll be no bother and, as I speak German, he will be company for me. I miss my brother and they are about the same age,' Louisa said, and Kitty heard the crack in her voice.

'If you are sure? Thank you for helping, I couldn't bear to hear his cry anymore and the soldier was only doing his duty, I know, but I think the boy has been punished enough by being so far away from home. I'll see you first thing.' Kitty gave Louisa and Josef a smile and turned towards the door.

Just as she was about to leave the hut, the door burst open, and the Scottish soldier and two others entered. Kitty noticed their puffed-out chests and threatening stance. She eased the screen around the patient's bed and Louisa bent and muttered something then stepped over to stand beside Kitty.

'A little quiet please, my patient is sleeping. Can we help you, which one is the patient here? Nurse Pattison is now off duty, but if it is serious, then I am sure she will be willing to stay and help,' Louisa said, her voice firm and in control. Kitty watched the soldiers glance at one another.

'We're just doin' our roun's, ma'am,' one said in a thick London accent. 'Scottie 'ere said we 'ad to check on the Jerry and take 'im back to 'is 'ut.' He nodded his head towards the Scot.

'His ankle is too swollen and painful. We asked him to move furniture and boxes for us earlier and he twisted it on uneven ground. I thought he had broken it, but we've both registered a severe sprain. I suggest you declare him out of service for at least three days. We'll give him light duties here when we see fit, and then return him to duty after the doc is satisfied. Thank you for checking on him,' Louisa said and gave them a dismissive smile. All three saluted but Kitty could still see suspicion on the face of the soldier who had helped her escort the boy to sick bay. She turned away and picked up a paper just to make it look as if she was doing something official, and then turned back to them.

'Right, that's me off duty. Night, all,' she said and swept forward towards the door. The soldiers stood to one side and once she was outdoors, they followed.

'Have a quiet evening, gentlemen,' she said and headed to her quarters. She didn't turn around and once inside she giggled to herself. Thank goodness for Louisa thinking the same way as herself. Neither of them had time for bullies and she personally felt a little peace knowing they had saved a young man from the inevitable taunting and humiliation he would have endured. No one bothered when women cried, it was a given thing in the female makeup, but when a man showed any sign of what was considered weakness they became an easy target, enemy or not. She'd witnessed it amongst friends and colleagues over the years and vowed never to allow it to happen in her company.

Chapter Eight

The following morning Kitty arrived on duty to find Louisa and Josef working on his English conversation. She smiled at the scene and wondered how many other cultures were coming together around the world regardless of the fact they were classified as fighting against one another.

'Good morning, you two. I hope you enjoyed a quiet night,' she said, addressing Louisa more than Josef.

With a start, Josef got to his feet but then remembered himself and sat back down sharing a theatrical show of pain.

'He's quite the comic,' Louisa said. 'He was good company, too. He is still emotional, but we have worked on a letter to his girlfriend, Ingrid. I'll get it sent out later today when our post arrives.'

Josef smiled at the sound of his girlfriend's name.

'He released her from their promise to remain a couple until the war has ended. Although she has already done it herself, he wants to cut the final tie and his thoughts are now about how to remain in Britain after the war. Apparently, several of the men are frantically learning the language in the hope they can find a way of staying.'

Kitty shook her cape free of leaves and placed it on a hook behind the door. She adjusted her apron and picked up a broom.

'You would have thought the last place they would want to live was in enemy territory, away from their families,' she said, sweeping up the leaves.

'Some have no families left and others like the more genteel manner of the British people. I had never really given it any thought, but apparently, we are not dictated to, but allowed to think for ourselves – the majority of the time, anyway,' Louisa replied. She gave a yawn.

'I'm heading off for some sleep. I'll leave you to it. *Auf wiedersehen*, Josef,' she said, waving at the young man who was tracing his finger on the tin cup Kitty had filled for him with warm milk.

'Goodbye, nurse. Thank me,' he said with a smile.

'Thank *you*. It is thank you, Josef. Remember?' Louisa replied, and turned to Kitty. 'If you are not too busy today, you can teach him a few more words. I am going to have a word with Private Rankin at the guardhouse and see if he will help the boy toughen up a bit or he won't survive here much longer. I suspect that if the war wasn't on, he would be one of the gentle kind, working with animals or children somewhere, so he's an easy target for anyone out for tormenting. Comes to something when we are both trying to save the enemy, eh, Kitty? We're as soft as he is,' Louisa said laughing and gave Josef a wave.

The morning was an easy one with only one man visiting for severe blistering of his hands. He grunted out a few words in German to the younger male POW and gained a smile as a reply. Kitty assumed it was along the lines of 'hope all is well' and warmed to the craggy-faced man.

'Do you speak English?' she asked as she applied a soothing cream to his raw palms.

He winced with the pain. His knuckles were swollen too, and she guessed he had chilblains forming on his hands.

'*Ja,*' he replied.

Kitty giggled at his reply, he was clearly teasing her.

'You will need to rest those hands for at least two days. I will write you a note and you'll need to come back tomorrow for fresh dressings,' she said.

'I work the farm,' the man replied.

Kitty had guessed as much and when she had finished dressing his hand, she picked up pen and paper.

'*Ihren namen?*' she asked in stilted German.

The man looked at her in surprise.

'*Mein name ist Frederich Schwarz und mein Englischer name ist Fred Black.*'

Kitty wrote a note to his group supervisor and handed it to him.

'Right, Fred Black, you will report here in the morning at eight. Your friend over there is learning English and teaching me a little German to fill the time. If the soldiers find nothing you can do, feel free to return and help us here,' she said and gave him one of her warmest smiles. Whatever had happened to Michael must not cloud her vision of peace in her life. If it meant lessons with the enemy, then she would find comfort there.

Two weeks later, Kitty and Louisa sat eating their lunch together. A generous slice of freshly cooked ham between two chunks of freshly baked bread, courtesy of a local farmer, was a welcome gift on such a wet and windy day. The sick bay was experiencing a quiet spell and the medical crew gave the unit a complete clean from top to bottom. Bandages were rolled neatly in rows and washed ones were drying over the line above the wood burner. A sense of calm filtered through the place giving Kitty time to go through her updated duties, read the latest articles of medical interest and write letters to her many friends around the country. Recently she had learned how to knit and was slowly transforming a moth-eaten cardigan into a hat, scarf and gloves.

Fred and Josef returned to their fellow inmates with renewed enthusiasm and formed a basic English speaking class, which thrilled both Kitty and Louisa. Over a period of time, several groups were formed to help the prisoners understand the British systems. It was interesting to hear the reaction of the enemy and their perception of Great Britain as a democratic country as opposed to a dictatorship. The more the men heard, the more the majority wanted to learn. Political debate groups formed whilst those with a musical or acting talent performed for the staff which lead to the creation of a theatre group. With the comings and goings of the men journeying to the village to work, some days it was hard to imagine the place as a prison camp with opposing sides. Even the Scottish soldier had mellowed, and Kitty often saw him laughing with his prisoners.

He once told her they were able to understand the Gaelic he spoke to them, and she was more than welcome to learn too if she wished. Kitty laughed and said she had trouble understanding his Scottish English let alone Gaelic and that learning basic German was enough, but that it was kind of him to ask.

'After lunch we need to fetch some things from the stores for sick bay – one of the German medics wrote out a list. The English lessons seem to be paying off,' Kitty said, watching Louisa pick at her food. She was unusually quiet. 'By the way, what are you doing on your day off? Are you still going home?'

'I've met someone,' Louisa said suddenly, causing Kitty to choke on a sliver of ham. 'I know I said I haven't got time for a man in my life, but this one is … well, different. He cares for me. He makes me feel special.'

Recovering from Louisa's confession, Kitty wiped her mouth free from crumbs and took a sip of warm milk before she spoke.

'Is he a local – not serving, or home on leave?' she said, assuming that Louisa had met someone in her hometown.

'He's not local but is living locally. He served, but is unable to serve at the moment,' Louisa said. 'Dad doesn't approve of me having a boyfriend, and Mum said she's sure he is a nice lad, but with him unable to serve she wants to meet him and find out why. I don't know why they can't just accept I love someone,' Louisa said. She pulled a piece of meat from her sandwich and placed it in her mouth, all the while looking at Kitty as if she held the answer.

Kitty sat in silence, mulling over Louisa's mother's words which hinted that her parents were worried that the new boyfriend might not be up to their expected standards. Was he an out of work, sick man? There had to be a medical reason for him not serving in the forces. She could understand Louisa's parents' hesitation. A mother is keen her daughter meets and marries someone who can be relied upon.

'What's his name?' Kitty asked.

'Eric,' Louisa replied.

'How did you meet?' Kitty watched as a flush of red flashed across Louisa's cheeks.

Realisation dawned on Kitty and she stared at her friend. Eric was a decoy name.

'No. No. Tell me it's not one of the soldiers you've nursed here. Someone discharged on medical grounds?' she asked.

'Not quite,' Louisa replied. 'But it is someone here,' she said with a shyness.

'Louisa! No. Stop it at once. You will lose your job and for what, a flirtation with a prisoner of war? Cut him loose and find one of the soldiers to walk you out to a dance now and then. Don't get into a—'

Kitty jerked back and stopped talking when Louisa rose from her chair, and it fell to the floor with a clatter.

'I knew I shouldn't have said anything. You just don't understand,' Louisa snapped back and began pacing the floor. 'Forget I told you.'

Kitty also stood up and put her hands on her hips, staring at her friend.

'I will not forget; how can I? We are not allowed to have relationships with the inmates. Rules, Louisa. Rules!' she whispered urgently.

Snatching her cape from the back of the front door, Louisa flung it around her shoulders so dramatically she would have made a great character in one of the camp shows.

'I had hoped you would be happy for me,' she said and

flounced out of the door. Kitty stood, stunned by the last few minutes of confession.

She went over her conversation with Louisa and tried to form images of the man Louisa might have enjoyed flirtatious moments with but could only bring Josef to mind as anywhere near Louisa's age. Even then, he was a good four years younger. After an internal debate with herself, Kitty chose to say nothing more to Louisa about the subject and to leave her friend to work out her own life. If it was a serious relationship, then it would become a discussion with senior staff and, if not, Kitty could only hope it would fizzle out without repercussions.

She pulled out a notebook and pen and started making plans for her Christmas visit to Trixie as a distraction. An idea for a small wooden toy for her friend, Meryn's, boy came to mind and she thought about which inmate she would ask to carve it for her. A beautifully carved pipe for her uncle already sat wrapped in brown paper and string in readiness for her next visit but, sadly, the prisoner of war who had made it had passed away suddenly. As an alternative, Kitty cast her mind to the young man she had seen working on a child's chair for one of the soldiers. Hans Dreiche had many artistic talents, and his work was a favourite amongst the local people. In addition to woodworking, he could charcoal images from photographs, creating portraits for those who had lost family to the war or those who were fighting. Suddenly she remembered the small photograph given to her by Michael of himself in uniform. Hans would be able to create an enlarged image for her and she decided to approach him that afternoon. It would be a Christmas gift to herself.

In return, she would knit him a hat and gloves. Money

never changed hands amongst the staff and inmates for security reasons, and because, although the inmates had their own camp currency to exchange for personal goods within the camp, actual cash was never given to them. No one would want to be found to have aided and abetted an escapee.

Scribbling down more notes, she pondered over Louisa's dilemma and about Belle – or Lizzie Belle, as Kitty had christened her in her mind – as both women had connections with the enemy in an intimate way and had brought about their own dilemmas. Lizzie Belle was supposedly working to bring about the downfall of the enemy's secret service and Louisa was intent on forming a relationship with a German. 'Thank goodness for Jo,' Kitty said out loud to the empty room. 'No complications there!'

The door of the sick bay opened. A British soldier, who normally stood guard outside the door for the end-of-day role call for prisoners, entered and looked around the room – probably to see who it was she had been talking to. On seeing no one, he looked back at Kitty.

'Nurse, can you take a look at my foot, please? It is giving me trouble and the sarge said to have a word with the medics,' he asked with a sheepish grin.

Kitty rose to her feet. 'Come in, and I'll take a look,' she said.

Once he was settled on a seat, Kitty examined the soldier's foot. It was red and inflamed and the skin was raw.

'It itches like the devil,' the soldier said.

Kitty washed her hands with carbolic soap.

'It is a fungal infection. I've recently been reading about them. It is where your feet are getting warm and moist inside your boots. Your socks look hand-knitted, your mum been busy?' she asked.

'My sisters. I've got so many pairs now, I've shared them with the others – even a couple of prisoners have a pair each, in exchange for pinafores for the girls,' the soldier said.

'Lucky you, I am a slow knitter so never rely on me for one sock, let alone two,' Kitty said with a laugh and placed a bowl of hot water in front of the young man. 'Pop your feet in there, I've only got disinfectant and carbolic soap, but it should help. I'll also wash your socks in it and give you a pair of regulation ones we have in the cupboard. Try and wash your feet when you can and dry them well. Keep the air to them and don't scratch when they are exposed. Tell the others to wash their feet and socks with this stuff too.'

As she spoke, Louisa came back into the building and nodded at them both.

'Sleet out there, we'll need more wood,' she said in a matter-of-fact manner, which told Kitty she was not forgiven for her earlier comments about Louisa's relationship.

'The inside windows of our hut were iced over this morning, winter is setting in,' the soldier said. 'Not sure about airing my feet nurse, the toes will drop off!' His laugh echoed loudly around the room and Kitty joined him.

'That's not funny, my granddad lost his toes during the Great War. Trench foot,' Louisa bit back from across the room, her voice filled with anger.

The soldier raised an eyebrow at Kitty and silently pulled on the socks she had given him. Kitty ushered him out of the door. 'Don't forget, tell the others to keep their feet as clean as possible. I will see what medication I am able to order in which might help with the itching. Come back in two days for me to check and soak them again,' she said quietly and closed the door behind her. She leaned her back against it, took a deep breath, and looked across in Louisa's direction. Her friend's shoulders were slouched and everything she picked up was slammed back down.

'Louisa. I know you are upset with me, but that poor kidney dish has done nothing to you,' she said, trying to make light of the situation. 'We need to talk about you and your beau,' Kitty added and moved over to the desk, picking up her pen and writing her notes relating to the soldier with the sore feet.

It was some time before Louisa joined her and when she did, she placed a steaming tin mug of tea in front of Kitty.

'Truce. Sorry for my mood. You touched a nerve and what with Dad going on and on about me falling in love with the wrong man … I didn't want to hear it from someone I consider a close friend,' Louisa said and sat across the desk from Kitty.

'Don't apologise. It isn't my business to interfere in your personal life, but it is a situation you need to seriously think about. My advice is to walk away if you can but, if not, try and find a way of holding out until the end of the war.' Kitty waited for an objection but when Louisa said nothing, she carried on talking. 'News of the war ending soon looks positive according to Private Rankin and friends. After what we've been through and for so long, it could only be a matter of waiting a few more months or one more year. By then you will know exactly how you feel about one another and can go through the correct authorities to be together. Think about it, Louisa. Don't bring trouble to your door if it isn't necessary.'

The hiss of steam was the only sound in the room for a while as the wet socks dripped onto the wood burner. Louisa twiddled with a loose curl of hair behind her ear and Kitty avoided talking as she could see her friend was deep in thought. Louisa was a good nurse; she would be a great loss to the Red Cross and the camp if made to leave.

'I've got an errand to run so I'll stop nagging and leave you to it. I am off duty until eighteen hundred, so keep the fire burning as I suspect it will be a tad chilly later in the evening,' Kitty said, before leaving the hut.

As she approached the workshop area where several prisoners worked, she looked out for Hans Dreicht who she found sitting astride a bench chiselling down a length of wood.

'Hans. Hello,' Kitty greeted him when he looked her way with a smile. 'Making anything special?' she asked as she watched his hands caress the wood.

'I have now finished the chair for the child,' he said, pointing to a small chair in the corner that looked newly varnished. It had raised embossed rabbits across the back and was a beautiful piece of carpentry. Kitty applauded his talent.

'With this new wood I am to make a tray with handles for Louisa's mother,' Hans replied.

Something in the way he said Louisa's name made Kitty refrain from saying anything else. His tone was soft, almost intimate when saying it. Kitty glanced around at some of the pieces he had made, which were sitting on a shelf. Squirrels, birds, small dolls and many other wooden pieces of art drew the eye to their intricate carved features. Small cameo pictures, a few larger ones and a partial drawing sat to one side. Curious, Kitty teased the partial drawing to one side and saw the outline of Louisa's face smiling back at her. Wide-eyed and undeniably happy, the young woman's features – although not yet fully formed – showed off a relaxed state. Louisa's eyes in the portrait creased into a softness, clearly looking at something which pleased her. Hans was the man Louisa had fallen in love with, Kitty was convinced of it; the clues were right there in front of her.

'You are drawing Louisa, as well as making things for her, Hans. Your talents have no boundaries. This is wonderful,' Kitty said casually as she pointed to the picture.

Face flushed, Hans glanced at Kitty and then looked away, concentrating on polishing the wood he worked on.

'Nurse Barker is very pretty,' Kitty said, using Louisa's formal title, reminding Hans of her friend's role at the camp. 'I am not surprised you wanted to paint her. She is a dedicated nurse; a good one. I would hate for her to leave, she's a good friend now and I'd be lonely without her.'

Hans continued to rub at the wood with tea dregs to stain it and Kitty could see his jaw clench tightly.

'Her family will love her surprise. I take it she has commissioned you to draw her as a Christmas gift for them,' Kitty said and watched the jaw clenching and face flushing continue. She guessed Louisa did not know she was his subject and it occurred to her Hans could also get into trouble for his secret drawing.

'She doesn't know, does she?' Kitty whispered and Hans turned to look at her, his face expressing shock.

'Maybe you had better draw others so as not to attract attention to this particular work, Hans. There are some who might not like it if you single out one of the female staff. Do you understand?' Kitty asked him. 'If I have guessed you have eyes for her, some of the soldiers might do the same and ask her if she knows about it. If it is a surprise gift for her, tell me and I can at least say I knew about it should anyone attempt to suggest something different. I'll happily sit for you so you can draw me, too. My uncle would love a picture. Be sensible, Hans. Be safe.'

Kitty gave him a smile as others in the workshop were starting to look their way.

'I would like to ask you to make something else for me as well. A gift for a friend's child. Maybe a carved aeroplane?'

Hans gave a brief nod. He didn't look at her and continued to work on his project.

'I will speak to Nurse Barker,' he said, his voice gruff with emotion.

'I will leave you to your work,' Kitty said and made her way around the room admiring the projects made by others in the workshop before leaving.

Chapter Nine

December 1944

Louisa's mood was not a happy one. It was evident by the way she snapped at her patients and colleagues. Kitty guessed Hans had spoken with her and several times during the week Kitty had to take her to one side to suggest she request sick leave and go home to her parents – away from Hans – but was rewarded by a biting remark each time she approached the subject.

By the Friday, Kitty had given up on trying to protect her friend and simply worked around her, doing her best to avoid the tantrums and sulks. She visited Hans for the portrait sitting and kept things as normal as possible. A welcome distraction was a letter from her friend Meryn. News of her and her son was always welcome.

Dear Kitty,

I hope this letter finds you as well as myself and Kedrick. I struggled to understand where in the country you were for a while and when the news came that you were now in Yorkshire and coming to visit us at Christmas, I cannot tell you how happy it made me, I do miss you. Trixie is very excited, but I have to remind her she is near her time and not to overdo everything, but in true Trixie style she reminds me she is more like my mother than a friend and she is quite adult enough to know when to rest. Stubborn is her middle name, but you know that so well. She has delivered six babies in surrounding villages this month alone and how she manages to walk from place to place I do not know. I am younger than her and when I carried Kedrick, by the end of the day I was ready to sleep. Trixie just keeps on going. Smithy tried talking to her, but she ignored him, too.

Your American friend Lewis Porter has paid us a few visits. I am told he has a different accent to us British, but as a deaf person I would never know what an accent is, so it makes no difference to me. He talks about you a lot in his notes to me; he is very concerned about you, and Trixie said he tells her he is worried you are experiencing too much for a young woman. He spends a lot of time with Smithy, they are a pair of chums nowadays. He is also very patient and plays with Kedrick whenever he can. He brings Trixie and Smithy gifts, which I get to enjoy too. He is good company when the days are dark and cold. I miss the pretty shores of Cornwall but not so much I would return to live there quite yet. Smithy pays me as housekeeper to the surgery and I enjoy growing vegetables in the garden, so my life is a good one. You have all been so kind to me since the Belle situation.

Tom and Maude write, and Maude stitched nightshirts for Kedrick from old ones of Tom's. I will take my son to see them one day and tell him about the way they cared for me. I know I rebelled when I found out I was pregnant, but they reassure me they understand how frightened I was.

Where has the time gone? Kedrick is coming up to nine months old and has a tooth! His dark hair has curls, which sit around his neck, and his eyes are so brown with thick, dark lashes and he has the sweetest smile. Yes, I know you are thinking I am his mother so I will always think he is the best-looking child on this earth, but Trixie will do the same, as will you one day. Please take care of yourself, Kitty. I am about to go foraging and I remember with fondness our blackberry picking days together.

Much love from us all.

Your friend, Meryn x

Kitty smiled at the letter and imagined Meryn enjoying life in the garden and cleaning for Smithy. She took pride in everything she did, and Kitty doubted the Stargazy Inn in Cornwall was as clean now as it was back when Meryn lived there. Wenna would do a good job, but Meryn had extremely high standards. She also baked a good pasty and Kitty could not wait to enjoy one when she visited. Of course, she also had the surprise of Annabelle Farnsworth's legacy and as she thought about it, she pondered over the truth of it all. If Belle never existed, then how could she leave an inheritance? The future would no doubt give the answer.

After reading Meryn's letter, Kitty had a pang of conscience for not writing to Jo and, not wanting to sit in the dismissive silence of Louisa, she moved beside a patient brought in overnight with a fever and drafted out a letter.

Dear Jo,

I hope this letter finds you well and you are safe. It has been a while now and I wanted you to know I have not forgotten you and to share what little news I have. My life here in Yorkshire is very different and far better than the home in Liverpool. It is strange working on healing the enemy, but also shows me they are human too. Very human. They have the same fears, family love and friendships as we do. Silly really, because some days I find it hard to imagine them as the same as us. Some of the prisoners are very young; we have one who is sixteen, and half the village nearby are falling over themselves to comfort him. I found a nineteen-year-old sobbing and it made me think about my cousin, the one I lost at Dunkirk, and how afraid he must have been. We think of men as the strong ones, but having seen the strength of women during this war, I am not so sure we aren't equal. Mind you, if I dared say as much to some of the soldiers here, I would soon be told my place, despite my rank. Don't get me wrong though, some of them have nothing but respect for how the women they know have stepped up and taken their places to keep the country running.

I aim to get to Trixie for Christmas; my leave has been granted. My colleague Louisa only lives a short way away from the camp, so she said she's happy to cover my duties and her family will collect her for her Christmas dinner. I will have five wonderful days! Meryn has written to me, and she said Trixie is overdoing things and that she is excited to see me. If only I could gather everyone I hold dear and we could all enjoy time together over the festive period, what a wonderful day it would be!

I plan to spend a longer break with my uncle back home in the spring. He is happy enough and he keeps in touch, which is good considering he is not a man of many words. He has a wit about his letters though, which tells me all is well. I never thought another woman would make him as happy as my aunt, but after her death he has survived and that gives me comfort, which is just as well because there has been no further news from Canada with regard to Michael. I write to him and live in hope. It is all I can do now.

My dear friend, please take care wherever you are and return to us safely. You are truly missed.

With affection,

Kitty x

After writing to Jo, Kitty sat and thought about her friend Sarah and the girl's quest to find her Jewish family. Kitty knew how desperate Sarah was and also knew how worried she personally would be if her uncle Frank was a victim of the persecution reported. Unimaginable was the word she used when she first saw reports filtering through about the atrocities, but it was more than just that one word she felt.

The thoughts stayed with her when she finished her shift and walked back to her quarters. Kitty looked around the camp at the German soldiers and understood why some of them were grateful to be captured. She would not want her name associated with the news that had been leaking either.

Despite having been through so many attacks and rescue missions it had never registered quite how much danger she had experienced and now she decided she must not allow her mind to focus upon any days other than the present. Nowadays Kitty found hope was not enough to survive on. She and hundreds of other people were the victims of war in so many ways, and after years of being told to hate their enemy, it was an adjustment to see that the majority of the prisoners she observed on a daily basis learned new paths of love and gratitude. Kitty had to find a way to survive emotionally after the war. Physical survival was out of her hands due to the random attacks on Great Britain, but she had to be realistic. As her thoughts tumbled over one another, Kitty was suddenly struck with the sense that her hoped-for life with Michael might no longer be a viable or realistic option.

The heart-breaking realisation that she was clinging on to the impossible broke down her protective barrier and she took time to allow the negativity of it all to explode from her in more tears than she had ever shed. Curling up on her bed, she released months' worth of pent-up emotions knowing regardless of what happened she would never forget Michael's warmth, the feeling of his hand in hers, the gentle smile he gave her just before he kissed her, the cheeky grin when he was about to play a prank or tease her gullibility with false facts.

The more Kitty thought of Michael, the more she realised how much she missed the little things about him, like how his eyebrow lifted to show how impressed he was when she completed a difficult rescue task. It was his way of communicating his approval and praise. She recalled his lips, white when hungry, pink after kissing, narrow and tight when angered – a rare occurrence. She longed to stroke the dark hairs on his forearm once again, and feel the firm muscles beneath his shirt, to hear his heartbeat as she rested her head on his chest. She wanted life back to before D-Day. Not necessarily before the war because that would mean she may never have met him, but to the days when they ambled along leafy lanes, cycled along the promenade, sat talking along a riverside watching a pair of moorhens skim across the water to build their nests. Even the moments spent rescuing someone from a bombed building had brought them close. She wanted those days back again, but Kitty's heart lurched when the memories brought to the surface the knowledge that those days were long gone.

Whichever country won, her hope of a husband and children would be clouded by the promises made with Michael, and it would be years before she would be truly able to release the love she had for him. Another man would have large shoes to fill.

After hours of restless sleep, Kitty awoke still tired from coming to terms with the sudden emotional barrage she had experienced, but she wasn't prepared for the war to take everything from her. It was time to start making plans for where she wanted to go after the war, and build on what she had learned during it, but Kitty knew in her heart of hearts she would never return to live in Parkeston. She was no longer the naïve girl she had been when she left the village environment and suspected she would feel suffocated by any expectations her uncle might have for her. She was all the blood family he had left in life now, and the present situation meant he had no voice on what she could do with her life, but it worried Kitty that he may become too overprotective if she returned to live under his roof.

Kicking off her covers and shivering her way to the bathroom, Kitty was reminded of her childhood baths in front of the living room fire, when her aunt would place a wooden clothes horse around the tin bath to give Kitty privacy whilst her aunt continued peeling vegetables for the family meal. Kitty knew she wanted to bring that element into her life after the war. To have a roaring fire with her children bathing whilst she peeled vegetables. She wanted a family man they all loved and adored to walk into the room making jokes and brightening up life in general. But Kitty sensed her children in the bath dream was just that – a dream never to be realised. Life had become far too complex to cling to dreams. It was time for Kitty to let go and find a means of healing her broken heart.

Chapter Ten

'Finished sulking?' Louisa's voice sniped at Kitty as they passed each other along the pathway to the medical quarters.

Kitty ignored the jibe and continued walking to work, trying hard to admire the patterned fretwork of spider webs laden with a light frost clinging to the metal railings surrounding the camp. Resisting the temptation to turn around and try to make peace with Louisa, Kitty stuck to her determination to keep her distance for fear of saying something she might regret.

'Thanks for gossiping about me,' came another snapping, harsh-voiced comment and, before Louisa could come at her with more nasty statements, Kitty's self-imposed restraint caved in. She turned around to face her. Although they were several yards apart Kitty could see the anger in Louisa's face. Behind her was the outline of dark, leafless tree branches reaching upwards and the scene was as stark and as menacing as Louisa's voice. A tremble of unrest and discomfort shimmied over Kitty's flesh.

'I've gossiped to no one. In fact, I've barely spoken to anyone recently, so keep your accusations to yourself. I've arranged our shifts to keep us apart and I've noticed I sleep alone in our quarters now, so assume you have made other arrangements.' Kitty inhaled and released a breath before she responded firmly and calmly.

'And that is supposed to mean what exactly?' Louisa asked.

'What I said, I assume you have moved home or have another place to stay,' Kitty replied.

'You mean with *Hans*,' Louisa said with heavy sarcasm. 'Just because your own man is sick in the head and not around doesn't mean you have the right to spoil the fun for others.' Louisa tapped her head with her forefinger to emphasise her statement about Michael's injury and Kitty's temper rose, but she refused to allow herself to have a public spat with an overdefensive colleague. She spoke with a steady voice, softer than she felt Louisa deserved, but firm enough to get her message across.

'Don't be ridiculous, of course I don't mean Hans. It is impossible given he's a prisoner of war. No, I just assumed you had returned home or are living with a friend off camp. I've tried protecting Hans from trouble, but I can't protect you if you turn against me for something I haven't done. Any gossip has nothing to do with me, so start looking at your behaviour and wonder who else might have noticed your attachment to him.' Kitty turned to continue the way she had originally been headed and walked away. Her hands trembled with the cold, and she tugged her gloves from her bag. Louisa had upset her with her accusations and it irritated Kitty to think her friend thought so little of her.

'If I find out it's you, I'll—'

Louisa never finished her spat-out sentence and Kitty continued walking trying to calm the pounding in her chest.

The day had started grey and miserable with the declining weather, and now it felt as if her mood had absorbed some of the dullness of the day. Not bothering to lift her drooping shoulders, or find something else in nature to remind her that the world was still beautiful, Kitty walked into the medical unit and simply nodded and spoke only where appropriate during the handover. She was in no way ready for small talk, she needed to calm down first.

Gathering items from a storage cupboard, Kitty set about packing gifts into boxes for the prisoners. Back at the end of November, local people had collected items to give to the prisoners for Christmas Day boxes, the effort organised by a team of volunteers who visited the camp. Kitty looked at the vast array of woollen socks, packets of cigarettes and bars of soap made from small pieces of leftovers mixed and melted together. Even well-worn books were treated as treasures to thrill on the big day, and she worked methodically placing the soap into small, knitted pouches made by herself and others on the Christmas volunteer team. She set up at one end of the ward, choosing to work alone, and after a while she found the work therapeutic after her run-in with Louisa. Thinking over their conversation, she realised that someone else inside the camp had obviously seen the pair looking cosy together. They must have mentioned it to another and then the gossip had landed at Louisa's feet, causing her to hit out verbally at the only person with whom she had shared her secret. It hurt Kitty to think Louisa thought so little of her that she would think her capable of putting a friend into a difficult situation.

Kitty packed at a methodical pace, steady and focused, but her mind drifted on and off assessing the reality of Louisa's accusation. It was clear that their friendship was fractured and beyond repair. Louisa's cruel words about Michael were unkind and there was no coming back from the hurt she had inflicted upon Kitty, so she decided she would leave the pair to their own devices and the suffering that would come once their prohibited relationship was exposed. Kitty understood that love cannot be stopped once it found hearts to bond together, but Louisa had a responsibility to keep Hans – and herself – safe from reprisals, which to Kitty meant keeping a distance until after the war.

'Can I help ma'am?' a male's voice said behind Kitty as she lifted one of the completed boxes into an empty cupboard at the far end of the room.

'You certainly can, Jimmy,' Kitty replied as she placed the box on the shelf. 'There's another fifty over there,' she said, pointing to a stack of boxes lining a wall. She turned around and gave him a smile. He was the first person she had spoken with when she arrived, and he had always watched over her from that day. It was discreet, but she knew he would be on the perimeter of any place she walked alone.

'Have you just arrived?' she asked.

'No, I've been on guard duty for the past two hours and on patrol before then,' Jimmy replied. He gave her a smile and looked around the room, which suddenly unnerved her.

'Not many patients at present. You must all be exhausted after the influenza spread so fast,' he said. 'I'm grateful I didn't catch it, but Scottie did and his chest hasn't been the same since. He's still on sick leave.'

'It certainly kept us on our toes, but thankfully we got through it without losing anyone. I thought I would make the most of the quiet and get these done,' Kitty said, lifting another box.

Jimmy followed suit and walked behind her. 'Is Nurse Barker not helping you?' he asked and something in the tone of his voice suggested what Kitty had feared the moment he said he'd been on patrol earlier – he had heard Louisa that morning.

'No, we work different shifts nowadays, spreading our expertise,' she said with a light laugh.

Lifting more boxes, Jimmy gave her a side glance and raised his eyebrows.

'I think it is probably wise; you keeping your distance,' he said.

Pushing her box into place and standing back to allow him to stack his, Kitty thought about how to respond. It was obvious he had heard about Hans and Louisa, and maybe even knew more than Kitty about the situation, but she could not be the one to clarify any suspicion he may have.

'Keeping my distance? We are on different duties and rarely see anyone, there's nothing wise about it on my part, I just do as I am told,' she said, keeping a steady, light tone when what she really wanted to say was for him to keep his nose out of other people's business.

'You both do so much with the prisoners, helping them with their hobbies. I saw a portrait of you one of them had scribbled out and several of Nurse Barker, but she was in mufti, not uniform like yourself,' he said. Kitty caught a hint of sly questioning in his voice, and it irritated her. She guessed he was trying to catch her out and get to Hans. Perhaps it was self-interest, and he had a soft spot for Louisa.

'We agreed to help when we were off duty. I wanted a picture in uniform for my uncle as a Christmas gift,' she said swiftly and began packing more boxes. 'I suspect Louisa wanted a few for family members but out of uniform. There, at last, I've finished, time to reorganise the medicine cabinet. Thank you for your help, Private Rankin.' Kitty's voice dismissed the soldier, and for once she was grateful to use her higher status to get herself out of a difficult conversation.

'Ma'am,' Jimmy Rankin said and turned heel after he had saluted.

For the rest of her shift, it niggled away in her mind that he might have been the one to drop the gossip around the other soldiers and staff on the camp. She needed to speak with Hans to warn him he needed to be extra cautious about Louisa's visits.

Chapter Eleven

As Kitty approached Hans, she saw him frown. She guessed she was not going to be a welcome visitor.

'Hello, Hans, how are you?'

His silence was deafening and he shifted his body away from Kitty as he focussed intently on the piece of wood he was working on in front of him.

'Ignoring me won't make the problem go away, Hans. Louisa is angry with me as well, but it is not fair. I have protected you both by keeping your secret. Someone else has seen you together and told others. You are at risk of being moved from the camp and Louisa will lose her job if Sister Craven finds out,' she whispered urgently whilst pretending to admire his work. Other prisoners looked on and she smiled at them, then returned her attention to Hans.

'You must stop Louisa from coming here again. Understood?' she asked.

Hans continued to work the piece of wood in his hand, ignoring her completely.

'I know you understand English *and* know what I am talking about, so do not be so rude. Things can become quite uncomfortable around here if you are found out. Wherever you and Louisa sneak off to for privacy, stop going there. Someone has seen you,' she whispered urgently.

She picked up a carved bird on the pretext of admiring it and turned it over in her hand. Hans laid down his work and took the bird from her.

She had been dismissed without him saying a word.

'Well, at least you can't say I didn't try to help you,' she said and walked towards another prisoner making a picture frame, then another staining a piece of cloth with a berry juice of some kind. She admired each item to keep her visit as normal as possible, then left the building. As she did so she spotted Jimmy Rankin walking away from a window at the far end.

'Busy on patrol I see, Private Rankin,' she called out and waved. She noted the flush of his cheeks and his blush confirmed he had followed and spied on her.

'My commissioned goods are coming along nicely, I'll have some lovely gifts to take to Yorkshire for Christmas,' she said with a cheery lift to her voice and walked towards him with the intention of leading him away from the building. 'Isn't it sad when the war brings out talents hidden by everyday life in peacetime. Do you have any hobbies?'

Jimmy Rankin walked beside Kitty towards her residential quarters and gave a low whistle, which Kitty recognised as a bird song.

'That's the only talent I have, given my army skills are no use anywhere else,' he said bluntly.

'Impressive. I am sure once the war is over you could get

work on a radio sharing those skills,' she said, still keeping her voice light and friendly. As they reached the huts Jimmy saluted her and walked away. Kitty watched as he strode towards the canteen, and she wondered if he was about to spread a bit of gossip about her visit to Hans. She also wondered if he was sweet on Louisa and if it was jealousy making him watch Hans so closely.

Back in her hut she pulled a chair beside the heater and wrote a short note to Louisa.

Louisa,

As I mentioned, you have directed your anger at the wrong person. I suggest you speak with Hans as he has also ignored my warning. I think a soldier is watching you both. I will not name him, but please know that I have good reason to mention this. You will lose your job and Hans will be shipped elsewhere and neither of you will be able to communicate with one another. I am only doing this as we were once friends and shared nice times together. I will make this the last piece of communication with you unless we are scheduled to work together.

Kitty

Folding the letter and placing it in an envelope she wondered how it could be given to Louisa without running the risk of anyone else reading it, eventually deciding that she would wait for Louisa after work and hand it to her personally.

Shortly after the shift finished, Kitty saw Louisa exit the sick bay and the two guards who checked staff in and out eventually moved away.

'Louisa,' Kitty called out softly.

With an over-the-shoulder glance, Louisa shook her head and carried on walking. Kitty rushed to catch up with her.

'Louisa, take this,' Kitty said, catching her breath and holding out the letter.

'I want nothing to do with you. You gossip about what you don't know,' Louisa said spitefully.

Still walking at speed, Kitty saw the night lights flick on as the camp prepared for the evening.

'If you won't read my note then listen to my words. I think a soldier in this camp is following your every move and is ready to get Hans removed as soon as he can. He spied on me when I visited Hans today,' she said in a rush.

Louisa stopped walking. 'You went to see Hans. Why?'

'To try and tell him to stop you both getting into bother and him being taken away. You know it will happen, Louisa. If you keep meeting in secret it won't do you any favours. Sister Craven is a stickler for keeping the rules. Anyway, Hans doesn't seem to care what happens to either of you,' Kitty replied. 'Sadly, he ignored me.'

'Good. I'll do the same,' Louisa said and brushed Kitty's arm aside as Kitty held out the letter again. 'I suggest we just carry on keeping our noses out of other people's business and you stay away from us both.'

Kitty watched as Louisa walked down the exit pathway of the camp. Kitty stuffed the letter into her coat pocket and returned to her room where she hauled out an extra blanket and settled down in a seat by the wood burner to read a copy of Dickens's *A Christmas Carol*.

About an hour in, a tapping on the door disturbed her reading. Puzzled, she hitched the blanket around her shoulders and opened the door to find Scottie standing beside Louisa. Or rather, attempting to hold Louisa upright.

'Scottie, are you ill again? And what are you doing with Louisa, what is the matter with her?' she asked.

'Sorry to disturb you, but this one needs a bit of help,' he said and nodded to Louisa, who was now leaning against his shoulder. Kitty looked out over their heads to check no one was watching this scene. 'Is she drunk?' she asked.

'The lassie's not in a good way. I've tried to walk her here, but had to carry her where we weren't seen. I ken she's not livin' on campgrounds, but I don't think her reputation will survive with the landlady she lives with if she were to return home like this. Help me get her inside… Err, sorry, ma'am, would you mind?'

Kitty stepped down the three steps and went to the other side of Louisa. As she took her arm, the girl's legs gave way.

'Hold ma rifle, I'll lift her in, just keep an eye oot,' Scottie said.

Once inside, Kitty closed the door and pointed to Louisa's bed. 'That's normally hers. Best she sleeps on it as it is closer to the bathroom. I'll fetch a bucket. She looks dreadful, where's she been?' she asked.

Scottie laid Louisa on the bed and retrieved his rifle.

'I think she has been sneakin' around with that Jimmy Rankin – Private Rankin. He seems to be wherever she is just lately. I've a feelin' she's enjoyed a drop of the strong stuff,' he said.

'Private Rankin has been hanging around me today, so I wonder if he is hoping to get closer to her by mixing with her friends. I swear he snooped on me through the window when I went to the prison woodworking hut to check on my Christmas purchases. It unnerved me if I am honest, where else is he peering through windows? His duty is to patrol, not peek,' Kitty said in the hope she could get Jimmy Rankin moved from the residential guard, thereby reducing the danger of Louisa being caught out with Hans. 'And if he is plying young women with strong drink, well, do we report it?'

Scottie walked towards the door. 'No, leave it with me. You'll not have any problem with young Rankin. Trust me. Hope the lassie's heid is braw by morning,' he said and left the building.

'Thanks,' Kitty called after him, noting all formalities had been dropped between them. He was a gruff one but over time Kitty had seen the softer side of him and by tomorrow she would ensure Louisa would always be grateful to Scottie.

Chapter Twelve

A harsh wind whistled through the gaps in the windows and Kitty pulled her bedclothes tightly around her. She was reluctant to get out of bed. Louisa had snored all night and twice she had groaned. Kitty had anticipated the worst, but Louisa had simply turned over in the bed.

After bracing herself to use the freezing bathroom, Kitty jumped out of bed, grabbed her dressing gown and tiptoed past Louisa. When she returned, she noticed Louisa had turned the other way and had her blankets over her head. Kitty went to the last bunk, where she had placed the spare bedding in the hope others might move into the unit, and pulled two of the blankets across Louisa. She dressed and placed the freshly filled kettle onto the small hob on the wood burner, then set about preparing a mug with Camp Coffee. She was not a fan of the sweet, syrupy, chicory brand, but it usually served as a hearty warmer before heading over to the canteen for breakfast.

A loud groan came from Louisa and Kitty watched as she

dashed from her bed to the bathroom. After several moments, Louisa rushed back to the bed and pulled the covers back over herself. Kitty wondered if Louisa knew where she was, but kept quiet, leaving her to sleep. The girl was not the friendliest person lately, even without a hangover, so she was probably best avoided when she had one.

Writing a note saying that Louisa was experiencing an upset stomach due to eating a slice of bad ham, she tiptoed out of the hut and took it to Sister Craven.

'Does she need to be taken into sick bay? Food poisoning can be quite debilitating,' Sister Craven asked after she had read the note.

Shaking her head Kitty smiled. 'No, I think I can help her before my shift and then watch over her afterwards. She should be fit for duty by tomorrow,' she said.

Sister gave a nod. 'In which case I will put her on duty with yourself and move Jenkins to the morning. It will give her time to recover. Don't go on duty this morning, stay and care for Nurse Barker. We have no inpatients, and the German medic will work in your place,' she said.

Not wanting to create a work problem, Kitty nodded her agreement. 'I'd best get back to her. If there are any changes I will report back. Thank you, sister,' Kitty said, and returned swiftly to her quarters.

Seated on the edge of her bed, a pale-faced Louisa looked up as Kitty entered the room. She scowled.

'What am I doing here? It's freezing,' she said in a grump and Kitty decided it best to ignore her. Walking over to her bed she pulled off her cape, grabbed her thickest cardigan and a blanket, then went to the wood burner and put more wood inside watching the flames rise before she looked across at Louisa.

'Scottie dropped you off here last night,' she eventually replied.

Louisa slid off the bed and swore loudly.

'Cold feet or headache?' Kitty asked sarcastically.

Louisa stayed quiet, looking about her floor space.

'Your shoes are cleaned and in your locker; they were in a bit of a mess,' Kitty said. 'The rest of your clothes are here, drying, as they were also a mess. You can borrow something of mine if you have nothing left in your wardrobe. There are spare woollen long socks at the end of the bed, but they are all I have to help until your stockings are dry. What happened to you, Louisa?'

Louisa said nothing as she reached to the end of the bed and pulled on the socks, then found her shoes. She wrapped a blanket around her and walked warily towards the fire.

Kitty poured a hot drink for her and held it out, but Louisa shook her head.

'I don't think I can face it just yet – thank you,' she said, though Kitty noted she had only added the "thank you" as an afterthought.

'Are you going to share what happened? You were extremely drunk,' Kitty said.

Curling up onto the chair beside the fire, Louisa shrugged her shoulders.

'Nothing,' came the blunt reply and Kitty stared at her.

'Nothing? You get so drunk you have to be carried back here by Scottie, pass out and I have to clean you up and dress you, but nothing happened,' said Kitty.

Louisa shifted in her seat and her bottom lip wobbled.

'Speak to me. You know I am not the gossip you accused me of being, so tell me what happened,' Kitty pleaded.

Giving a loud sigh, Louisa rose to her feet.

'Jimmy Rankin tried to kiss me,' she said. 'He gave me a drink of lemonade and tried to kiss me. I slapped his face, and he pushed me over. He called me dreadful names. My lemonade tasted normal but once I finished it, I knew there was a problem.'

'Where were you?' Kitty asked.

Louisa was studying the clothes Kitty had laid out on a vacant bed.

'Behind the empty units just beyond the canteen,' she said in a softer voice.

Kitty watched as Louisa tugged on a corduroy skirt and navy jumper.

'Suits you better than me,' she said as Louisa pulled the socks above her knees.

'Thanks, I'll bring them back when I am next on duty,' Louisa said.

'We're on duty together tomorrow afternoon, Sister Craven thinks you are currently recovering from food poisoning,' Kitty said.

Walking back to the fire, Louisa sat back down and pulled a blanket over her legs.

'Thank you. I don't deserve it,' she said. 'Your letter was a kind warning, but I am stubborn. My parents tell me as much.'

Cupping her hands around her mug, Kitty gave a brief nod.

'What you said about Michael was cruel, but I think you have just lost your way and I am willing to try and help you. Right, so you were behind the empty units. What were you doing there? Let me guess, waiting to meet Hans?' she said.

'Not really. I was sent a note to meet him, but when I got there, Jimmy was waiting and said he was a friend of Hans and that Hans had sent lemonade as a treat and that he was sorry he couldn't get away for his evening walk after all,' said Louisa.

'Jimmy knows. He also fooled you into being alone with him. Louisa, he mustn't get away with it! We must tell Sister Craven. Getting you drunk under false pretences, that is sly,' Kitty said, her anger rising.

Louisa pressed her hands together as if in prayer. 'Please, don't say anything to her. Hans will come off worse than me. After I pushed Jimmy away, he left. It's over. Forgotten,' she said.

Kitty got up from the chair and walked around the room, pacing up and down. She looked outside and checked the weather. Thick fog loomed across the fields and did nothing to entice her outside for a walk. She inhaled the fresh air and closed the door.

'Brrr, it's getting colder. I think Scottie will be dealing with Jimmy. He suspects he got you drunk, and you have been courting in secret. He said I was not to worry about reporting Jimmy, he was going to deal with him. It might be best if we leave him to the army and make sure you stay away from Hans to keep him safe,' Kitty said, deciding to take charge of the situation while Louisa was in a calmer state.

'You must be lonely in here,' said Louisa, looking around the bleak hut. The only bright area was Kitty's space where she had a crocheted blanket of many colours her aunt had made laid out on the end of her bed.

'I've got used to it, but some days it would be nice to come off duty and speak to someone,' Kitty replied, sipping her tea and watching Louisa over the rim of the mug.

Louisa yawned and stretched.

'If I go home and fetch my things, I can come back to stay. Keep you company,' she said.

Kitty pointed to Louisa's bed.

'You are going nowhere. If you are seen wandering about, there will be questions. Stay out of sight and sleep. Give me your address and I will go and fetch your things. I assume you don't live too far off camp?'

Louisa nodded.

'Write a note for your landlady and I'll get back as soon as I can.'

Louisa climbed into bed and Kitty prepared herself for the weather outside.

She didn't relish a walk on such a day, but Louisa needed support, so reluctantly she headed to the address Louisa had given her. Once she arrived, she was shocked by the conditions. The camp quarters were far superior. Louisa certainly had a stubborn streak if she was prepared to live in squalor.

'She owes me eight shillings if she is moving out,' the landlady said bluntly and held out her grubby hand.

'She is moving out. Here, I have three and that is all you will receive. I cannot believe this corner of the room is worth even that but, believe me, I will not be returning to bring more money. I will also be informing the army not to use your property to billet their men – I suggest you clean up before you take in another tenant,' Kitty said, using a superior voice to get her point across. She drew on the Annabelle she once knew and her distaste of Mrs Smith's property when they first met –

which was a proverbial paradise in comparison to the room she stood in now.

'Don't give me your hoity-toity ways here. Gimme the money and get out. Her things are over there. Tell her I don't want to see her or her man around here again!' the landlady said in her strong Yorkshire accent, but Kitty understood every word. Her blood ran cold. Louisa had had a man visiting. Surely not Hans?! Grabbing Louisa's bag, Kitty shoved Louisa's belongings inside and rushed from the house.

Once inside the camp gates, Scottie strode over to greet her.

'Let me carry that for you. How's yer patient?' he whispered as they walked past his colleagues in the guard room.

'Better than I thought. I told Sister Craven she had food poisoning, and we are both off duty – well, Louisa is, I am her nurse for the day. Back on shift together tomorrow. That bag is me bringing her back here where she needs to be. The place she stayed was a rundown farm – or should I say a room in a pigsty. Disgusting. I need a bath, ugh.' Kitty shivered and Scottie laughed.

Taking the bag from him and entering her hut, Kitty heard the snores of Louisa and put her finger to her lips.

'Thanks, Scottie. Come back when you are off duty. We need to talk, and I feel I can trust you. She's sleeping it off, so I will read my post and enjoy some time off my feet.'

Chapter Thirteen

Opening a letter from the orphan twins David and Peter Gaskin was always a joy for Kitty. They wrote of antics on the farm with their adoptive family and of their little sister. Eric, the orphan who had joined them and was now their brother, also wrote to her telling of his affection for his newfound family and of the animals he cared for every day.

This time around there was a little picture of a cow drawn by the boys' sister. The children were growing up fast, and Kitty hoped she would get time to visit them and the city of Durham, which meant so much to her and Michael, in the summer. The war had changed and taken so much from so many, but the Gaskin brothers, Eric and the other children she had cared for at Fell Hall had all found new parents and, when they wrote to Kitty, their letters shared nothing but positivity. She fed off their positivity to get her through the hard times. It was all she had to cling to, and the boys always made her laugh.

Kitty laid back on the bed remembering the day she first

met Stanley as a patient with his damaged leg. He and his wife, Jenny, were so kind opening up their home to the orphaned children, until cancer took Jenny, and Stanley committed himself to fighting the enemy.

She rarely heard from Stanley now he was heading up things in the RAF, and since Jenny died, he appeared to have cut ties with the past. Kitty still wrote him letters but never expected many in return.

A groan from Louisa disturbed Kitty's thoughts. She looked across the room and smiled.

'Headache arrived?' she asked her friend who was holding her hands to her head. Louisa nodded her reply.

'I've brewed a pot of tea, fancy a cup?' Kitty asked and again, Louisa nodded.

She shuffled up the bed and leaned against the pillows.

'Did you manage to collect my things?' she asked.

Kitty walked over with a mug of steaming tea and handed it to Louisa.

'I did. I had to hand over three shillings to pay off the landlady – what a dreadful woman she is! I bumped into Scottie, and he asked after you. He is coming to speak with us both soon. Drink your tea. I'll fetch us something to eat from the canteen,' she said.

'I don't deserve your help,' Louisa said.

'That's a conversation for later, drink your tea,' Kitty replied.

———

Upon her return she found Scottie standing outside.

'No reply?' she asked as she approached him.

'Nae. I guessed you were oot. Food?' Scottie said, nodding towards the packages in Kitty's hand.

'Bread and cheese. I recall my uncle swore by a bread and cheese sandwich when he had indulged in a few beers,' Kitty said with a laugh and opened the hut door. Louisa sat on the edge of the bed dressed in her own clothing.

'Hello, Scottie. I think I have you to thank for bringing me home last night,' she said and gave Scottie a beaming smile.

'Aye. You needed the help,' Scottie said shyly and Kitty was taken aback by his sudden change in personality from the robust Scotsman to the humbled male, and she wondered how much he had helped Louisa, how much neither of them had told her.

'Tuck into these and we can talk about what happened and what you want to do about it,' Kitty said and passed Louisa her sandwiches.

'Jimmy is packing 'n is waiting to be shipped out. Th' laddie is trouble. He'll be gone before nightfall,' Scottie said.

Kitty shared a sandwich with him and pulled out a chair by the fire.

'We are grateful, aren't we, Louisa?' she said.

Louisa swallowed her mouthful and wiped her mouth.

'I am grateful for last night – not that I can remember much about it, and I'm grateful to you both for looking out for me. If my parents knew the bother I brought about for myself, they would have me home and working a mundane job somewhere else.'

Kitty busied herself around the room and left Scottie and Louisa together for a while. She had to approach the business about Hans without creating another problem for Louisa and needed a moment to think. She heard Louisa laugh and decided it was time to get the situation sorted out.

'Louisa. I think we need to have a serious talk about your relationship and how far you want it to go in the future. We can move messages around, but sooner or later there will be questions and consequences. As you know I think you are heading down the wrong path,' she said in a soft voice.

Scottie rose to his feet, and Kitty noticed he looked agitated. 'I will see myself out. Jimmy will be gone soon, and I am not sure I am wanting t'take a message to him, nae after the way I found you. I need to stay away from him. If you want to keep speaking with him then you will have to find someone else to help,' he said and walked to the door.

'Wait! Louisa, you had a man visit you at your lodgings, the landlady told me. I am sorry to do this in front of Scottie, but it needs to be addressed. Was it Jimmy?' Kitty asked with urgency in her voice and glanced at Louisa then over at Scottie who also looked to Louisa, waiting for her to answer, his face registering something Kitty couldn't quite put her finger on.

'It wasn't Jimmy,' Louisa eventually said and lowered her head. Kitty gasped.

'Was it...' she asked.

Louisa nodded.

'Good God! Scottie, there is something you should know and because of what Louisa has said there is a serious breach with a prisoner leaving the camp and being out.' She turned to Louisa. 'Was he there all night?' she asked her.

'He came at eleven and left at four-thirty in the morning,' Louisa said her face flushed with shame.

Scottie switched his head between the two of them.

'Are you tellin' me you were collodin' with an enemy prisoner and nae Jimmy?' he asked Louisa. She nodded.

'Did Jimmy find out and blackmail you?' asked Kitty, thinking she already knew the answer.

Again, Louisa nodded.

'He followed Hans one night and threatened to report him unless I met with him, too. He came to the lodging house, but the landlady turned him away as I was on duty. That's when he said about meeting for a drink. I did it to protect Hans,' Louisa said and looked at them both. Kitty glanced at Scottie whose face was now a dark shade of red.

'Scottie found you in a bad state, had Jimmy…' Kitty asked, but Louisa shook her head.

'I pushed him away and threatened to scream when he touched me. He slapped me and called me names, and then I must have been sick and passed out. Please, don't tell on Hans,' Louisa pleaded and looked at Scottie.

'I have to,' he said quietly and put his hand on the door handle. 'I won't say where he went or who he went to see, but we have to hope Jimmy keeps quiet.'

With a sudden movement, which made Kitty jump, Louisa slid from the bed, grabbed her hairbrush and dragged it through her unruly mass, then threw it onto the top of the locker.

'No. Tell on me too. Take me to Sister Craven. Kitty isn't involved in this and she tried to stop me but I never listened. If they find out she knew, she will lose her post and she's a good person. A good nurse. A friend I lost thanks to my stubborn ways. Sister Craven will hear about this but not about Kitty, promise?' Louisa said, moving away from the bed and grabbing her cape from her locker. 'Let's get this over with. Jimmy is not someone who will keep quiet.'

Kitty heard the defeat and resignation in her voice.

'Maybe it is for the best. For you and Hans. And thank you for thinking of me, too,' Kitty said, walking over to Louisa and embracing her.

'Scottie will take care of you; he's got a soft spot for you,' she whispered in Louisa's ear, then she let go of her and turned to Scottie.

'Thank you for protecting us,' she said and watched them leave.

Chapter Fourteen

The days ticked by, and Scottie had not returned with news of Louisa. The message to the sick bay was that she was unwell and had returned home for a recovery period. But Kitty had noticed Sister Craven had crossed Louisa off the working roster for all of the Christmas period, through to the end of the year.

It frustrated her that she couldn't find Scottie or contact Louisa to find out what was happening. She made a brief visit to collect her Christmas gifts Hans had made when she received a message from the workshop supervisor that they were waiting for her, but Hans was nowhere to be seen when she arrived, and she assumed he had been removed. Kitty didn't linger in the room as she felt all eyes were on her. Did the prisoners know she had learned about Hans and Louisa? She wasn't prepared to find out. Louisa had created an uncomfortable situation for Kitty and her Christmas trip couldn't come around fast enough.

Hitching a lift into the village, Kitty spent her day off tracking down postage stamps and writing paper, followed by a long conversation about the food shortages with the lady serving in the small grocery shop who greeted her with a friendly, ''ow do?'

'Very well, thank you,' Kitty replied and continued picking out a few apples to take back with her.

Her purchase led to a discussion about how the prisoners worked hard at vegetable production for the village, and then the woman said the local gossips had heard rumours of an escaped prisoner frightening a nurse from the camp and the woman wondered if it might have been Kitty. Taken aback by the sudden change in conversation, Kitty did her best to dismiss the story by saying the rumour spreading was wrong and all that had happened at the camp was that a young soldier got into bother with his superiors for not working hard enough and was moved to another division. She laughed it off and shifted the topic of conversation by sharing stories of the woodworking skills of many of the prisoners and of how she had commissioned gifts from them for her loved ones. She wondered if the woman had shelf space for some of the smaller items to sell for the prisoners leading up to the festive period, and so took the opportunity to ask.

'My Dolly would be thrilled to find one of those waddling ducks you mentioned beneath the Christmas tree. Duck mad she is, and I know a few of the boys in the village would beg for an aeroplane. I think I can accommodate a few items,' said the woman once Kitty had finished describing what she had seen the men make.

'There are so many other things. Some of the men even have embroidery skills that put me to shame,' Kitty said. 'I will speak to the officer in charge of such things and send him your way. It is hard for people to see the prisoners as no different to us, but when you work caring for them at their weakest point, you realise.'

The woman and two others who had joined them agreed.

'Mind you, he's still determined to take all he can – that Hitler. Dangerous man. Only the other day my Bill told me about those Doodlebugs, V1 – or was it a V2? – anyway some kind of contraption that's killing men from his unit in Antwerp. Thank goodness my man lost his leg and was sent home weeks ago,' one of them said. Kitty thought the man was probably not of the same opinion as his wife about his leg, but she understood the woman's relief that he was home and safe.

'Where you from, nurse?' one of the women asked Kitty with a friendly smile. 'You've got an accent I've not heard before. Southerner, are you?'

'East Anglia. My accent is a soft Essex compared to some who are closer to London,' Kitty said. 'Yours takes a bit of getting used to, but I'm learning,' Kitty said with a giggle and the women joined her with their laughter.

'You courting?' one of the women asked Kitty.

'Give over, Lil, the girl has come to shop not be interrogated,' the shopkeeper said with a laugh.

Kitty felt the warmth of friendship fill the room, something she had missed for some time and was not ready to walk away from, so she was more than happy to share a little something about herself with the village.

'I'm Kitty. Nurse Pattison to those on the camp. And yes, Lil, I am courting. Well, not so much at the moment, but I have a fiancé. A Canadian doctor named Michael,' Kitty said with great pride in her voice.

'Ooh, is he one of those Canadians abroad who have kicked Hitler's behind? Look here, in the newspaper. I was just reading about them.' The shopkeeper tapped a copy of the regional paper and Kitty skimmed the story. The mention of Michael's old division caught her unawares and she hitched a threatening tremble in her throat.

'He was part of them once, but was … um, badly injured, in the head. He's recovering back in Canada, but he trained here in England and considers this as his home. He joined the British Army to serve in the medical corps. We met in Birmingham and joined rescue teams together. Sadly, he may never recover but I live in hope,' Kitty said and a large teardrop dripped onto the counter, just missing the newspaper.

'See what you and your questions and newspapers have done? Poor girl, come here and cry it out,' said the quieter of the women and pulled Kitty to her. After a few seconds of allowing herself to take a breath, Kitty stepped out of the woman's arms.

'I'm sorry ladies, I haven't done that in a while,' she said with a flush of embarrassment. 'It's only that my friend from the camp has recently returned home unwell, so I think a bit of loneliness found its way inside me.'

'Bless your heart, you don't worry yourself about it, we've all been through enough. You are welcome here anytime, understood? Don't fester away up there with sad thoughts, it's no place for a girl like you. Feel free to come and see me anytime. I'm Gladys,' the shopkeeper said with a beaming smile.

'And if Gladys is busy, I live at the end of the street. My girl wants to be a nurse, maybe you can speak to her, point her in the right direction. I could do with the money at home and wanted her to work the factories, but if she wants to volunteer, then life is too short for the young'uns not to follow their dreams. Goodness knows we have to get our country back on its feet, and our men need our help. I'll manage without her, but I'll miss her and that's a fact.'

The woman speaking gave a loud sniff and Kitty hoped she wouldn't cry as the tears were not too far away in her own eyes again. Some were for Michael, but the majority were happy tears. The company of the women around her had given her a warm feeling of friendship again.

'Aw Jane, your Betsy is a darling, she is kind and a born nurse. We'll miss our babysitter,' Lil said.

Kitty had an impulsive moment. 'I'm happy to babysit when I can. I love children. I nursed and cared for many orphans before being sent here. Send a note if ever you need someone and I'll let you know if I am on duty,' she said so fast it left her breathless.

She felt all eyes upon her and gave a brief smile.

'We will have to keep you a secret, Miss Kitty Patterson. Once the village hears of someone willing and able to care for their kiddies, you will never have a day's peace,' Gladys said with a loud laugh.

'I rarely have time for myself, but when I am off duty I have very little to do. I am spending Christmas with my dearest friends in Pinchinthorpe, but unless I am drafted into extra duties, I sit and knit, write letters or go for a walk. Today, I was determined to visit the village and I truly think I was sent this way to meet you all, thank you for befriending me,' Kitty said.

'I believe in fate. I read the leaves, you know,' said Lil.

'Not that there's many left in our teacups nowadays,' Jane said with a laugh. 'But when Lil tells you something, don't disbelieve her. After seven boys, she predicted a girl, and my last was just that, and the sweetest thing she is – a true blessing.'

'Maybe you can read mine one day,' Kitty said politely, not sure she wanted to know what the future held for her as each day brought about a new challenge.

Kitty's walk home an hour later was a slow but pleasurable one. The weather was pleasant although wintry. Woodsmoke filtered across damp fields, crows called out, and a robin tweeted in the hedgerows. Everything Kitty encountered brought with it a contentment, and although she could have waited for the bus or a lift back to the camp, she was pleased she had chosen to walk and fill her lungs with crisp, fresh air. Her heavy basket was laden with treats for her and the Christmas boxes she had mentioned to her new friends, and the weight of loneliness had lifted from her shoulders, but Kitty still longed to see her closest ones and news from Jo was much needed.

Chapter Fifteen

B ack at the camp Kitty saw Scottie at the guard gate and waved.

He saluted her back, which was unusual when he was alone.

As she approached the guard unit he gave a slight shake of his head and stepped out to ask for her identification.

'Keep it formal. I think they're peepin' on me. Ah don't want ye caught up in anythin'. Jimmy's likely told lies about us,' he said. 'Word is the lass in not comin' back.' Scottie spoke so fast Kitty could barely keep up with his accent.

She nodded and took her identity papers from him.

'Speak soon,' she said and walked away. She knew it probably tormented Scottie to not be able to offer to carry her heavy basket, but she understood that Louisa, Hans and Jimmy had put them both in a difficult position and keeping things formal for a while made sense.

Calling into the post room, she was delighted to see a letter from her uncle, and two via the Red Cross, meaning Sarah had written to her – or maybe even Jo. The upbeat feelings she'd had inside since meeting the local women were given a renewed burst and she rushed back to her quarters and placed everything on the bed in readiness for a relaxing few hours. Before she settled down to read her correspondence, she went to speak with the workshop supervisor about the prisoners selling more of their work in the village.

On approaching the unit, Kitty noticed a guard on duty outside, which presented as unusual.

'Afternoon, ma'am. No entry I'm afraid,' the young guard said firmly and moved in front of the entrance.

A loud noise from inside the workshop made her peer around him to try and see through a window, but he took a sidestep preventing her from getting closer.

Kitty gave him a quizzical look.

'What is going on, private?' she asked.

'Sweep through inspection,' came the blunt reply and Kitty guessed she had received all she would hear, and decided to ask Scottie when she saw him again. Her stomach rumbled and Kitty smiled at the soldier.

'Time for the canteen then, I think. I'll speak to the supervisor when I see him again, it was nothing urgent,' she said flippantly and walked towards the canteen wondering what was going on inside the place where Hans had fallen in love with Louisa.

Sipping on a vegetable soup, Kitty sat alone listening to the clatter and chatter going on around her.

'May I join you, ma'am?' a young soldier asked.

Kitty nodded and continued enjoying her meal.

'Another Christmas and we are no better off than in thirty-nine,' the soldier muttered.

Kitty gave him a sympathetic smile.

'My friend Scottie said we are getting closer to winning the war,' the young man said and stared at Kitty when she looked up at Scottie's name.

'Is that the guard at the front gates? He said much the same to me once,' she said, careful not to show she knew Scottie as a friend too. 'I'm surprised you understood him, I struggle with his accent,' she said with a light laugh and returned to concentrate on her food, hoping he would do the same.

'I get him to write things down for me sometimes. Like this note for instance.'

With a sigh, Kitty took the note he held out to her.

'Give a laugh as if I've shown you something funny,' he said.

She gave a giggle, not too loud but enough to suggest what the soldier had mentioned, that he had shown her something funny, then turned her attention to the note.

I need a medical check on my arm. Tell my friend what time you are next on duty. Buchanan.

Kitty smiled inwardly. Scottie had used the name of the place she told him she had once nursed, a Scottish castle he knew well.

'She's funny,' she said and then lowered her voice. 'Early shift. Seven to four, tell him ten o'clock. Your girlfriend has a great sense of humour,' she said, finishing off the conversation with a slightly louder voice.

The soldier gave a laugh and continued eating his food. Kitty lifted her tray and gave him a smile before walking away.

Back in her room she went to her letters and settled down to read them. The peace was only disturbed by the spitting of wood on the burner and Kitty eased open the letter from her uncle.

Dearest Kitty,

I hope this letter finds you well. News from here is that two more lads from the village have grieving parents, which spurred me into writing to you.

I have enclosed a postal order for five pounds as a Christmas gift. Put it into a fund for your future. I can hear you gasp and tell me off but, before you put it into your savings account, treat yourself to something. A new dress, handbag, something you young women always hanker for.

I am spending Christmas with Doreen. I want you to know I loved your aunt very much, but I think I have found a different kind of love with Doreen. She is a good woman and I have spoken to her son James when he came home on leave. I asked him for permission to ask his mother to marry me. He gave us his blessing and I hope you will, too. Your aunt would approve my choice and decision, but only if you gave us your blessing. I will ask Doreen on Christmas Day. I am also letting you know we will more than likely live in her house as it is the larger one. I will give you good notice in case you would prefer to move your things yourself. I wish for you to be at our wedding, and I will let you know as soon as we have set a date. Of course, she has to say yes first!

My dear girl I miss you and know I am always your loving uncle. Be safe and come home to us soon.

Uncle Frank.

Kitty folded the letter and held it against her chest. She wished her uncle nothing but joy in his life, the sort of joy he ensured she had over the years after her parents were killed. Instead of writing to him, she would send a telegram in the morning.

Moving on to the first of the Red Cross letters, Kitty lifted out a single sheet of paper and her heart lifted with excitement when she recognised Jo's handwriting.

Kitty,

How the devil are you? Thanks for your letters; they arrive at random times but are always welcome. I am on the move again but my holiday on foreign shores is never short of excitement. Fireworks and wine. The hotel is cramped and there are far too many guests for my liking, some have four legs, but we get by. We are static at the moment thanks to a few holidaymakers ahead parking their tanks in the way, but we are healthy, and I am in the company of good people. I must say life in America sounds exciting and when this darned war is over, I intend to find out for myself. Come with me, let us go on adventures around the world and kick up our heels before you decide to settle down and have those babies you and Michael want. Talking of your fiancé, I truly hope you always hear nothing but good news about that man. He is a good doctor.

Any news from the crew in Cornwall? What about Trixie, has she slowed down yet? Smithy must be pulling his hair out with her as I bet she is not listening to a word he says and delivering everyone else's babies right up to the point she delivers their own.

Time to fire up and dish out the endless cups of coffee to the thirsty American soldiers.

Much affection my dear friend,

Jo x

Kitty recalled Jo working the drinks vehicle when she and Michael were on a mission and embedded the image in her mind. She had no intention of allowing herself to think of her friend in the thick of the fighting in France.

Opening the second letter delivered by the Red Cross, Kitty sat back to read of Sarah's news.

The handwriting looked different and when Kitty ran her eyes to the bottom of the page she gasped. It was signed 'Lizzie'.

Kitty,

    Thank you for your friendship when we last met. It is always good to have someone from home sending you on your way.

    We are all well here.

    I have a favour to ask. Whenever you visit our mutual friends, please take a walk in the gardens and think of me with kindness. They are always beautiful at Easter.

    I wish you good health,

    Your new friend, Lizzie.

Belle, or Lizzie as she was now known, had written to her from France too!

'What a cheek!' Kitty said out loud to the ether.

She read through the short letter again. Lizzie wanted her to sit in the garden when she next visited Cornwall and the Stargazy Inn. Then she noticed the word 'gardens'. Lizzie wanted her to go to Trebah Gardens and remember Annabelle Farnsworth in a better light.

'I don't think so, Belle … Lizzie … whoever you really are,' she said, looking at the paper.

However, she did think a visit to her friends at the inn for

Easter might be nice, depending on where she might be in the country herself. Kitty did have a feeling that with Louisa gone, she was going to be at the camp for the duration.

Chapter Sixteen

K itty's stomach turned over with anxiety when she saw the summons to see Sister Craven in her office after duty. Had something happened regarding Louisa? Was Kitty herself in trouble for the relationship between Louisa and Hans? She tried hard to concentrate on the steady stream of men walking through the door with minor ailments.

At ten o'clock she saw Scottie walk in and waved him over to her station.

'What appears to be the trouble, Private McLennan?' she asked, pointing to a seat for him to sit down.

'Ach, it is probably nothin' but my ankle is troublin' me, nurse,' he said, saluting before he sat.

'Slip off your boot and sock and let me see,' she said.

'I washed the foot and am wearing fresh socks, so don't look nervous,' Scottie said in a loud voice and Kitty laughed.

As she knelt down to inspect his foot, Scottie leaned down on the pretext of looking at it too.

'Your friend is not comin' back. She's in the family way and her parents are coming to find out why she moved out of quarters. Jimmy must have told on her and Hans, the sly b—'

'Thanks, I think I can make up my own name for him,' Kitty whispered before Scottie had time to curse his way through the conversation.

'No doubt they will ask me about it. I've been summoned to speak with Sister Craven at four,' she said, then followed on with a slightly louder voice. 'No swelling. Just a mild sprain. Tighten the boot and it will support you. No running for a week,' she said with a smile as she knew one of Scottie's pet hates was the training hikes they had to take. 'I'll give you a note for your officer, come back and see me tomorrow just so I can check the bruising,' she said.

Scottie pulled his sock and shoe back on and stood up.

'Thank you kindly, nurse.'

Kitty handed him his note and he left. Now she knew what Sister Craven would be asking, she was a little less nervous and more prepared.

At five minutes past four Kitty knocked and entered Sister Craven's office.

'Sit down, Nurse Pattison,' Sister Craven said, and Kitty sat on the seat indicated to her in front of the sister's desk.

'Nurse Barker,' Sister Craven said. 'She left residential quarters some time back.'

Kitty gave a brief nod. 'Yes, sister, she said she had permission to do so and left,' she said.

'Did she give a reason?' sister asked.

Kitty shifted in her seat. On the walk to the sister's office, she had compiled several responses to questions, all offering the truth.

'We had a falling out about a relationship she was forming. I shared my concerns, and she didn't like what I had to say,' Kitty said, squeezing her hands together in her lap to stop them from trembling because she knew the truth would have to be told. If Louisa was expecting Hans's baby there would be trouble for both lovers and for Sister Craven and the senior soldiers involved with guarding the POWs, but Kitty was not prepared to lie. Louisa had been warned on more than one occasion, and the situation was getting worse by the day. With Jimmy involved, and wanting to keep Scottie out of it all, Kitty knew there had to be a point where the problem had to have an ending.

'These concerns of yours, were they based around the man she was seeing?' Sister Craven asked.

'Yes, sister. I pointed out the consequences of continuing the relationship, but she didn't want to hear my opinion. She moved onto a farm on the edge of Malton. A disgusting, rundown building I later found out, when I went there personally to retrieve her things after I persuaded her to come back on camp to live. I paid the landlady three shillings she said was owing, and the woman told me Louisa had had a man visit her there – at night.'

Kitty took a deep breath and looked over at Sister Craven. The woman's usual pink shade was now pale.

'Do you know who the man was, Nurse Pattison?' Sister Craven asked with a level of demanding to know in her voice whilst staring at Kitty, who felt it was almost a challenging stare.

'No. I don't. Well, I don't know for certain, but I have an

inkling it was someone from the camp. One of the prisoners.' Kitty held her breath. She had said it, told a version of the truth. 'I suspected she liked this man when he asked her to pose for a portrait. I approached him and warned him off quite some time before Louisa and I fell out, but neither of them would listen,' she said.

Sister Craven wrote something on a notepad before looking up at Kitty and offering a soft smile.

'Thank you for your honesty, Nurse Pattison. As you can appreciate, this is a serious problem and I do wish you had come to me earlier, before this dreadful event took place,' she said.

Her words infuriated Kitty. Sister Craven sounded as if she was prepared to have a finger point at Kitty for not reporting her suspicions and Kitty was not happy about being blamed when all she had done was try to help.

'I am sorry you feel that way, sister. However, I only had my suspicions and when both denied it, I thought nothing more of it. I cannot sit and take the blame for anything that followed. I lied about her food poisoning, yes, but it was because I did not know what Jimmy Rankin had done beyond suspecting he had attempted to drug her. When she recovered she told me she was moving back into quarters and was going to think about who to speak to about what had happened,' Kitty said without drawing breath and her temper teetering on the edge, giving her tone an annoyed ring to it that she had not intended.

Sister Craven continued writing on her notepad and it gave Kitty time to calm down and unclamp her fingers. She sat in the silence of the room and reflected upon what had just happened. What with the Belle spy situation, then her Lizzie secret, Meryn and her baby's father abandoning her, Michael's injury, and her aunt's death, Kitty hoped the Louisa drama she found herself involved in would have a supportive family outcome and life might finally leave her to follow a calmer path.

She watched as Sister Craven laid down her pen.

'I have given it some thought, Nurse Pattison, and my view is that you had your suspicions, aired them with both parties who chose to ignore you. In your innocence, you assisted Nurse Barker after finding out she had been duped by Private Rankin. Please consider the matter closed.' She smiled reassuringly at Kitty. 'I must ask for your discretion. It is best you distance yourself from the situation and have no contact with your colleague. What you have told me is much the same as what Private McLennan told his sergeant. He said he found her drunk and took her to her quarters where you offered her nothing but wise words and kindness. He reported his concerns about Private Rankin potentially having made an attack on Nurse Barker, which led to the investigation.'

'Thank you, sister,' Kitty said, rising to her feet, relieved the meeting had a final outcome. Her hands stopped trembling and as she went to leave, the sister called her back.

'I am sorry but I did not realise you were alone in quarters; I am wondering if it might be best if I arrange lodgings outside of camp. There will not be a replacement for Nurse Barker as the sick bay is not busy enough to warrant another nurse and as the German medics have become a useful support to our doctor when the beds are full, I plan to keep you on permanent day duty. What do you think about taking a room in a pleasant house and being granted a bicycle to transport you to work?'

Kitty knew the question was not a question, it was a telling.

Sister Craven was removing her from camp to make life more comfortable for them both. Kitty was not sure whether to be offended by the fact that the sister thought she might be tempted to follow Louisa's path, or to be grateful she was to have company in a pleasant home. Or at least that is what Kitty hoped would be the end result of her agreeing to live under the watchful eye of a landlady.

Sick bay the following morning was stale and stuffy, and the sunshine and promise of fresh air lured Kitty outside for a short spell. As she opened the door she noticed Scottie walking towards her.

'Good morning, Private McLennan,' she said pulling her cape closer around her. 'Chilly this morning.'

Scottie gave a smile. 'Morning, nurse.' He moved closer and gave a glance around, then lowered his voice. 'Ah hear it's a' brushed under the door mat. Ah just happened to be on guard duty outside my sergeant's office, ah think he arranged it, so he did nae have to make' up a fairy-tale to keep me happy. The folks were told unless they want a scandal they had better take the disobedient daughter home with them. The camp has done all they could to halt Louisa getting into bother but she was not prepared to listen or obey. They more or less said she had pushed herself on the prisoner and flirted with Jimmy. I'm feelin' sorry for the lassie, but there's some you canna help see the way,' he said.

Shaking her head, she gave a brief look about before speaking. 'I am being moved into lodgings in the village. They are covering up the scandal and removing any possibility I might become a victim or trouble on the camp. I'll be cycling to work. That should be fun in the snow, but at least it will be day shifts only,' she said.

'At least I can stop worrin' about you,' Scottie said and walked into the sick bay. Kitty followed and made a quick inspection of his faked sprain, then dismissed him with another note for an extra two days free from hiking.

'Thank you for worrying about me, Scottie. I hope we can meet again without drama and suspicion. At least I know what a hero looks like up close,' she said. She gave him a tap on his knee when what she really wanted to do was hug the bear of a man with a growl in his voice and a heart as big as his beloved Scotland.

'Ach, it was nothing,' he said and stood tall. 'Always ask for me if you need anything, you hear, anything. I miss my sister, you remind me of her, she joined the Navy and I hope someone is watchin' out fae her wherever she is in the world.'

Kitty saw him out of the sick bay and watched him stride away. Never in a million years would she have chosen him as a friend, but she knew he was one, and one she could trust.

Chapter Seventeen

Kitty jumped from the truck outside her new home and Scottie handed down her kitbag. He joined her at the door of the end-of-terrace cottage holding the small suitcase filled with items to take to Trixie's.

'Thanks, Scottie. The house looks nice; clean windows and tidy garden,' Kitty whispered as she knocked on the door. 'You can go, I think I will be fine here.'

Scottie gave her a nod and a gentle touch of her arm. 'Don't forget lass, if you need me...' he said, and Kitty smiled at the fact he had dropped the formal ma'am now they were away from the camp and spoke to her as a friend.

By the time he had reached the truck, the front door of the house opened, and Kitty turned to look at an elderly lady dressed in a green tartan skirt and a green jumper leaning heavily on a walking stick. The skirt made Kitty smile – Scottie would approve – and she turned to give him a quick wave goodbye before addressing the woman she assumed to be her new landlady.

'Mrs Stamp?' she asked.

'That's me, and I take it you are Nurse Pattison. Sister Craven spoke to me about you being alone when you are not on duty. Come in, you will never be alone in this house. You are my only tenant, but the curious will keep coming. My granddaughter and her three will be the first, you mark my words.'

Mrs Stamp spoke all the while as she ushered Kitty through the neat hallway towards the stairs. Her accent was definitely Yorkshire and Kitty guessed she was probably born in the village.

'Your room is at the front. It used to be two, but my son knocked them into one years ago. The bathroom is downstairs but there is a private toilet at the end of the hallway up there,' she said, pointing up the staircase. 'I'll put the kettle on while you take your things to your room. I sleep down here, in the back room, as my hips can't cope with stairs anymore.'

Entering her room, Kitty felt a sudden rush of emotion. The eiderdown draped over the bed was identical to the one from her family home. The welcome could not have been any warmer. The room was large and airy, with well-structured oak furniture, and spotlessly clean. Her aunt would have approved. Unpacking her things and making use of the small closet toilet at the end of the landing, Kitty was ready to go downstairs and get to know Mrs Stamp.

She tapped on the kitchen door and entered. Another spotless room.

'Come in. Sit down my dear,' Mrs Stamp said with a kindly smile.

'Thank you. And thank you for allowing me to stay in your lovely home,' Kitty said with genuine gratitude.

A delicate cup painted with roses was placed in front of her and in the saucer were two plain biscuits.

'You are more than welcome, Kitty. When Sister Craven came to me to enquire after the room and explained you were alone in an enormous hut with your only friend no longer working there, I told her I was more than happy to accommodate you. Your reference from her is glowing. You might prefer not to return after you hear my house rules, but I am certain we will get along and be good companions in no time.'

'Thank you. I enjoy a quiet home and my work at the camp. My fiancé is injured and recuperating in Canada, my best friend is driving in France, and my other friends are in Cornwall and Pinchinthorpe. My colleague recently left and there is to be no replacement so Sister Craven has been extremely kind in finding me somewhere like this,' Kitty said sweeping her arm around her. 'And you are kind to take me in.'

Mrs Stamp gave a sigh.

'I am sorry about your fiancé. I have a feeling you will be a good fit in my home, Kitty. More tea?' she asked.

———

'Mrs Stamp's order?' Gladys said as Kitty stepped inside the grocer's.

Kitty burst out laughing.

'Gracious me, I only moved in an hour ago. The tongues have been wagging fast! Yes please, she asked me to pick it up. I will use my ration card if you could add a few extra things please, Gladys,' Kitty said.

'Lil found out from Mrs Stamp's granddaughter that a nurse from the camp was moving in and we all hoped it would be you, Kitty. And here you are with your bright smile. Mrs Stamp is a good woman, and you will be a good companion for her,' Gladys said, and tapped the basket in front of her. 'Be careful with this, there are two extra eggs from my own chickens, one each for your breakfast. A "welcome to the village" gift.'

'That's kind of you, Gladys. Thank you. I have a feeling I won't be so lonely anymore, take care,' Kitty said as she left the shop. The short walk to her new home was one filled with smiles and the odd 'How do' greeting from passers-by. As she slipped her key into the front door she heard children laughing and Kitty realised it was a happy sound she had not heard in a very long time.

'Here she is, everyone meet Kitty, my new tenant,' Mrs Stamp said as she entered the kitchen, and Kitty smiled at the three children who were looking up at her from beneath the large table. A young girl of around ten crawled out and jumped to her feet, taking the basket from Kitty.

'Granny said you were pretty, she is right. I wish I had curls in my hair,' she said.

Kitty giggled. 'Thank you. When the air is damp my hair curls. Apparently, my mothers did the same.'

'Why are you here?' a little boy who Kitty guessed was around seven in age said as he joined his sister. 'Did you have a bomb on your house?'

'Clive, no bomb talk tonight. I told you, Kitty works just outside the village as a nurse. Irene, put the basket in the pantry for now, there's a good girl. Now, let me get to your little sister before she brings the tablecloth down with her,' Mrs

Stamp said and went to bend with difficulty to the floor to retrieve a crawling child.

'Let me, Mrs Stamp,' Kitty said and knelt down, putting her arms out and allowing the baby to crawl into them.

'That's Alice, our baby sister,' Clive said.

Kitty stood upright with the baby tugging at her hair. She eased the little plump fingers away.

'It's lovely to meet you all,' she said.

'You haven't met me yet,' said a short, slim woman in her early thirties walking in through a door off the kitchen. 'I'm Pat, the mother of these three. Granny, I've brought a few logs inside as I noticed your basket is nearly empty.' Pat held her hand out to Kitty. 'Granny is a stickler for time, so make sure you are up at six every morning to fill the basket – she'll have you chopping logs in no time.' Pat winked at Kitty.

'Less of thy cheek, young lady. Get these children home and tell that husband of yours to have a good journey back to barracks,' Mrs Stamp said and gave her granddaughter a hug.

'Nice to meet you, Pat,' Kitty said, handing over Alice.

When the family had left, Mrs Stamp eased herself into a large wing-backed chair and sighed.

'That poor girl is worn out. Her mother-in-law lives in the next village and is in a sorry state – not long for this world – and my Pat's husband has finished compassionate leave, so must return to barracks and head for France in the morning. Pat works factory hours making goodness knows what for the Air Force, and the children come here for an hour to give her a break twice a week. I teach them English and sums, well, what little I can remember and read to them. It is the least I can do as my son passed away and his wife remarried and moved to

India. Pat chose to stay with me until she married. We tick along,' she said.

By the evening Kitty and Mrs Stamp had exchanged life stories and eaten a meal of mutton stew. Kitty went to bed with a positive mind and a contented belly.

Chapter Eighteen

The temperature had dropped overnight, and Mrs Stamp insisted Kitty wore several layers of clothing for her journey to Pinchinthorpe. She gave Kitty a small packed lunch to take with her.

'Take this bait box and flask. I've travelled on the bus for several miles at this time of year and it is not a warm journey. Especially near the moors,' Mrs Stamp said and handed Kitty a pair of navy-blue knitted gloves with a pretty cream cuff edging. 'I've not wrapped them for Christmas as you need them now. Have a safe journey and I look forward to hearing about your Christmas with your friends.'

Touched by her generous gift and kind words, Kitty felt a swell of emotion towards her landlady.

'They are pretty, and I will make good use of them, thank you so much. Merry Christmas for tomorrow. Enjoy your time with the family,' Kitty said and hugged her.

The short time she had lived with Mrs Stamp had brought Kitty nothing but contentment and a calm she had longed for in her life. At work Kitty smiled and gave her best to each task sent her way. She cycled there and back with a struggle at first, but soon she felt fitter than ever and looked forward to springtime when her surroundings would share their beauty.

In the evenings she read out loud to her new friend, and they both worked on a large jigsaw of an apple orchard in springtime. Whenever Kitty returned home from work Mrs Stamp greeted her with a beaming smile and Kitty's tea of cheese on toast was served on the dot of five. Kitty ate her main meal at one o'clock at the camp, so Mrs Stamp insisted on serving Kitty a tasty tea, much as a grandmother would a grandchild. Some days the young children visited, and a packet of cards entertained them all.

A few days before Kitty was due to visit Trixie, Scottie had returned from leave and brought back a wrapped package from Scotland. His mother had made a large batch of shortbread and he chose to share some with Kitty and Mrs Stamp over his colleagues. His generous gift was well received and treated with respect. Mrs Stamp served the biscuits on one of her best plates with a small glass of sherry for an early Christmas celebration together. When Scottie returned to the camp, Kitty sat reading beside the fire, and Mrs Stamp darned socks belonging to the children. As they sat in the comfortable silence Kitty forgot the war and fell into a simple evening of friendship without a care in the world.

On the day of her trip to spend Christmas with Trixie, the bus arrived on time and Mrs Stamp waved her off, insisting the short walk to and from the bus stop would make her appreciate the warmth of her home.

Mist rolled across the hillocks and fields on either side of the bus, thickening in the narrow lanes. The bus driver took it steady, and the conductress predicted another night of thick fog.

Kitty relaxed in her seat putting her trust in the female driver and glanced at the other passengers nearby. Elderly men and women, a few women dressed in various uniforms and three soldiers either chatting or looking out of the window. All were releasing clouds of vapour as they spoke.

Her journey was to take about two hours and Kitty ensured she had plenty of reading material in her bag.

By the time they made it to the outskirts of Guisborough, the fog had thickened, and the driver became concerned about the darkening skies.

'My last stop with be the next one, but I am not sure if the local village service will be running. There's one thing driving in a blackout, but this pea-soup sky is deadly.'

Kitty's heart sank when she heard the driver call out the news.

'Excuse me.' She beckoned to the conductress. 'How far is Pinchinthorpe from the last stop? If the bus isn't running, I will have to walk,' Kitty said.

'Ee lass, in this fog you are taking a chance walking there. It is a good half hour,' the conductress replied.

When they arrived at their final destination, the driver wished them all a Merry Christmas and despite the gloom outside the bus gained a cheery air when everyone returned the festive greeting.

Kitty alighted from the bus and with a sigh headed to the bus depot across the road. To her disappointment, the clerk informed her the last bus for Pinchinthorpe left an hour previous and due to the adverse weather conditions there would be no further buses until daylight the following day –

around seven in the morning, depending on the fog. The taxi was also avoiding travelling into the countryside.

Kitty had no choice but to walk. She hitched her kitbag into a comfortable position in her left hand and did the same with the heavier suitcase in the right. After establishing the directions, she took a slow but steady walk in the limited visibility. Fortunately, it was not dark and some areas between hedgerows were free from the fog and Kitty could just about establish where she was in the narrow road. Most of the time it was in the centre as she was doing her best to avoid the ditches on either side.

Halfway down one of the roads she heard the thrum of an engine and moved to the right side of the road, stepping to the edge and lowering her bags. She took the moment to rest her aching arms. The noise grew louder, and Kitty anticipated it to pass her by within a few seconds. Her judgement was correct, and the black Ford chugged on by. Envious of the driver sitting in the dry, Kitty smoothed her dripping hair away from her face and picked up her cases. She walked on a few feet and came across the car around a bend. The driver stood beside it and waved to her as she drew closer.

'I thought there was someone standing there, but dared not take my eyes off the road. Darndest thing this fog. Do you need a lift somewhere? I'm heading through Pinchinthorpe,' the man said and tipped his hat in a polite fashion. Kitty could tell by his voice he was not local as he had an accent which suggested he was upper class. She took a few more steps and saw he was around her age and dressed in RAF uniform.

'I am afraid I am rather damp and would ruin your car, but it is kind of you. I am heading for the doctor's surgery on the edge of the village,' she said. 'Visiting friends.'

'The car is not mine and I am certain the Air Force will forgive me if I help a damsel in distress. Climb in. You are quite safe. Charles Armstrong, pilot extraordinaire at your service,' the man said.

'Kitty Pattison, a grateful Red Cross nurse,' she said with a laugh.

The last part of her journey was spent listening to Charles chatter about what he called his 'adventures in the sky'. His bravery was not lost on Kitty though he made light of the dangers he had faced. By the time he had finished telling her about skimming the belly of his plane along the runway home, it was time for them to part company.

'When you are up there Charles, know there is a Red Cross nurse down here extremely grateful your parents brought you up a true gentleman. Good luck,' she said and went to open the door.

'A kiss will be a good luck charm, Kitty. On the cheek,' Charles said with joviality in his voice as he leaned his face towards hers.

'Cheeky Charlie,' she said, pushing his face away and clambering out of the car. She laughed as he jumped out to assist her with her bags drooping his shoulders in playful disappointment. Once he placed her bags by her feet, Kitty reached out and planted a gentle kiss on his lips.

'Take that with you Charles and stay safe,' she said as she walked away.

'Be happy, Kitty Pattison. May the rest of the war be kind to you!' Charles called out and waved. He tooted his horn as he drove away, and a sadness washed over Kitty as she watched him disappear into the fog. His chances of surviving the war were slim, and although some would tell her she was frivolous and wrong, she was happy to have given him his good luck wish. Every hero deserved knowing someone was grateful for their bravery.

The short walk to the surgery was chillier with thicker fog rolling from the hills and Kitty walked as fast as she could, excited to see Trixie, Smithy, Meryn and baby Kedrick once again.

Chapter Nineteen

'Kitty!' An excited Trixie tottered towards Kitty with her arms out wide as Kitty stepped into the residential side of the surgery.

Taking a step back and looking at her pregnant friend, she placed her bags on the floor in readiness to embrace.

'Look at you, Trixie. You are blooming!' Kitty said.

'Smithy keeps singing "Roll out the Barrel" whenever he sees me!' Trixie said, stroking her pregnant mound with affection.

Kitty laughed. 'And he still lives?' she asked with a wide smile and eased her wet shoes off with a shudder. 'The fog makes everything so wet and drab,' she said.

'Go and hang your coat up in the kitchen, it will dry faster in there. You know where your room is; go and change out of your damp things and I'll pop the kettle on,' Trixie said and waddled her way down the hallway. Kitty smiled at her friend's back. As tiny as Trixie was, her hips showed signs of widening and Kitty imagined her with a child on each hip later on down the line. Trixie was born to be a mother.

Once upstairs she entered the room she had stayed in for Trixie's wedding the previous year. Kitty loved the guest room with its wide windows overlooking the hills, except today there were no hills to see so she pulled the curtains to, shutting out the gloom.

The room was warm and cosy with a fire lit in the grate, and her journey was soon forgotten, apart from the short trip in the car with Charles. Any serving member of the forces Kitty had enjoyed a conversation with was never forgotten. She stored snippets of their words in her mind, and transferred them into a little notebook for future reference, never wanting the spirit of friendship to die, even though the chances are the person had not survived the war was probable. Later that evening, when she pulled out the notebook to write her memory of Charles inside, it fell open onto the pages about Belle before she became Lizzie. Kitty shivered and closed the book. Some memories needed to be kept at the back of the mind.

Rough drying her hair with a towel and laying her damp stockings and dress over the back of a chair in front of the fire, she quickly pulled on a pair of wide-legged trousers, a woollen jumper, and socks. Brushing her curls into a tidy state, she rubbed a small amount of moisturising cream onto her face and rushed downstairs to join Trixie.

The kitchen welcomed her with its array of dishes for food preparation, baby clothes drying on wooden racks hanging from the ceiling and an ironing board piled with neatly ironed cot and pram sheets. Kitty's heart swelled with joy. Trixie was preparing her home for her child and doing so with such precision the army would happily employ her in their laundry rooms.

'My word Trix, you are organised!' Kitty said to her friend now sitting down at the kitchen table pouring out tea for them both.

'I can't stop myself,' Trixie said. 'I was warned I would become extra fussy about my home nearing the end of the pregnancy, and have seen it in my patients, but never dreamed it would happen to me. And woe betide anyone trying to move something from its place. It is not worth the argument.' She laughed.

'Can I help you with anything?' Kitty asked.

Trixie put her feet with slightly swollen ankles onto a sagging pouffe.

'You can start by telling me all about your life at the Liverpool home and the camp. And anything else you would like to share... I never get to chat with you like this and for now, it's my treat for Christmas,' Trixie said and sipped her tea.

An hour later Kitty had filled Trixie in on what had happened with Louisa, but did not divulge her meeting with their old colleague Belle, or how she had become Lizzie the Secret Service spy. It was meant to be kept a secret and for the safety of both her and Lizzie, she was not prepared to share it even with the most trustworthy friend.

'I did hear from Belle before her sentencing,' Kitty admitted. 'It is most odd. She has left the inn and all of her personal items to me, with a financial share to be given to Pots, Wenna and Meryn. I will hear from a solicitor when it is all to be formalised. To be honest, I am not sure it is true, but then I am also not sure about Belle being a spy for the enemy, it all seems a bit surreal,' Kitty said.

Trixie shifted in her seat and rubbed her back, then settled back dismissing Kitty fussing around her with cushions.

'I'm comfortable enough, thank you. I am pregnant, not ill,' she said, laughing. 'I cannot believe what you have just told me about Belle and the inn. Good fortune for you all if it is true, but as you say, Belle and her situation was strange. Time will tell if the solicitor gets in touch, then you will know if Annabelle Farnsworth has done something good for others for a change. As you know, I was never fond of her and am amazed by how tolerant of her you were. Some days I thought Jo was going to explode with Belle and her frustrating ways.'

Kitty sat listening, but not wanting to keep the conversation going about Belle for fear of slipping up and sharing the secret, she changed the subject.

'Is Meryn not around?' she asked.

Shaking her head Trixie struggled to her feet. 'She is fetching the last of the shopping for tomorrow. The village is small, but the queues are long, and everyone fusses over her and Kedrick, so it takes her a while to get there and back. She is so excited about you visiting. If you'll excuse me for a moment, I must pay a visit; this baby sits on my bladder. Thank goodness for indoor facilities!' she said, laughing once more as she left the room.

Sitting back in her seat, Kitty allowed the peace of the room to wash over her and reflected upon her luck with both her new home and her loving friends. She closed her eyes and enjoyed the moment.

Chapter Twenty

'Now there is a sight for tired eyes on Christmas Eve.'

Smithy's voice filtered into the room and Kitty jumped to her feet.

'Smithy! You are looking well, how wonderful to see you! Trixie looks ready to burst,' she said. 'Not long now and your child will be here, it's wonderful. Wonderful.'

As they embraced, Trixie came back into the room.

'I see, just as I turn my back...' she quipped and walked over to her husband.

He leaned down and gave her a peck on the cheek and their affection tugged at Kitty's heart. She quashed the envy as soon as it tried to spoil the moment.

A rustle outside the door told them Meryn was back from her shopping trip and Smithy pulled open the door to help her in with her bags. She beamed at them as she entered and as soon as she had placed Kedrick's pram to one side, she rushed to Kitty and held her close.

Once they had finished embracing, she pulled out her notepad from her pocket and wrote her welcome. She pointed out to the pram and mimed Kedrick was sleeping. Kitty made the movement of cuddling a baby. 'I can't wait to hold him,' she said slowly and facing Meryn so she could read Kitty's lips. Meryn nodded and indicated he was a heavy weight.

'I'll leave you ladies to it, and it is wonderful to see you again, Kitty,' Smithy said and left the room. Meryn turned her attention to the shopping bags and Trixie spoke while her back was turned.

'When the siren goes, I struggle to get out of bed, so Smithy has to run to wake Meryn and grab Kedrick. Bless her, she comes to help me once she is up. We muddle through, but there are days I wish I could speak with her instead of writing everything down. The wonderful thing is that Smithy has started learning British Sign Language along with Meryn, and I have picked up a few words, so there is hope. Meryn also teaches Kedrick. At birth, Smithy carried out his hearing tests and he is a hearing child, it is going to make a big difference to Meryn if he can communicate with her. It is wonderful to watch her signing words and see his little face light up as she helps him learn. He signs for his feed already,' Trixie said and eased herself back into the armchair. Kitty sat on the sofa opposite.

'I have never thought of learning it myself, maybe I should try and then I would be able to speak with her too. I will get her to teach me a few words while I am here. It is a shame she missed out as a young girl after her accident. I am happy she is here with you both,' she said.

A loud burst of male laughter disturbed the peace of the

room and Trixie shook her head. 'Now here is someone who has become a good friend to this house. He helps Smithy on many levels,' she said.

Kitty smiled. 'It was a good day when Lewis came into my life. I will always hold him dear,' she said and waited for their American friend to fill the room with his presence. Kedrick gave a loud cry and Kitty jumped to her feet, but noticed Meryn continuing with her chores.

'How will this work when you have your own baby, Trixie? You will be exhausted when they both need attention,' she said.

With a loud sigh, Trixie nodded. 'Smithy and I have discussed this, and we were wondering if it was better for her to return to Cornwall where Wenna and Pots could watch over her again. With Belle no longer alive, and now with the news you have given me, I am thinking it might be best. We'll talk about it with Smithy, put him in the picture about the inn and her income, then maybe speak with Meryn. I could get a woman in from the village, but she would have to sleep in, and I am not sure we can afford the cost,' she said, pulling a face of regret. 'I feel dreadful thinking she might feel unwelcome here, but it simply is not the case; I just cannot physically help her for much longer. If she was hearing…' Trixie gave a sigh and for a moment Kitty felt a twinge of guilt for asking a lot of her and Smithy by encouraging them to take Meryn on in the first place.

Kitty touched her friend's arm. 'I think what you have suggested is a good idea. I can write to Pots and Wenna, and explain both the Belle situation and the difficulty here. I know they will help Meryn and Kedrick, and must miss her. Don't fret, Trixie, you have given her a good home and care, but it is time for you to think about your own family.'

Meryn turned around and they both smiled at her. She pointed to the pram and then her chest.

'Her milk tells her Kedrick will be waking for a feed soon. She is a good mother, and it is fortunate she cannot always hear the few comments about the colour of the babe's skin. I've also heard people suggest Lewis is the father and comment on how loyal he is to her, so that in itself is a good thing. She's a hard-working girl and we will miss her if she leaves, but I think it will be for the best. Thank you for understanding, and for being such a good friend to us all,' said Trixie.

Smithy and Lewis brought laughter into the room with them when they came through to the kitchen. 'Hello, Lewis, how are you?' Kitty said, rising to her feet. 'You are looking well.'

Lewis stepped forward and shook her hand. 'Mighty fine, Kitty. I am mighty fine.

Lewis had brought with him a large hamper of treats – including several packets of chewing gum, and a selection of beers from the American base, which were gratefully received – and he received a round of applause when he placed an array of wrapped gifts onto the table.

'You are so generous, Lewis, thank you,' Trixie said and stroked her hand across the goods with affection and amazement.

'You have been generous in opening your home to me. We treat friends for the holidays,' he said, giving a nod to all in the room.

'Now look at who has grown again this week!' he said,

mouthing clearly to Meryn who was holding Kedrick in her arms. Meryn nodded shyly and handed the baby out to Lewis.

Kitty watched Lewis bounce Kedrick on his knee, and understood what Trixie had meant about people thinking he was the father of the boy. Not so much the fact both were of white-black parentage, but because of the clear bond and affection between the two. It also didn't go unnoticed when Meryn and Lewis looked at one another. If romance hadn't bloomed already, it was going to flower in the near future and Kitty decided she needed to take Meryn to one side for a chat, then she would have a private word with Lewis about the situation in the home, and Meryn's possible return to Cornwall. The conversations could wait until after Christmas but needed to be had before she returned to the camp. It was not something she wanted to put into a letter as Meryn would need reassurances and possibly comfort. Kitty also knew Meryn would be upset if she thought she was a burden, and would need to hear directly from Trixie and Kitty that that was not the case.

Laughter and friendship filled the room and by seven in the evening, Lewis had left armed with gifts from them all, including an apple bread pudding made with Canadian apples. Trixie and Smithy had received a box of them from a grateful patient, and Trixie had set to work in making gifts for families in the village, ensuring there were several to be enjoyed in her own home.

After Meryn had cleaned the kitchen, she took Kedrick from Kitty who had enjoyed snuggling him in her arms as his eyelids drooped. Before he fell asleep, Meryn settled Kedrick with his last feed and told Trixie she would be up early to prepare the two large chickens for the oven in the morning. By eight o'clock Trixie had dozed off in the chair and Kitty and Smithy insisted she went to bed too. Smithy had created a bedroom in a room off the surgery back parlour to save Trixie from climbing the stairs.

'See you in the morning,' Kitty said, hanging a small sock of treats for Meryn and Kedrick by the fire.

Chapter Twenty-One

'Happy Christmas!' Smithy called out when they all gathered in what Trixie declared to be her 'best room'. It was a bright and cheery room with paper chains and lamps strewn across the ceiling. Kitty had brought them from the prisoners at the camp.

The shortage of Christmas decorations and the gloomy news of food shortages called for creative inspiration. They had used old magazines for the lamps and old newspapers painted in a variety of colours for the chains and Kitty had spent evenings knitting small bags in bright colours to hook onto the tree. Inside each bag was a surprise treat. Seeing Trixie and Meryn's faces light up with delight was worth the few camp coins spent on something in use for only two days a year.

She and Smithy had worked through until late evening after Trixie had gone to bed. Smithy had pulled the small pine tree he and Lewis had tracked down from its hiding place behind the shed and the two of them decorated it as they shared hushed whispers of excitement that they had got away with decorating the room as a gift for Trixie. Smithy's other gift to his wife was a small piano, and after enjoying an egg and bacon breakfast in the kitchen, they returned to the room and sang carols.

The whole house fended off the war by creating an atmosphere of warmth and friendship until the shrill sound of the telephone from inside Smithy's surgery cut through the jovial atmosphere and everyone stopped what they were doing.

Smithy turned and addressed his wife. 'Emergency no doubt at this time of day and being Christmas – or it could be old Grandma Hawkins in pain with her bunions or giving me the latest update on her haemorrhoids. Sorry, folks, got to take the call and go either way,' he said as he brushed his wife's brow with a kiss and rushed from the room. 'Forgive me,' he shouted as he pulled the door to and entered his surgery. In what seemed no time at all, he was back in the doorway and addressed Kitty.

'Kitty, quickly, it's a telephone call for you,' he said.

A bewildered Kitty looked to him then gave Trixie a panicked glance and frowned.

'Is it my uncle Frank?' she asked anxiously, rising quickly from her chair. 'He has your surgery number for emergencies. Please let him be well, bless him,' she said as she rushed from the room following Smithy. Trixie called out reassurances all would be well she was sure, as they left.

Kitty snatched up the handset. 'Hello? Uncle Frank, how are—'

A crackling sound on the line stopped her from continuing. She heard a cough followed by a faint voice. 'K-Kitty?'

Kitty's heart lurched and her stomach turned somersaults. 'Michael? Is that you?!' she exclaimed. More crackling on the line disrupted any response and she listened with intent in disbelief.

'Is it really you? Michael, my love I can hear you.' She could barely hear her voice over the sound of her heart pounding in her chest.

'Kitty. I can hear you too. I love—'

The line went dead. All crackling stopped and Kitty swung an anxious glance at Smithy. She held out the handset.

'It was Michael. He's gone,' she said in barely a whisper and pressed her ear to the telephone again, in the hope of hearing her fiancé's voice. When she heard nothing, she replaced the handset gently with a trembling hand into its cradle, releasing a deep sigh of frustrated resignation. Teardrops slapped onto the leather panel on Smithy's office desk and spread like scattered glass, and Kitty leaned forward to support herself, allowing the tears to flow free.

'It was Michael. He spoke to me. I heard him – I think he tried to tell me he loved me. Where is he, Smithy?' Kitty asked between sniffles, her sobs growing louder as she shuddered with deep emotion. No matter how she tried to control her body shakes, they took over.

Smithy walked over to her, placed his hand over hers and gave a warm, comforting smile. 'It was him, Kitty. Calm down – you are not dreaming. I could not believe it myself. Santa sent you a very special Christmas present,' he said.

'But… How did he speak to me – I mean, is he better? He sounded weak. He knew who I was! Is he coming home from Canada?' Kitty asked, rushing her words. She stared at the telephone willing it to ring again. 'Do you think he is going to ring back – we got cut off. Ring them back, Smithy.' All the time she spoke Kitty paced the floor, her tears subsiding and giving way to an agitated state of impatience.

'Slow down. Sit down. I doubt he'll get to call you back.' Smithy pointed to a chair and Kitty did as he suggested. 'Michael is improving. Apparently, a new doctor stopped the old-fashioned therapy and is using a more modern approach and fortunately, it's proving to work. Michael has rallied round. I'll show you the letter with the medical article the army doctor sent me – we've kept in touch since Michael was shipped out. I've offered our home should Michael need to return to civvie street. He will need a lot of support. He's my best friend but with no family in England, you must be prepared. He might want to stay in Canada. But we have to wait and see,' he said kindly and laid his hand on Kitty's shoulder. Kitty leaned her head sideways and absorbed the warmth of his touch on her cheek. Her head was spinning with confusion. Just as she had tried to put Michael into a memory box and move forward without him, he calls her out of the blue and reminds her he is still alive and thinking of her.

'Thanks, Smithy. It was wonderful to hear his voice again, I know I must be extremely patient,' Kitty said with a light laugh.

'And of course, we all know you will be just that,' Smithy replied with a hearty laugh. 'Let's go join the others and see how my wife is doing with her feast preparation.'

Kitty stood up and walked behind him towards the door. 'I don't know how she does it, but I swear Trixie could feed a thousand of us on just one potato!'

'That's about all there is in the food cupboard nowadays; that and bottles of forbidden home-brewed concoctions the patients give us. Lewis's generosity with his Christmas gift means this Christmas is a good one for this home and we are truly grateful to him, but roll on the day I can go and purchase a decent whisky or brandy. Trixie keeps hinting about surprises, but I think it will just be how she carves a slice of ham ten ways!' Smithy said and let his laugh ring out.

Both were still laughing when they entered the kitchen. Trixie was perched on a chair by the table and smiled at Smithy and Kitty as they entered the room.

'Well, was it your uncle or someone with bunion pain?' she asked and followed her question with a wide knowing grin.

Kitty shook her head with a smile. 'It was Michael! He spoke, Trix, he spoke to me,' she said and clasped her hands over her mouth. 'It was wonderful to hear his voice again.'

'That's wonderful, Kitty! Before you know it, he will be home where he belongs,' Trixie said.

Kitty gave a little pout of the lips. 'I keep thinking maybe he is where he belongs. Canada is his home after all,' she said in a quiet voice.

Smithy gave a cough. 'With you over here, he is bound to want to get to you the moment he is fit enough. Don't think like that, Kitty. Enjoy Christmas Day,' he said.

Kitty pointed to Meryn's coat and smiled. 'Time to get ready for church,' she said, and Meryn smiled back.

'I miss hearing the church bells announcing Christmas service,' Trixie said as she handed Meryn a warm pram blanket for Kedrick's pram. 'I often wonder if we will ever hear them again.'

'We said the same only last Sunday. We've never heard them here but they were always ringing out in our hometowns,' Smithy said, then turned his attention to Trixie. 'Are you coming to church, my dear?'

Shaking her head Trixie smiled at him. 'I will take the opportunity to sit quietly and read whilst the meat cooks. Goodness knows when I will get the opportunity to do it again. Five days to go and all thoughts of reading in the warm, quiet kitchen will be a thing of the past,' she said with a laugh.

Kitty and Smithy agreed. A knock at the door broke the conversation and Smithy walked towards it and pulled it open.

'Tradesmen's entrance. Appropriate given what you are wearing,' he said to the person on the other side.

'Dungarees help when maintaining my vehicle, I'll have you know, young man,' came the haughty reply, and Smithy burst out laughing. He stepped to one side and gave a theatrical bow. 'Introducing the one and only, Jo! Our very own Christmas surprise,' he said with a loud guffaw of a laugh.

Kitty threw her coat onto a chair and rushed to Jo.

'Jo, oh Jo! You are home from France!' she said and hugged her friend.

Trixie went to get out of her seat, but Jo put up her hand to stop her. 'Stay where you are, Trixie. My word girl, are you impersonating a plum pudding?' she said, dodging Trixie's hand after she said it.

'Bringing cheek into my home, who do you think you are, Joanne Norfolk,' Trixie said, and accepted a kiss on the cheek from their friend.

Jo turned to Meryn and waved, then looked at Kedrick and put up a thumb. 'Lovely lad,' she said, and Kitty giggled. Jo was not one for babies, so Kedrick was quite safe from cuddles and kisses.

Smithy wrapped his scarf around his neck. 'I'll go to church with Meryn; you three catch up and then we will feast and have fun when we return. I'm sure you are happy to forfeit your reading time, Trixie. Have fun, ladies,' he said and helped Meryn outside with her pram.

'I'll pop the kettle on,' Kitty said and set about laying a tray of cups and saucers.

'Sit down, Jo.' Trixie patted a seat beside her. 'Tell us about France and doughnuts, and Kitty can tell you about her telephone call. Ouch! Even baby is settling down for a good chinwag,' she said.

Kitty gave a sigh of contentment as she handed out the cups of tea to her friends. 'Here's to the three of us. Merry Christmas, girls,' she said and settled down to enjoy their company.

Chapter Twenty-Two

B oxing Day was a quiet day of sombre reflection. Jo had left to return to her unit, and when Smithy returned from home visits with the news that Hitler's forces had carried out air attacks bombing the northeast and Durham with V1 and V2 rockets on Christmas Eve, a sadness swamped over them all. Christmas was over and the reality of war once again reared its ugly head.

Trixie and Meryn sat rolling the decorations and storing them in old hat boxes, Smithy read his newspaper, and Kitty set about writing letters to Stanley, seeking reassurance that the Gaskin brothers, Eric and their family were safe. She also wrote to gather news from Nelly, her landlady friend who had helped her when she visited Durham city. The room was quiet as they all reflected on the sad news. Only Kedrick rested in ignorance and Kitty hoped he would never truly know about living through the war and that it would be over before he understood it all.

After a solemn meal of cold meat and pickles, Smithy

received a telephone call to attend to a farmhand trapped beneath the wheel of a tractor.

Not wanting to sit around all day, Trixie suggested she and Meryn took Kedrick out for a walk but as the fog rolled in thicker they cut it short. They returned home to find Trixie had taken a call about a difficult labour for a young woman on the edge of the village and had left them a note on the table to say she had gone to assist.

Meryn scribbled a note.

I will go to her. I know where it is, she will need help.

Kitty glanced over at Kedrick asleep in his pram, his rosebud lips already smacking gently in readiness for his next feed. She left Smithy a note to tell him they were with Trixie.

'We'll both go. You can feed Kedrick there when he wakes, and I can support Trixie. We'll take it in turns,' she said, and gave Meryn a little smile as the girl studied Kitty's lips. Meryn nodded and pulled her gloves back on and they both lifted the pram outside into the fog.

As they walked steadily through an uphill winding path between two fields, Kitty heard a sound and put her hand across the pram handle to stop Meryn from walking. She looked directly into Meryn's face.

'I hear something,' she said.

The fog muffled and confused the sound, which drifted back and forth across the hill to their right.

'Which way is the house from here?' she asked.

Meryn pointed in the direction of the sound and moved her hand to suggest a curve in the road.

'Another road around the corner takes us up there?' Kitty asked her and Meryn nodded.

'I think I can hear the girl so the house must be close,' Kitty said.

Meryn frowned and shook her head. She held up her hand and spread her fingers.

'Another five minutes, is that what you are saying?' Kitty asked.

Giving another nod, Meryn released the brake of the pram and started pushing it towards the turn in the road at speed. Kitty followed and continued to listen out for the noise. As they turned the corner another dark shadow of a treelined lane came into view. The fog filtered between the trunks and made the view ahead of them hazy. The temperature was noticeably cooler. Kitty had no doubt it was a pretty lane during the daytime and beautiful in the spring, but right at that moment it had a sinister look about it that made her uncomfortable. Kedrick stirred in his pram and Meryn tugged his blanket closer to his face. Kitty shivered. Daylight had disappeared and the lane grew darker the further they walked.

The noise sounded out again and Kitty stared to her right and focused upon the place she thought it came from, which she noticed was a shepherd's shack. She stopped, tugging at Meryn's arm.

'Over there,' she said and pointed at the building.

Meryn shook her head and pointed to a pinprick of light on their left. The house where Trixie was visiting.

The noise sounded out again and this time she heard words, which meant it was not an animal calling out. Trixie!

Pulling at Meryn's arm she pointed and turned to speak to

her. 'Trixie. It is Trixie calling for help. The girl must be in the hut. Can you get the pram over the field?'

Meryn shook her head. She pointed to the house and her breasts, then the hut.

'Yes, you feed him, and I will help Trixie,' Kitty said and waved Meryn forward.

Stumbling across the muddy field, Kitty's legs grew tired as the mud on the bottom of her shoes grew thick and clumpy. Twice she slipped and the mud clung to her gloves. Once she reached the hut, she pushed open the heavy door and found Trixie on her back on top of a mound of hessian sacks.

'Trixie!' Kitty called out and her friend looked over at her, her face pinched in pain.

'Kitty. Thank God you have arrived. My labour started this morning, but I knew I had at least a day to go given it's my first baby. I was heading back home after delivering the baby at the house, but slipped on some mud and the pains grew worse after I hit the floor, oooh.' Trixie puffed her way through her words and breathed away her painful contraction. 'This baby is determined to come sooner than I thought,' she said and laid her head back once the contraction had finished.

'So, you decided a shepherd's hut over a ditch is where it is to be born?' Kitty said with a light laugh. 'No chance of getting you home, I assume?'

Another contraction interrupted the conversation and Kitty had her answer.

'We can do this, Trixie. I'll look for more sacks to put over you and keep you warm, then we will get you ready. If it had been yesterday I would be expecting three wise men and a donkey to appear, but we will be grateful for the roof over our heads,' she said, trying to keep the banter light as she made her way around the dark room, looking for anything which might help. Her knee knocked into something, and she felt her way around it, hitting her hand against something metal. She bent down to discover an old metal travelling trunk and eased the lid open. She felt around inside and lifted out a tin mug, a small iron kettle and a large tweed overcoat. Kitty tugged the coat free hearing other items fall to the bottom of the trunk. She went back and laid the coat across Trixie whose wails of pain had increased.

'It's probably grubby but it is another layer of warmth for you. Keep going Trix. I've found the smallest kettle and a tin mug, but nothing of use aside from the coat so far,' Kitty said.

Settling down beside her friend she took Trixie's hand. It was cold, and Kitty felt around her own pockets for her gloves. 'Put these on, it'll save me rummaging around your coat pockets looking for yours,' she said and eased the gloves onto Trixie's hands.

Time ticked by and the outside grew so dark Kitty knew it was sunset even without the sun to prove it. She hoped Meryn had fed Kedrick and could return to help soon. Just as she eased back against the wall of the hut, she heard a noise outside and jumped to her feet. She pulled open the small door and saw the shadow of two people walking across the field. One was shielding a lamp and the soft glow could barely be seen but Kitty took great delight in seeing it grow closer.

'Hello,' she called out, knowing only Meryn's companion would hear.

'Ay up. The lass made herself clear and here we are,' a male voice boomed out.

Inside the hut, the lamp was placed close to the floor, and

the man stepped out to check no light could be seen from outside.

Meryn stroked Trixie's warm brow.

The man stepped back inside. He was large and Kitty guessed he was the farmer or shepherd.

'I'll carry her t'house,' he said bluntly and moved towards Trixie who chose that moment to let out her loudest groan and draw her knees to her chest.

'Hmm, maybe not,' the man said and looked at Kitty.

She shook her head. 'Trixie's going nowhere,' she said.

'I've a grandson turned around the right way thanks to the doctor's wife, so what can I do for her?' the man asked.

'She's born to be a midwife, now it's her turn to be a mother, so I will need blankets, including a soft one for the baby, and warm water so I can wash my hands where I fell in mud. We will also need drinking water for Trixie, clean scissors for the cord, towels, cloths – anything to make them comfortable once baby is born,' Kitty said.

'Leave it with me. Good luck. I'll leave the lamp, I know my way,' he said and rushed back the way he had come.

Aside from Trixie's groans and the birds outside calling in the late evening, the hut was silent. Within approximately thirty minutes the man who had introduced himself as Bernard returned armed with two large flasks of hot water, three blankets, a bundle of baby clothes, towels and bowls. He also produced a wrapped package from one pocket, which held a large pair of scissors.

'Wife scrubbed 'em clean,' he said and gave a nod towards Trixie. 'How's sh'doin'?'

'It won't be too many hours now,' Kitty said. 'Her husband

is on call to a serious tractor accident, so I am not sure if he has seen our note to tell him we are all at your house yet.'

'He'll find it when he finds it. The bairn of the deaf girl is sleeping and m'wife is making soup for me to fetch down to you, so I'd best get back,' Bernard said and raised his hand in a farewell wave.

'Kitty,' Trixie's soft voice called out.

Rushing to her side, Kitty knelt down and took her hand. 'I'm here,' she said.

'Push. I need to push,' Trixie said, puffing in and out.

Kitty patted her hand and then looked over at Meryn.

'It's time, keep holding her hand,' she said, and Meryn nodded.

Kitty lifted back the coat from Trixie's legs and eased away her stockings and knickers, noting spots of blood and the wetness of where Trixie's waters had broken. She raised Trixie's legs into a comfortable position just in time to see the mound of the baby's head.

'I see the head, Trixie. Your baby is on its way. You're the midwife, you do what you know is right and I will take my guidance from you. Not long now, my lovely,' she said and Trixie gave a moan as she moved her body forward to bear down.

After a strong push she leaned back and caught her breath ready to lean into the next contraction wave. Kitty kept her eye on the crowning head and silently thanked the farmer for his lamp. A sudden movement from between Trixie's legs showed the baby's head had entered the world.

'Keep going Trixie, the head is out!' she encouraged with excitement and awe. 'You are doing well, keep pushing. Clever bean! She's here, you have a daughter, Trixie. A little sandy-haired girl!'

A soft moan of approval came from Trixie as her child cleared her lungs, and Meryn clapped her hands in delight.

Meryn wiped Trixie's face with water from a flask and then grabbed a baby gown and blanket as Kitty cut the cord, tied it off, washed it clean and wrapped the end in a clean flannel.

Handing the baby to Meryn to dress quickly and keep warm, Kitty helped Trixie pass the placenta, and wash the area clean.

Suddenly the rush of the moment was over, and Meryn handed Trixie her first child.

'Oh Trixie, you were incredible,' Kitty said as she tidied away the dirty linen and covered Trixie's legs with a blanket, keeping the grubby coat clear from both mother and child.

'So were you,' Trixie said. 'I couldn't have done it without you at the busy end.'

Kitty knelt beside her. 'You would have had to if we hadn't have found you, but I am honoured you think so considering you are the midwife amongst us,' she said and leaned in to kiss Trixie's forehead. 'I am so proud of you.'

A loud knock on the door startled them all.

'Can I come in?' Bernard's voice called out.

'Come in and meet the star of the show,' Kitty called out.

Bernard entered with a large crate in his arms.

'What were yee blessed with?' he said cheerfully to Trixie, smiling down at her and her child.

'A girl with hair the colour of her daddy,' Trixie said softly. 'And thank you for your kindness.'

Bernard gave a wave of his hand dismissing her thanks.

'Best tell the doc to start savin', daughters come with

weddings and are expensive. Maybe we can save a few bob and marry her off to the lad at my house,' he said with a loud belly laugh. 'Congratulations, lass. Now, do you feel fit enough to walk a few paces to the edge of the field? I've got the horse hitched to the cart and can take you home. The wife's warmed a few more blankets and she's pushing young Kedrick down from the house as I speak. She'll wait by the cart for us. No rush, but I think warmth is called for now,' he said.

Chapter Twenty-Three

After the flurry of arriving home, getting Trixie into bed, weighing the baby and writing up in-depth records to keep Trixie happy, Kitty left Meryn organising the room for mother and child, whilst she prepared the thick rabbit stew the farmer's wife had made for Trixie's recovery.

Their kindness knew no bounds and Kitty soon learned of the respect and affection held for Smithy and Trixie in the area. Although she tried not to envy them the stability of a home life it tugged at her now and then and forced her to reflect on her own life. Roaming around Great Britain was not ideal, granted she was doing good things to help those in need during the war, but Kitty knew she had lost out on so many things because of her travels, and one of those was a permanent home with a man to hold her tight at night. As she prepared Trixie's tray, she shook the thoughts from her mind, especially the ones of Michael threatening to upset her, and headed to attend to the exhausted new mother whose life had just been turned upside down for the better.

'Rabbit stew to build you back up. Orders of Bernard's wife,' she said to Trixie who was leaning back against the pillows.

'Is Smithy back yet?' Trixie asked hopefully.

Kitty laid the tray across the bed in front of her and shook her head. 'Not yet, but knowing him he has escorted his patient to hospital. I don't think it will be minor injuries he has had to deal with. Eat up and before you know it he will be home and fussing around you and his daughter. I can't wait to hear what you are going to name her. Bless her, she's a little poppet,' Kitty said cheerfully, looking over at the bassinet beside Trixie where the baby lay.

The kitchen clock ticked around to ten o'clock at night before Kitty finally heard Smithy's voice calling out thanks to someone and a vehicle drive away. She jumped to her feet and rubbed her eyes, preparing herself to spring the surprise.

Smithy stepped through the back door and looked pale, tired and extremely muddy.

'Smithy, was it bad?' she asked in a whisper watching him peel away his coat.

He nodded. 'He never made it, poor boy. He was thirteen and slipped in front of the tractor. Trixie in bed?' he asked, looking at the door leading into the surgery part of the house and to where his bedroom was.

'She is, but she is awake and desperate to see you,' she said. 'Wash and change in here, it's warm and there's plenty of hot water,' Kitty said and gave him a gentle smile of encouragement. She went to the pile of ironing waiting to be put away and pulled out a fresh shirt, trousers and jumper for him.

'I'll leave you to it, and go and see if Trixie needs anything.

She is extremely tired. Then I'll brew you a pot of tea and bring it to you. Sit with Trixie a while, she will bring the joy back into your life again,' she said, her stomach churning with excitement as she tried not to give the game away.

She went to Trixie and helped her brush her hair and then lifted the baby from her bed and placed her into Trixie's arms.

'Smithy will be in any minute and he hasn't got a clue. He's had a bad time of it and seeing you with your little one in your arms will be just the tonic he needs tonight,' she whispered, and Trixie giggled.

Trixie motioned to Meryn to join her on one side of the room when she heard Smithy outside the door. He opened it slowly, and Kitty watched him intently as his face registered what he was seeing. He rushed to Trixie's side.

'You've had the baby? When? Oh, Trixie, what do we have?'

Kitty's eyes filled with tears as Trixie held out the babe and Smithy took it from her.

'Meet your daughter,' she said. 'Meet Rosemary Katherine Joanne Smith,' she said, and Kitty gasped.

Smithy kissed his daughter's brow. 'Hello, my little Rosey. You have my mother's name and that of two very brave ladies we are blessed to know and love.'

He turned to Kitty. 'We had names ready and how wonderful you are here at Trixie's side for the event,' he said.

'Event is the word, darling,' Trixie said. 'Sit down and I'll tell you all about it.'

Kitty nudged Meryn and they left the room. It was time to leave the little family alone for a while.

'I can't hear you,' Kitty called out above the noise of two children crying out for feeds. Kedrick rattled a wooden toy he'd received for Christmas, and Kitty cursed whoever had bought it for him.

'I have a patient to visit and will be an hour maximum and then you can get some rest. I will watch over Trixie for you. Her sweats have reduced thank goodness. I think the remedy for flu worked. I'll be back soon,' Smithy said as he picked up his medical bag and left the house.

Trixie had spent the last five days fighting off a chill, which at first threatened to go to her chest. Smithy said it was from lying damp in the fog for so long and would have been much worse had Kitty not found her. Fortunately, Rosey was a placid baby only crying when she wanted a feed, which seemed to coincide with Kedrick's mealtimes. Trixie was too weak to feed her baby and Smithy reassured her the feeds she had given were enough to give their daughter strength to fight any infection she might have come in contact with. He brought home formula and Kitty took over the feeds during the night. Both reassured Trixie she would soon be back to breastfeeding her daughter and it was a temporary measure to help them both through a tough time.

Meryn walked into the kitchen with an empty bowl and held it out to Kitty.

'She managed porridge, that's good,' Kitty said. 'Maybe she can offer one feed today.'

Pulling out her notepad Meryn scribbled out a note.

She is not hot. Smiling. I will fill the bath.

'A good idea, Meryn. Feed Kedrick first. I will feed Rosey

and then we will get Trixie freshened up,' Kitty said and patted Meryn's cheek. The girl had worn herself to exhaustion keeping the home running and fretting over Trixie.

Two hours later Kitty and Meryn settled Trixie in a seat by the window and stripped her bed, remaking it with fresh linen. Rosey slept in her basket beside her mother and the fretful days of the end of December slipped away.

'New Year's Eve, can you believe it, Kitty?' Trixie said, her voice still husky from her illness.

'Let's hope 1945 brings us good news. I have been granted two more days' leave to help you. Smithy arranged it with Sister Craven, but then I have to go back to Malton. But enjoying the end of the year with you on the mend already suggests the new one will be off to a good start,' Kitty said, patting the creases in the bedding. 'Smithy is out on a call but will be home soon. When he comes I will take Kedrick out for some air and Meryn said she will get started on the meal. We have another rabbit thanks to Bernard; I think you will have a long friendship with that family.'

Pushing the pram through the village, Kitty smiled and chatted with the local people all wanting to express their joy at Trixie giving birth. The news had spread quickly, and the pram filled with gifts for the family. By the time she had finished her walk and was heading home, Kitty's mood was low. Her hopes of receiving the same congratulations were slim and a stark reminder she was rolling through her twenties with no future to speak of, and that had never been her plan. Her spirits lifted when she saw Smithy's car parked on the grass verge beside the house. His cheerful nature always kept her in check, and she wanted to discuss Meryn's return with her and gain Smithy's support for the plan. She also noticed Lewis's army vehicle parked ahead, and smiled. Rosey would no doubt have received a generous gift from him. He had a big heart when it came to children; she had witnessed it with his interactions with Kedrick.

Parking the pram in the old coal house, she lifted Kedrick out and entered the kitchen. Meryn moved from the sink and dried her hands before taking him from her. Kitty went back to the pram and collected the packages. As she went to step back inside the kitchen she heard Lewis and Smithy laugh, then she heard another male laugh and knew it in an instant.

Michael!

She looked at Meryn quizzically and then over to the door leading into the best room of the house, and Meryn nodded with a beaming smile. Dropping the gifts onto the table and not waiting to remove her coat, Kitty dashed into the room. All three men turned to look at her, two were in uniform, but she was only interested in one face that looked at her with a lop-sided grin.

'There's my girl,' Michael said and held out his arms.

Kitty stood still, her legs threatening to give way. She wanted to rush into his arms but memory of the frail man she had once kissed goodbye to prevented her from doing so, and she struggled with the want for his arms about her and the fear of hurting him.

'Sweetheart, it's okay. I am fit and well. Come here,' Michael said and moved towards her.

Once enfolded in his arms Kitty released all emotion and allowed her sobs to break free. She heard the click of the door and knew Smithy and Lewis had left the room. Once she was able to cope with the fact Michael was in the room with her and fully fit, she took a step back to look at him.

'Don't worry, I'm still handsome,' Michael said with a cockiness to his voice.

Kitty grinned. 'Hmm, I'm not so sure,' she teased. 'Are you back on duty? Have the British Army given you full clearance?' she asked, not wanting to hear he might be sent away to foreign shores again.

'I am classified fit for desk duties within both the Canadian and British Army, and I am here in the UK to facilitate the transfer of a sick Canadian officer back to Canada,' he said and pointed to a chair for Kitty to sit down. He sat in the one opposite her. 'I have problems with balance sometimes so running and standing for long periods tend to be an issue, but all other faculties are fully functioning. Given the state I was in, that is a miracle. The electric treatment was horrendous, and the new guy could see it caused me huge problems with trying to use my limbs, so he tried a rehabilitation method using muscle strengthening and medication to help with the violent headaches I suffered. His patience and my stubbornness were a great combination. I wanted to surprise you, hence the limited information sent to you and Smithy.'

Kitty listened in amazement, pinching herself to be sure she wasn't dreaming.

'You said the Canadian Army had declared you fit, but you are in the British Army. I don't understand,' she said.

Michael gave a gentle sigh and Kitty sat upright in her seat. 'Michael?' she asked anxiously.

'The British Army retired me from medical duty, but offered me a desk post. At the same time, the doctor who treated me was part of the Canadian Army and he arranged for them to agree with signing me up as a medic with a desk post, which means I am now a member of the Royal Canadian Army Medical Corps. My job is to secure hospital beds for our injured and allocate their treatments accordingly. Doctor Sansom, who helped me, has an ambition to use me as a living and walking specimen I think. He has written papers on my recovery and his interventions. I have attended several case conferences with him where he explains his methods. We are helping soldiers who fought on the beaches, just like me,' Michael said, giving her a smile and reaching out for her hand, but she kept them gripped together in her lap.

'In Canada,' she said.

Michael tilted his head in agreement. 'In Canada.'

'So, you are going back?' Kitty said, her voice barely a whisper.

The silence of the room was his answer.

Kitty jumped to her feet as a temper brewed inside her and caught her by surprise. She pounded the floor from door to window and back again.

'I am to know you are fit and well, working again, but leaving me. Leaving me to nurse the enemy, knowing they nigh on blew out your brains. You sit here and smile as if it is a good thing.' She took a deep breath and waved Michael to remain seated as he went to stand up. 'You alive and well is a good thing, but leaving me to live in Canada? That's the reason you are here, isn't it? To tell me you are returning home,' Kitty said with a resigned sigh of realisation. She turned to the window and looked outside. It was as gloomy as ever, but she could not stop staring out at the damp, grey sky. A touch around her waist told her Michael was standing behind her, but she refused to allow herself to be drawn into a kiss. She slid from his arm and moved away, turning to face him.

'In some ways, it would have been kinder if you had not come to see me, Michael, do you understand? While you were in Canada it hurt me. The loss of you broke me, but I always held out hope you would return to me, and we would fulfil our dreams after the end of the war. But now, now I have to watch you walk away again, and this time you will not return. You will not make plans for a future with me. Instead, you will live your life without me,' she said and stared at him in disbelief.

'I had no intention of leaving you again. Kitty, I want you to come *with* me. To live in Canada with me … as my wife,' Michael said, running his fingers through his hair and Kitty could see his hand tremble.

'But you are leaving me. The war is not over. I still have work to do to help my country through it, I cannot abandon it to fill my own needs and desires. We are in a crisis. If you had not been shot we would still be here, planning and meeting whenever we could. I accepted it when you were injured because I thought if you did recover you would return to this country and remain here.' Kitty drew a breath and raised her hands in the air in despair. 'Yes, you mentioned Canada as somewhere to visit once the war was over, and I foolishly thought we would go together as a married couple, fall in love with the place and live happily ever after out there. I had not imagined you coming back to ask me to return and live there without ever visiting, whilst there is still a war raging around us. It's too much to ask of me, Michael,' Kitty said, resigned to the fact that once he walked away it might be the last time she ever saw him. But she had to make a stand. It was clear he had not taken her feelings on the matter into consideration.

'The army decided what my job was to be, and I have no choice in the matter. Even if I had, I am enjoying the post and wanted to share my life with you out there. You would be safer, and we would see each other every day. We could marry sooner than we thought. Sweetheart, we could begin again, a fresh start. Have a family like Smithy and Trixie. You have nothing here to hold you. Come with me.'

Kitty stared at Michael as his words registered. The anger festered but she would not allow it to rise.

'I have my uncle. Friends. I will soon own an inn, which is as crazy as it sounds, but I have a mixed-up life here and when I saw you I thought you were the glue to hold it together again, but you have not given me a thought. You have not considered how I have had to hold myself together not knowing the state of you. Even that call on Christmas Day made me think you were still a broken man. I had to think about how I was going to get to see you again once the war was over. I had to get up every day and wonder if you had *died*, and all the time you were happily being a specimen for a doctor, sitting at a desk where you could have written me a letter explaining everything. But no, you turn up and expect me to be so thrilled that I pack my bag and abandon my life here. I am sorry, Michael, but I think it best you take back your ring,' Kitty twisted the ring from her finger and held it out to him.

'Go back to Canada and do great things. I will always love you, that will never change, but I cannot follow you into the unknown and abandon others I also love, people who put me together again after your accident, people who I need around me to help me be the best of me I can be. I do not want to be a letter on their doormat forever. Once this war is over I want to be part of their lives, not hundreds of miles away,' Kitty said, with a courage she never knew she had.

'But I love you,' Michael said, his words emotionless, simply a statement of fact.

'What exactly does love mean to you, Michael? For me, our love was something so precious that for a year I wrapped my body and soul around it to protect it until you returned. As I see it, for you it was something you could set aside until the time felt right to reconnect with me once more. I wasted precious time worrying myself sick about you. Every day for a year I wrote to you but what did I get in return? Merely a letter from a nurse with scant details. Nothing from *you*.'

Michael rose to his full height. 'I called you here on the telephone,' he said with an indignant rise in his voice.

Fighting the urge to put her hands on her hips and square up to him, Kitty stared at him.

'Yes, and I thought, well … for me that call was a miracle, but for you, it was a teasing prank. How could you have done that to me, Michael? How did you find the strength to ignore me for nearly a year? You are not the man I once knew. I'm sorry but *that* Michael would never have left me tormented with worry. I doubt I will ever be able to forgive you for what you have put me through.' As she spoke, Kitty sensed an unexpected moment of closure approaching. 'You allowed the war to divide us and it is a pain I will have to live with, but like you, I will recover and find a way to cope with what I've learned today. But it will be without you in my life, Michael. I loved enough to deserve and receive at least one letter about your life changes.'

Handing back her engagement ring tore at her heart but

Michael's thoughtlessness hurt more. He had been well enough for travel and work, but had not given her the courtesy of a letter to end her worry and torment.

Her hand trembled as he reached out to take it and in that moment Kitty knew it was over, she had to let him go.

'I will leave, Kitty. It is evidently too much to ask for you to forgive my stupidity in thinking this would be a wonderful surprise. But know this – I love you and will try to find a way back into your heart. Smithy told me time and time again about how you were only just coping, and of how worried about you he was. Of how he was prepared to open his home and tend to me, but I pushed it to the back of my mind. My life was so busy with the new posting I barely took it all in. My Kitty is strong, I told myself. She will cope,' Michael said, and Kitty heard the pain in his voice as he tried to express his goodbye.

She fought with her feelings and composed her thoughts before she spoke. Kitty knew there was an easy way out and that was to accept Michael was home and life could move forward, but she could not bring herself to find forgiveness over the shock of him not considering her feelings in their relationship and in planning their future.

Don't give in, Kitty. If he can do such a thoughtless thing and not understand the consequences, he might not be the man you thought he was – walk away, save your heart – it's broken enough.

Eventually, she found the strength to say her piece without her throat constricting with emotion.

'I did cope, but finding out I did not need to allow my mind to fall into such dark places where I wanted to die if you died, is not what I want to hear. Please go, Michael. Send letters if you must, but like the ones I sent you time and time again, they might not get a reply,' Kitty said and waved her hand towards the door. 'It's clear you really don't know me at all.'

Once the words were released Kitty's chest tightened and she could feel the air in her lungs bursting in her throat and it ached. A dizziness took hold, and she took two deep breaths to calm herself.

Michael remained standing by the fireplace and not wanting to churn the same words over and over, Kitty rushed from the room. She brushed past Smithy and grabbed her coat, pushing off her indoor slippers and shoving her feet into her outdoor shoes.

'Get him out of here,' she whispered as she walked out. She passed Lewis smoking a cigarette outside the back door as she raced down the road away from the village.

Lewis called out after her, but she ignored him. When she reached a clearing in a hedge she rushed through and into the field where she let out the loudest scream. A scream of a future lost.

Chapter Twenty-Four

February 1945

The weeks that followed her break up with Michael were an emotional journey Kitty had never thought she would experience. She had always thought if Michael was never in her life again it would be because he had died or been killed. She never imagined they would part on such terms as they had or that he would lie to her for so long, claiming it was to protect her.

Mrs Stamp and Scottie were supportive and encouraging, and Sister Craven gave her several projects to keep her occupied after Mrs Stamp approached her with her concerns over Kitty's welfare.

After she had left Trixie's home, Smithy wrote to say how angry he was when he also found out the truth about Michael, and how sorry he was to have been involved with the tormenting prank. Kitty wrote back and reassured him he was not in the wrong, only Michael could be blamed for what had happened. Trixie wrote to say she had spoken with Meryn, and she had agreed that returning to Cornwall would be an ideal move after they had experienced one particularly hectic day which had ended in tears. It was organised between Trixie and Kitty that Kitty would meet Meryn at the Stargazy Inn as soon as Kitty had leave again, and Meryn wrote to confirm she was happy to move back to Cornwall, and that, Lewis being Lewis, he had contacts who could help with transport. All was arranged for the middle of February.

News of Germany struggling to overcome its enemy was a regular topic of conversation and Kitty often wondered if the war was nearing the end. She also pondered her career and wondered if she would continue working as a nurse. She questioned whether it would have the same appeal after the war, or if there was something else she could consider. She rarely thought of anything else to replace her life within the Red Cross, but she did wonder where in the country she might live, and knew being an innkeeper was not for her.

Once Kitty worked her way through the painful memories and could focus on her work and life without constantly thinking about Michael, Kitty moved into February with the determination to overcome distracting thoughts, and found a project suggested by Sister Craven where she spent her days off helping prepare homes for families in need of new accommodation. She grew used to the smell of carbolic soap and cabbage soup and encouraged the prisoners to keep making small items of furniture and toys to help everyone through the process of rebuilding their lives.

Mrs Stamp and her granddaughter made quilts for beds from scraps of material and Kitty forged forward with her knitting efforts creating jumpers, socks and cardigans from rewashed wool. It was as if her life was on repeat but without an injured fiancé in the midst.

A letter had arrived from Michael expressing his regret over their parting, and although it brought on a bout of tears, Kitty was able to fold it and put it into a box holding his other letters. She knew if she clung onto the past, the future would become a void she moved through without vision. Helping the children of the displaced families gave her stability, a reason to get up and spend valuable time with them. She made their lives more comfortable and reassured them that everything would work out for the better, hoping upon hope the same would happen for her.

Scottie never allowed her to wallow from the day she told him about Michael. He had listened to her rant and vent her anger, but never said a word against Michael or suggested reasons as to why Michael might have done what he did. He listened and then distracted her once she had finished. After a while he started inviting her to the cinema and dances, and Kitty never refused. She enjoyed his company. When they first met she had judged him, but over time she understood he had values and a method of coping with having the enemy who had killed so many of his friends, under his watch. They grew into a comfortable friendship, and she soon became aware he had also experienced heartbreak over what he had considered a solid romance.

Mrs Stamp enjoyed his company and willingness to help with the maintenance of her home. The children, although shy of the large man at first, soon warmed to him and he brought a different dimension into all of their lives.

Then came the change Kitty anticipated. She had heard rumours of Scottie's unit moving out and a fresh one arriving after the German town of Dresden was bombed and news of its devastation filtered through. She knew it was time for the camp to have a change of guards, but had not wanted to think about the possibility of Scottie leaving too. On their last evening at Mrs Stamp's house, Scottie asked if he could write to her and if Kitty would do the same. He was returning to Scotland. Waving him goodbye from the cottage gate was not as sad as she had thought it would be and Kitty and Mrs Stamp stood and watched the children chase him down the road, laughing and cheering him on as he pretended to be Mr Wolf.

'He's a tender giant. He'll make a good woman happy one day,' she said with a wistful air about her. Kitty turned to her and put her arm across her shoulder.

'He is and he will. We will miss him, but my toes will thank me for not dancing with him for a while,' she said, laughing, but deep inside another emotion stirred. Her friends came and went, she made new ones and they moved on, and the same had happened with her first love. Time needed to stand still to allow her to catch her breath. Too much had happened since 1939 and the whirlwind surrounding her life had finally caught her and lifted her from her feet. She watched Scottie turn around and wave from the end of the street and, in that split second, Kitty knew what changes she needed to make to turn her life around.

Rising from her bed the following morning Kitty stretched out and listened to the cheery calls of the birds outside the window. The house was silent with a waft of bacon drifting from the kitchen below. Mrs Stamp was a force to be reckoned with when she put her mind to doing something which gave her pleasure, and today's was to cook her last breakfast for Kitty. Kitty's heart sank when she thought of leaving such a welcoming home, but her honest talk with Sister Craven had opened up a new opportunity.

After a day of discontentment at work, she had requested a meeting with Vera Craven, and was granted one within the hour. Kitty confessed to feeling at a loss when at work. There was not enough to keep her occupied. Although she wanted to remain part of the Red Cross, she explained about Meryn's situation and of her inheritance. Michael and their separation also became a topic within the conversation when Sister Craven suggested there was more upsetting Kitty than not having enough work to do. Kitty gave her account of what had happened and asked for Sister Craven's help and guidance. After offering words of support, the woman gave Kitty a list of career options available to members of the Red Cross, and they discussed at length Kitty's unrest since leaving the intense role she had had in the rescue divisions. Forty-eight hours later Sister Craven had arranged for Kitty to collect four orphans aged three to six years, from Derby. The children were victims of the Christmas Eve bombings and Kitty's task was to escort them to Cornwall. Kitty offered accommodation at the Stargazy Inn until their official Red Cross attendant from St Ives was free to escort them to their new homes. Kitty sent a telegram to Wenna warning of her pending visit with the children.

After she handed the children over, Kitty was to report to White Cross prisoner of war camp at St Columb Major, and await further orders. Sister Craven reassured her she would not stay there for long, and that she was waiting for confirmation of another posting, which she felt might suit Kitty's need for a new challenge.

Taking in the scenery as she travelled to Derby in a vehicle filled with Red Cross staff heading for various towns and cities en route, the atmosphere was upbeat and buoyant. February showed signs of warmth, and the hedgerows and ditches edged the streets and lanes with new life. Word was slowly getting through that the battles being fought abroad were weighing heavier towards the positive for Great Britain and her allies. Once in Derby, she saw a large crowd of children and staff waiting for their arrival and the next stage of their journey. Kitty's four children consisted of a snot-nosed three-year-old boy and three girls aged between five and seven. Two of the girls were sisters and squabbled for most of the journey despite Kitty's attempt to keep them calm. Other staff members travelling with them also had struggles with their wards and the driver spent most of his time yelling out for quiet. By the time she arrived at the inn, Kitty was exhausted and grateful for the mother hen figure of Wenna taking charge of the children.

'Well, here you are my lover, and you look ready for your own bed,' Wenna said using the Cornish endearment Kitty had missed hearing for so long.

'Wenna, you speak the truth!' Kitty said. 'But I need to speak with you and Pots later on. I have news and so much to tell you.'

'Are you telling me you own this place and Belle mentioned us in her will?' Pots asked, his mouth opening and closing as he puffed on his pipe.

'I am, Pots. I've a letter from the solicitor confirming it all now and have returned the papers he asked me to sign as her executor. Both of you, and Meryn, will have a regular income from a trust fund she set up, and I own the building and its contents. I am not sure who has inherited her pub in St Mawgan, but I bet they are as shocked as we are. It's all legal and nothing to do with her spying conviction,' Kitty said, sitting back in her chair sipping on a red berry cordial made by Wenna.

'Will you sell it?' Wenna asked and Kitty could see the anxiety on her face.

With a soft shake of her head, Kitty smiled. 'No, I am keeping it and would like you both to continue as you are. I am committed to my war work and am about to receive a new posting, which I have a feeling will keep me busy until the war is over. After which, who knows what will happen?'

Prior to breaking the news about Belle, Kitty had told them about Michael. They had also discussed Meryn and Kedrick's pending arrival and exchanged various stories until Kitty found the right moment to share Belle's extraordinary letter but refrained from telling them about the reincarnated version named Lizzie. As Kitty sat with her friends she tried to feel a sense of home, sitting in the inn she now owned, but could not see herself living there.

Chapter Twenty-Five

The following morning the four orphans left with their guardian and Meryn arrived with Kedrick shortly afterwards.

Wenna had set up Meryn's old room for Kitty at her request and Meryn had use of the master bedroom, which had more space for Kedrick's cot. Her reward was the smile on Meryn's face. Meryn was back in her home.

That evening, Wenna was sitting with her feet up enjoying some time off and listening out for Kedrick. Meryn moved around the inn clearing tables as if she had never left and Pots chatted from behind the bar with the many servicemen who had arrived for a tipple. She watched as her three friends moved around the inn and instinctively knew they were the ones who were the heart of the business and building.

Kitty's only concern was Kedrick. Having witnessed the attitude of white soldiers towards their black colleagues, Kitty worried that Meryn would experience torment from the men. She expressed her concerns to Wenna who reassured her the village now had more than one or two children whose fathers were Black Americans. No one tolerated any kind of fighting between the men and the inn still had a policy of everyone being free to drink there. Kitty was not to worry.

Before she left for the camp, Kitty went through the belongings Belle had bequeathed her. She found it strange that the original owner still lived, but could never claim the items. Picking out a few brooches and necklaces, she folded them in a handkerchief with the intention of finding a way to get them to their rightful owner – Lizzie, Belle … whoever she was had chosen those pieces intending to wear them, or maybe she had inherited them from her family. If what she had told Kitty was true, Lizzie had given up everything to become Belle – or was it Belle who had given up everything to become Lizzie? Either way, Kitty felt it right she had something to hold onto of her past. If the interpretation of the letter she had received from Lizzie was correct, then she would be visiting the area at Easter, and Kitty assumed it was a huge risk for her to take. There was a possibility Kitty could not meet with her, but she would find a way of getting the jewellery to her.

Thinking through the future of the inn, she made the decision to give it up completely. Everything other than the few items she had chosen were to be divided up between her three friends, and the inn was to be left to Meryn. After breakfast, she went through to speak with Pots about her decision to get the solicitor to draft up the papers making it official, and he agreed Meryn needed something stable in her life to help her bring up Kedrick. He was more than content with the clause stating he and Wenna would retain their salary and trust fund, plus his room and right to stay living in The Stargazy.

Once satisfied all was as it should be, Kitty sent the letter and left for her new posting, content that everyone she held dear was now settled and where they should be. Now it was time for her to concentrate on her own life, and accept the invitation to her uncle's wedding in June, for the answer to his proposal had been a resounding 'yes'.

During her first full day at White Cross, Kitty couldn't help noticing that the camp and prisoners reminded her of the camp at Malton, as did her duties. As such, it was a disgruntled Kitty who arrived to eat her supper in the canteen. The noise pounded inside her head, and she struggled to find a quiet place to eat in peace.

Her quarters were a shared house filled with women from all walks of life and on her arrival she had walked into a catfight over a sliver of soap. She dreaded going home after her meal as it took only seven minutes to walk there and so gave Kitty no time to unwind.

When she reached home, she climbed the stairs to her room on the third floor in no mood for an untidy roommate, but that's exactly what she found.

Clothes not belonging to her were strewn across her bed, a bed which had looked neat and well-made when she first saw it that morning. Now she had to step over an array of shoes and magazines and clear the way to her own wardrobe. She scooped up the clothes and threw them onto the bed opposite, pushed all four pairs of shoes underneath it, and made the decision not to bother clearing herself a space on the dressing table. How one person could make so much mess was beyond her. Just as she put down her suitcase, the bedroom door opened and a tall, slim girl walked in wearing nothing but a towel.

'There is not a drop of hot water to be had, so don't get your hopes up about a shower,' she said and the hairs on Kitty's arms shimmied to attention. The scene reminded her of the first time she had met Annabelle Farnsworth, even the other woman's voice had the same plummy tone.

'That's a shame,' replied Kitty, and returned to her unpacking, not wanting to interact with someone who had no consideration for others.

'I am going to put in a complaint. Ghastly place. The sooner I am out of here the better. Daddy will be horrified when he hears where they have sent me, he will get me somewhere decent to stay,' the girl complained.

'I hope you get your wish,' said Kitty and continued to tidy her area in readiness for the evening as she intended to stay in her room and unwind.

'There's a dance on in the village, you coming?' the girl asked, throwing clothes over the back of the chair when they were no longer contenders for the evening's attire.

'No thanks. I'm exhausted,' Kitty said, secretly thrilled the girl would be out for a few hours.

'It will be fun, you should come,' came the reply, but Kitty chose to ignore it and pulled out a small embroidery project she had chosen to attempt as a thank you gift for Mrs Stamp.

An hour later she sat on her bed and enjoyed the quiet. The girl, whose name she still didn't know, had left with a group of five other girls just as lively and noisy, and Kitty was convinced she heard the house sigh with relief when they all left.

She gathered up the girl's clothes, and hung them up in the wardrobe, then cleared the floor area in front of the bed, all with the intention of ensuring limited noise when the girl came home.

By morning it was obvious the girl had not returned that night, or was sleeping in another room, and Kitty washed and dressed for work in peace.

On arrival at the camp, Kitty could see a queue of army trucks easing their way slowly through the entrance. Another batch of prisoners had arrived, which would mean medical checks for them all, so she headed to sick bay to set up the trollies and await her orders for the day.

'Pattison?' an orderly called out.

'Here,' Kitty replied.

The man blushed when he saw her. 'I'm sorry, ma'am, I was told to look for someone with the surname Pattison, I was not told it was a nurse,' he said.

'I am Nurse Pattison, so we will assume you have found the right person. Now, what is this about?'

'You are to report to the front gate at eighteen hundred ready for transfer. Orders came through an hour ago,' the orderly said and gave her a grin. 'Let's hope it's somewhere warm and sunny for you, ma'am.'

Working her way through the day checking and cleaning wounds and infections on the newly arrived prisoners, Kitty pondered over her new posting. Sister Craven had told her that the stay at White Cross would be a temporary one, and Kitty cursed herself for unpacking her bags. She finished duty at sixteen hundred hours and rushed home in the hope of getting a shower with hot water. Her luck was in, and her room empty aside from her own property. Once showered and packed she went to the communal room and filled her flask with hot tea, and then made her way to the entrance of the camp.

To her surprise, Sister Craven stood by the gates talking with a guard. When she saw Kitty she waved and smiled.

'Surprised?' she asked.

Kitty placed her bags on the ground and put her hands on her hips. 'What are you doing here, sister? And yes, it is a pleasant surprise,' Kitty said. The guard picked up Kitty's bags and put them in the back of a Land Rover parked to one side.

'Our driver will be joining us soon,' sister said. 'There are blankets but from what I have just been told, Scotland is unusually warm for the time of year,' she said.

A stunned Kitty stared at her. 'Scotland?' I am going back to Scotland?' she said.

'You are. *We* are. It will be a little sensitive for you, Kitty, given that it is working with the Canadian forces and you were engaged to a Canadian, but I am sure you will overcome any emotions when you get involved with the work. There are several forestry camps where the lumberjacks – and Jills – are working, and we are going to check they have all they need and tend to any minor injuries or illnesses. Are you up for the challenge?' Sister Craven asked.

A bemused Kitty responded with a grin.

'Just when I thought I could relax,' she replied with a laugh.

The journey to Scotland was long and interrupted by long queues of military vehicles travelling in the same direction, but Kitty and Sister Craven spent the time learning more about one another and Vera Craven's reason for taking Kitty under her wing. In Kitty the sister had seen herself, someone who overcame anything life threw her way, and she wanted to spend time with someone not afraid to face life and who was always thinking of others. In Vera Craven, Kitty could see some of herself later down the line, but she made a silent vow not to become so focused on others that she forgot to learn to love and lead a family life. Vera Craven was devoted to being a spinster and prior to the war had cared for elderly relatives.

'You will be based at Nethy Bridge where it has been reported several men have pneumonia. Most of the original lumberjacks were sent to fight abroad, and those remaining struggle with the climate – not the cold but the damp, despite the majority of them belonging to the navy. I will be touring around collecting reports from other bases and will be back at Nethy Bridge in a fortnight for yours. I have secured you a room in the village with a widow who is much like Mrs Stamp.'

Kitty took in all instructions still in a daze. Since leaving Mrs Stamp's home she had not stopped travelling and the last place she had expected to be posted was on a camp for Canadians in Scotland.

Vera Craven had definitely given her a challenge to overcome. Memories of Michael and their time working in Scotland came flooding back and she struggled to suppress them. She was thankful she had not been sent back to Buchanan Castle and the military base where she and Michael had spent precious time together.

Chapter Twenty-Six

March 1945

The forest pine smell lingered on her clothing long after she had finished her two weeks assisting the sick and recording their medical needs. Many local women worked in the forest and were proud to be called Lumberjills. They worked as hard as the men, were admired for doing so and were an important support to the remaining Canadian lumberjacks.

Kitty recorded her findings for the Red Cross and, when they took a break, she enjoyed chatting with the women, learning how determined they had once been to show the men they could match their skills, and no longer needed to prove themselves equal. They were as strong in mind as they were in body.

Kitty learned much about Canada and the lives of the men from Newfoundland and British Columbia who were stationed in Scotland. Sometimes listening to their soft accents made her wistful after Michael once again, and she struggled with what had passed between them.

The more she spoke about the country, the more she knew that, when the war ended, she wanted to visit, and so she wrote down advice, tips and places the men thought she would enjoy visiting. Some offered her their addresses and told her she was welcome to visit and meet their families. Her evenings were spent trying to understand the Scottish landlady who spoke in a broad native tongue at great speed, and she went to bed totally bemused every night.

Once the posting was over, Sister Craven and five other nurses arrived to collect her en route to the military base at Edinburgh Castle. Kitty made them laugh when she mentioned she would never be able to live in a three-bedroomed house again having experienced life in two Scottish castles. They were told they would remain in Edinburgh for at least four months, which was not well received by Kitty, but she kept her counsel knowing Sister Craven would be good company and the other girls were friendly enough.

After receiving a rare letter from her friend Stanley Walker-Fell, Kitty asked for a meeting with her mentor and when Vera Craven listened to what she had to say and gave her approval, Kitty felt the weight of the world lift from her shoulders. By the following afternoon, she had had her notice accepted by the Red Cross and Kitty had officially stepped down from her role as a nurse within the association.

It was time to return to Brancepeth.

Dear Stanley,

I am delighted you are returning to Fell Hall and the RAF have left it in good condition. As I have said to others, the end of the war feels so close.

With regards to your proposal, I accept!

I have already given notice as I have completed a recent stint in Scotland and was awaiting fresh orders. My mentor and senior sister is understanding and fortunately knows I have been through a lot recently, so made no waves in trying to prevent me from leaving. It will be strange no longer being part of the Red Cross, but will be wonderful to be able to help them establish new homes for the displaced children. Caring for children is definitely my calling. I have tried to fall in love with all kinds of nursing, but my heart will always go out to an orphan in need.

I am beyond excited and ready to accept a mission so close to my heart.

I will be with you on Friday, the twenty-third of March.

Kitty

Dearest Meryn,

I hope everyone at Stargazy is well. It has been a busy month for me as I have worked in the Scottish forests on a medical posting. I have exciting news but will save it for my next letter.

I am writing this one to say I have signed all the legal papers granting you the ownership of the inn and you are now officially the landlady and property owner. I know you will run it with pride, and you have earned every brick.

My congratulations also to you and Lewis on your engagement! How wonderful for you both, and I'm so pleased to hear that he intends to return and live in Cornwall once he is discharged from the army. I hope the inn will bring you both happiness in the future.

Give Kedrick a big kiss from me. I will come and see you when I am back that way, but my next trip must be home to my uncle to celebrate his wedding in June.

Take care, my dear friend, and give my love to Wenna and Pots.

Kitty

Dear Trixie and Smithy – and of course, Rosey,

I hope you are all well. Thank you for your lovely letter, which arrived today and thank you for asking me to be Rosey's godmother. I am delighted to accept and God willing I will make it to the christening.

Yes, it is wonderful news about Meryn and Lewis, and I am delighted they have chosen to remain in the inn once married.

Scotland was a surprise posting and stirred up memories of Michael. I have decided to write to him as he has not stopped writing to me since we parted. I skim read the letters and push them into my keepsake box, I have to protect my mind as well as my heart. I will write and ask him to stop sending them so often. Sister Craven said I must use the letter to express the pain he caused so he can see it in ink and absorb it better than my emotional outburst at the time. She has become a great confidante and supporter of my career, but makes me face my past, telling me it will strengthen my character. I am not sure how much more strength my character needs, my life so far has pushed my emotions over the edge and back again.

I heard from Jo, and she is still roaming Europe in her entertainment truck. She has hinted about opportunities for her in

America after the war, and of how happy she is despite her surroundings.

The war must end soon. The news of yesterday's surrender by thousands of German troops is heart-warming to say the least. Is peace on the horizon? We can but hope.

I have exciting news and will write to you in a week or so to tell you all about it – or I might have use of a telephone and will be able to talk to you. Either way, wait for my news before you write to me again as I will be able to send you my new address.

Take care, with affection your friend, Kitty x

Michael,

I hope this letter finds you well and still enjoying your life in the Canadian Army.

Your letters are becoming a struggle for me to read considering the hurt you caused; however, I thank you for making the effort to apologise.

I recently had a posting in Scotland working with Canadians and the place and people stirred up strong emotions for me. I am struggling to come to terms with how we ended our engagement. Hopefully, when the war is over the reminders will fade and we can both move on with our lives.

I need a clearer mind, hence me writing down my thoughts of us and of our broken-down relationship. I am told it will be therapeutic.

I struggle to forgive you still. I struggle to understand why you chose to put me out of your mind when you had come through a full recovery. I struggled to live without you in my life.

I also struggled to think about a future with another. I still have those struggles; they are with me every day.

There, I have told you my feelings and so hope you understand my request for you to slow down or stop writing the letters.

Kitty.

My dear uncle Frank,

I will be home for your wedding and will shop for a new hat to wear with my best Sunday outfit, which has not seen the light of day for over a year and has only been worn once.

I have exciting news and know you will be pleased to hear that I will be working with Stanley once again. I am returning to Fell Hall in a few days to care for orphans once more. I am no longer a working member of the Red Cross, but I will be working with them to help the little ones adapt to a new life. I will explain more when I am settled in. I cannot wait to surprise those devilish Gaskin boys, and meet their new sister at last.

The world news is showing signs we are winning this war or at least have a stronger hold on the enemy troops, but it has come at a great cost to so many – and specifically to us with the loss of my dear cousin.

Spring has brought beauty to the countryside, and I heard a cuckoo sing today. Let's keep our fingers crossed for sunshine on your wedding day.

Much love to you both,

Kitty x

Kitty's letter-writing day was followed by a trip to the hairdresser and exchanging her uniform for a tweed suit and blouse which felt liberating.

Chapter Twenty-Seven

S tanley stood waving at her as her train pulled into the station. Kitty felt well-rested and ready to embark on her new challenge in life. She stepped down from the train and smiled as her friend limped his way towards her.

'How wonderful to see you again,' he said and held her in his arms. Their friendship had not altered despite not seeing one another for over a year.

'It feels like coming home,' Kitty said, her voice muffled against his shoulder.

'I have a good feeling about this, let's talk as we walk. I can manage one bag,' Stanley said when he released her. 'It is a good day today, very little pain.'

Kitty handed him her kitbag as it was lighter than her suitcase, and she knew better than to refuse him.

'I am sorry you were released from the RAF, I know how much it meant to you,' she said as they headed towards the Fell Hall grounds.

'It was time for me to be realistic. I had a fall that injured my leg even more and I could not take pain relief on the hour, so when the force said they were moving out of my home, and I was approached about releasing it for orphans again, I had a think about what sort of set up I could manage without committing to the home being commandeered again. It's wonderful that you are in a position to help, too,' Stanley said.

Once inside the house, Kitty knew her decision had been the right one.

'Oh, this definitely is good timing for me. Gracious, I was thinking back to the first time I saw your home. Do you remember that horrible man, Mister Evans, who had to assess you before you were allowed to leave the hospital? What did he know about life away from the clipboard restrictions?'

If Mister Evans had actioned his thoughts Stanley would still be considered too crippled to be around children and never would have accomplished the dream he and Jenny had of supporting orphans from the area. Kitty had fought his corner and won. Sadly, with the loss of Jenny to cancer, Stanley needed something else to keep him going, but at least the RAF gave him back his pride and dignity. Closing down the home to orphans was hard for him, but now the place would hold new hope for them all.

She took her bags to her old room before re-joining him in the dining room where a tray of tea and a batch of scones sat in the middle of the table.

'This brings back memories,' Kitty said, rubbing her hands.

Laughing, Stanley pulled out a chair and sat down. 'You will be pleased to know Daphne is back in the kitchen, and the RAF kept Jack on to keep the gardens, so the four of us will eat supper together tonight and catch up. What is the news on Michael?' he asked.

Kitty's hand trembled as she poured the tea into his cup. She had forgotten to tell him about Michael and his question caught her unawares.

'Michael recovered. Sadly, it took him a year to tell me,' she said.

Stanley frowned at her. 'I don't understand,' he said.

Kitty sliced into a scone and took time to spread the butter and jam. 'He chose not to inform me he was fit and well, and working a desk job in the Canadian Army. He transferred on a medical discharge from the British Army into a doctor's team in Toronto. Even on Christmas Day he pretended to be sick and confused, when in fact he was in England waiting to escort a patient of importance back to Canada. When he did drop by a few days later I had the shock of my life,' Kitty said not holding back the bitterness in her voice.

'So, he is in Canada?' Stanley asked.

'With the engagement ring, yes. I was so hurt, Stanley. What sort of man does not let his fiancé know he has survived the horrendous injuries she tried to nurse him through? He has become career minded and if I am honest with myself, after all he has been through, he deserves to live life how he wants. I am coming to terms with it and being here in Fell Hall is the best cure for a broken heart, I can tell you!' Kitty said and knew she had spoken the truth. Fell Hall, orphans and Stanley were going to be her future even after the war had ended. There were hundreds of children needing help and the Walker-Fell Home for Children was a steppingstone for many. As the newly appointed matron of the home, Kitty was ready to nurture and comfort those whose lives had been shattered by the war. Both she and Michael had found their place in the world, and standing looking out at the gardens that evening she knew it was meant to be and Michael was her past.

The following day Stanley called Kitty into the main sitting room. He sat freshly shaved and wearing civilian clothes, which Kitty could see were good quality even if clearly pre-war in their style.

'Sleep well?' he asked.

'Like a log, it is as if I have never been away,' Kitty said. 'Breakfast was pure luxury. Seated on padded chairs and only a blackbird song disturbing me.'

'Daphne and Jack have brought down the boxes from the top rooms. The RAF were not allowed to use that part of the house as it was used for my personal property. Amongst the boxes are Jenny's sewing things and bolts of material she had purchased before the war. Her hobby was dressmaking, and a lot of the curtains in the home were made by her. I couldn't bear handing them over to anyone after her death, but I am ready now. Daphne took a couple of bolts, and I thought you might like the rest. You could make yourself some dresses as I don't want uniforms around the children, or perhaps something for your uncle's wedding, and then with the leftovers, maybe a few items for little girls. I am not sure boys will want to wear the florals in pink and yellow,' he said with a laugh.

Kitty smiled at him. 'That's very kind of you, thank you.

With the clothes rationing and lack of choices, the material is gratefully received. I will use it wisely,' Kitty said.

'I have also given your situation with Michael some thought.'

When Kitty went to object Stanley put up his hand to stop her interrupting him. 'Hear me out,' he said. 'Michael had a severe head injury and, as you have told me, he has changed. His thoughtlessness was not a trait of the Michael you knew before his accident, but he did say he still loved you and that counts for something, surely?'

Kitty gripped her hands together tightly, as she always did when confronted with a discussion based around Michael. She felt her shoulders tense.

'But he did not love me enough to share the incredible news of his recovery. Don't you see, Stanley, I never featured in his thoughts at a pivotal moment in his life. I have been told men do not think the same as women, they do not express their emotions as we do, but surely, if he loved me, he must have missed me, wanted to hold me and hear my voice again. Anyone, male or female, would have wanted to share something so incredible as recovering from near death.' This time it was Kitty who put her hand high to prevent Stanley from interrupting her words. 'I had to battle daily with worry, all while nursing the enemy, and driving myself to thinking the worst was going to happen.'

Stanley stood up and stretched his legs. Kitty watched as he lit a cigarette and his brow creased deep in thought. He reached out for an ashtray and placed it on the table nearby. She knew he was thinking through her words. Stanley had always been wise and she looked up to him and accepted his advice, but this time she saw him struggle to find the right words of wisdom.

'Perhaps he wanted to protect you. It's our job, as men. We don't always understand the thoughts of women, especially if they do not tell us how they feel and instead expect us to find out through their actions,' he said at last.

Kitty put her hand to her chest. 'I understand that, but Michael knew my thoughts; I wrote them in my letters to him every week. I am not condemning him, just his actions, and if this is the man I would have to live with as his wife, how will I trust he will be the man I loved when we first met? For better or for worse is for those who have already given their vows. I have not – nor will I. True love walked away from me the moment Michael made the first decision not to communicate with his fiancé, the one thing which would have had me begging to go to Canada and be with him. Now I need to do what he has done, focus on my future – alone if need be – and I cannot allow the pain of what has happened to eat away at me. I have lost a lot of people in my life, and accept he is one of them, though I will always be grateful for how he helped me through my innocent years and taught me how strong and capable I am as a woman,' she said and lowered her hand.

Stubbing out the tail end of his cigarette into the ashtray, Stanley looked her square in the face, his expression serious.

'Kitty, I do believe you have given this thought and made your decision. Listening to you, I have an inkling it is the right thing for you to do, but please do not shut him out entirely. Let him know where you are and don't close the door on him yet. He must have been frightened and confused, or as you say, there must have been something else convincing him it was best not to tell you about his recovery until it was complete.

We won't talk of this again. I can see you are here for the right reasons and will respect your chosen path to recovery. You have a special place in my heart, Kitty, and I will support you as you have always supported me,' he said and, as he went to turn towards the door to leave, Kitty swallowed down a choking sob brought on by his words.

'Thank you for understanding, Stanley,' she whispered.

Chapter Twenty-Eight

Modelling a dress in front of Daphne and awaiting approval of her choice of style and fabric, Kitty's patience was stretched to the maximum. She had forgotten Daphne was a perfectionist and would study the most minute details at length.

Kitty fidgeted from one foot to the other.

'Keep still, pet. How can I check the hemline is straight if you are dancing around?' Daphne said with the impatience and fussing of a mother hen.

'And is it straight? Or do I have to wear one flat and one heeled shoe?' Kitty asked, laughing.

Her days since the talk with Stanley had been filled with laughter but she knew the next day would be one bringing children burdened with sadness and fear.

'Yes. It is well made, and you look bonny,' Daphne said.

'I have the perfect hat and bag to go with it already, so that is my wedding outfit complete. I have four dresses for work and am just finishing a skirt for a child. Jenny had a good stash of elastic. I am going to bring the machine downstairs so I can work and watch the children, maybe even teach a girl or two how to use it,' Kitty said.

A rush of air from the back door blew through the window beside her.

'I just love spring and the freshness it brings,' she said and left Daphne to her meal preparation.

As Kitty walked through the large entrance hall she caught sight of Stanley standing tall on a stepladder holding a picture against the wall above the fireplace of her favourite room, the lounge with the large sofas and windows overlooking the gardens. It was the place where Jenny's portrait always hung.

'Taking it down or putting it back?' Kitty asked as she entered the room.

'Putting it up. It will look better in here than in the dining room,' Stanley said and Kitty leaned in for a closer look.

'Oh, it's a new one, not—'

Stanley cut in. 'Like you, I have to make changes in my life. This is Fell Hall when my great-grandparents first had it built. It will do until I find something else to hang there,' he said and hitched the picture high onto the hook. Once down from the stepladder he folded it and stepped back to look at the picture. The place she now called home looked magnificent and she imagined Stanley's grandparents looking at the same picture with pride.

'Perfect,' she said. 'I approve. New beginnings. As my uncle once said, we must live our lives the best we can and it will work out right in the end.'

Jack called out for Stanley from the garden and Stanley gave Kitty a guilty glance.

'I took the ladder from the shed, and he forbids me from

climbing it since my last fall, but I cannot be mollycoddled by my gardener no matter how much of a friend he has become. He fusses more than Daphne.'

Kitty laughed. 'Quickly, open it up again,' she said and helped him lean the ladder against the wall. As Jack's footsteps stomped across the hall she scrabbled up the steps and turned around to Stanley whilst holding onto the top of the steps.

'Is it straight now?' she asked loudly.

Stanley bit his lip to prevent himself from laughing as she winked at him.

'Perfect,' he replied.

'Ah Jack, what do you think? The original back in its place,' he said to Jack as he stormed into the room red-faced.

'I, um … it looks good. Have you finished with the steps, only I need them for, um … I need them,' Jack said, staring up at Kitty then over at Stanley.

Kitty clambered down and brushed the skirt of her dress back into place.

'All done, now forgive me but I must go and take the dress off before it is ruined. It's my wedding outfit for my uncle's big day,' she said as she walked out of the room. Had she stayed she and Stanley would have laughed and given the game away, and just for a short while it was good to have a little light-hearted fun. Although, she was going to have stern words about him taking risks by climbing ladders without someone to help him. There was a difference between being independent and being stubborn, but her first job was preparing to greet the first of the children arriving that morning.

'Just one more step and you will be inside. Don't be frightened little one,' Kitty said in her softest voice as she coaxed a six-year-old girl into Fell Hall. The vastness of the house appeared to have overwhelmed the child and she trembled as she refused to follow the three other orphans inside.

As Kitty glanced up at Daphne ushering the others into the dining room where the table was laden with sliced apples and carrots, and jugs of milk, the girl turned and ran across the garden. Kitty followed at a steady pace knowing the girl could not get out that side and that Jack was nearby, tending to the chickens in their fenced-off run.

Eventually, Kitty caught up with the girl who sobbed against a wooden fence.

'Agatha, let me help you,' Kitty said.

The girl buried her face into her arms and continued sobbing.

'Let me tell you something that might help. My best friend's name is Joanne, and she drives a Dolly Donut van. Do you know what a doughnut is? It's a scrummy cake.' Kitty's ploy of distraction worked as the girl looked at Kitty from beneath an arm.

'Yes, it is a cake. Now I think Joanne is the luckiest girl, but I also think you children might have a little luck too. She wrote to me and said she is coming to visit in two days and guess what, she usually brings doughnuts as a treat for those who live here. Now, if you step through the door and let me sign you in, it will mean you are entitled to whatever cake we have in the house on any given day, so that could mean a doughnut if Joanne manages to get her hands on some. What do you say, will you come wash up, and eat a snack before we settle you into your room?' Kitty kept the stream of conversation going, knowing from her personal experience of when she was orphaned that it helped. Her aunt had done much the same for her, distracting the mind to dissipate some of the fear.

Kitty held out her hand to the girl and gave her a warm smile.

'You can call me Kitty. The other lady you will meet is Daphne, she is the cook and housekeeper, then there is Jack, he is around here somewhere, collecting the eggs for breakfast, I expect.' Kitty watched the girl's eyes widen. 'Yes, we have eggs here every day. You will have one in the morning if you decide to stay with us,' she said and was rewarded with the warmth of a small hand sliding in hers and gripping her tightly around her fingers.

'Mummy and Daddy used to call me Aggie,' Agatha said in a way Kitty took to understand no response was needed.

The walk across the grass to the main entrance was a quiet one and the little girl gripped her hand tighter as they reached the front door where she stood and shook her head. She sank to the floor and Kitty did the same, sitting beside her in an awkward position but not wanting to make any sudden movements. She remained seated on the gravel hoping it wouldn't be too long before she could enjoy a more comfortable seat.

Just at that moment Stanley walked through the front door and glanced their way.

'Not coming in, Kitty?' he called over.

Kitty shook her head. 'Not yet. We are admiring the garden first aren't we, Aggie? This is Mr Walker-Fell, but he likes to be called Stanley. It is his house, aren't we orphans lucky he lets us live here?'

The little girl looked up at her and her eyes widened in amazement.

'I was your age, around five actually, when I was told the news about my mummy and daddy, and my baby brother,' Kitty said, moving her aching knees into a better position. 'It was the saddest and scariest moment in my life. I do understand.'

To her relief the little girl stood up and looked over at Stanley.

'Do you get bombs here?' she asked.

Stanley joined them and Kitty rose to her feet but before she could speak Stanley crouched down as best he could and gave Agatha's nose a gentle tweak.

'I have actually just come to tell Kitty that the German Army are weaker, and our Air Force have hit them hard. My pilot friends have made a big difference to the war, and I think we are much safer now. We don't get bombs here but I will show you our special bunker below the house where you will be taken if there is the slightest hint of a plane belonging to Mister Hitler flying across the water. We will protect you, Agatha. *I* will protect you,' he said with such tenderness Kitty welled up and had to compose herself.

'Stanley protects us all. He is a kind man and I believe in him, which is why I live here too,' she said.

Agatha held out her hand to Stanley. 'My Grandy had a walking stick and a wooden leg. I'm hungry, can I eat now?'

'I think we can manage to find something in the dining room, let's go see,' Stanley said, and Kitty watched as he limped away still holding Agatha's hand like a kindly father – or in Kitty's case – loving uncle. Something stirred in her as she watched the pair disappear into the dining room. A moment of glimpsing into her future, wanting what she had just witnessed, the combination of thoughtful words and trust. A powerful expression of healing.

Chapter Twenty-Nine

The honking horn of a vehicle coming down the driveway two days later had Kitty and Stanley laughing and the children rushing outside to see who was making the noise. Jo had arrived.

Aggie, looked up at Kitty. 'Is this her; the lady who might bring cake?' she asked.

Kitty knelt down. 'It is. That is Jo, my best friend. She is noisy, and is sometimes on the grumpy side, but she always finds me no matter where I live,' she said.

Jo jumped from her vehicle and pulled a box from the backseat.

'Happy Easter! Who's for doughnuts?' she called out and was immediately surrounded by three of the four children. Aggie stood looking up at Kitty and smiled.

'She brought some!' she exclaimed.

'Go and grab one before they all go, quick!' Kitty encouraged. Aggie had held back from the children at times but slowly, as the little girl learned they had also lost their families, she found the courage to join in with games and her crying spells eased. If Stanley was around she followed him, and Kitty suspected his artificial leg and stick gave her a strange comfort, reminding her of her grandfather.

'Hello again,' Jo said and gave Kitty a swift hug after handing the doughnuts over to Daphne. 'I had a touch of déjà vu as I drove here. You look well.'

Kitty linked her arm through her friend's and guided her inside.

'I am well and I am happy here – it was like coming home. Stanley is good company, and the children keep me busy,' Kitty said.

Jo stopped walking and stepped in front of Kitty.

'So long as you are not hiding from your true feelings about breaking up with Michael,' she said. 'I know you and of how you will always put others first but this time you must not, this time you have to look out for yourself. We will speak later. I have something to tell you.'

Later that evening, when the children slept and Stanley snoozed in the armchair, Jo indicated to Kitty to step outside. They pulled on their outer coats and walked to the end of the garden and sat on the bench overlooking what was once the rose bed but now sported bean canes in rows.

'I had a conversation with a mutual friend when I was in France,' Jo said once they finished chatting about how beautiful the garden must have looked at twilight before the war and victory garden vegetables took over the flower beds.

'A mutual friend in France?' Kitty said, questioning Jo's statement.

'Lizzie.'

Jo's reference to the woman they once knew as Belle threw Kitty and she leaned back against the bench in disbelief.

'I don't know anyone called Lizzie,' she said, not wanting to break a promise made.

Jo snorted at the reply.

'We both know it isn't true. I can't say much myself except that I am heading to Cornwall and then back to France soon, which means I will see her again; we will need to trust one another out there,' Jo said and grabbed hold of Kitty's hand. 'There isn't time to play a round of Guess Who, and we both know who she was in her past life. As I said, I can't say too much except that you need to know where I am headed next as there will be no communication for a while. She knew I was coming here and sent a message for me to pass along – forget Easter and the gardens.'

Kitty stared hard at Jo. The resident blackbird called in the evening with great enthusiasm, and then the realisation kicked in.

'You have joined her,' she said with a strangled cry. 'You're part of—'

Jo put her hand across Kitty's mouth to prevent her from saying anything else.

'As I said, I am heading for Cornwall and then back to my duties in France,' she said bluntly.

Kitty pulled Jo's hand away. 'We both know it isn't true. I know what you have done - what you've signed up for, I'm right. I know I am! Listen, tell her I've signed the rights to the pub over to Meryn. Tell her good luck and I have kept back a few items of jewellery for her – maybe you could take them to her? I cannot believe you have signed up for something so dangerous,' she scolded.

'I was approached when I returned to Britain some time back and went through training. When she walked into the room her face was familiar but had dreadful scars across it.'

Kitty gasped.

'She has been through much and managed to retain her French disguise, convincing her captors and managing to get out of France. When she saw me she took me to one side and told me what had happened and about you. No wonder you didn't stay in Liverpool long, it must have spooked you. She is not who we thought she was, and is incredibly brave,' Jo said. 'Anyway, I had already signed the Secrets Act and was too far into my training to walk away. I've told you too much already, but I know we can trust one another. I will leave soon and no fuss, understand? Keep her jewellery, I will tell her where you are and if she wants to find you, she will. Now, no more chatter. Give me a hug for good luck and thank Stanley for his hospitality, and do me a favour and write to Michael. You still love him, I know you do. A love that deep cannot be buried just because he is a man who tried to protect you in case he relapsed. He wouldn't have wanted to build up hope for either of you until he was sure. I spoke with Smithy about you and Michael, and he agrees, you need to give Michael a chance.' Jo gave a brief smile. 'Oh, and Rosey is a pretty little thing, isn't she? And that's me saying something nice about a baby. See, the war has changed so much! Now, forget I visited. Keep doing wonderful things,' Jo said with a light laugh but Kitty struggled to find any humour in her words.

'Don't distract me with baby talk, you fire wise words at me and then expect me to watch you walk away into … I can't even bear to think about it. You had better come home in one piece, Joanne Norfolk!' Kitty said this with a passion so fierce she had to suppress the rest of it bubbling inside. She pulled Jo tightly to her and fought back the tears. Despite her bravado, there must have been a smidgen of fear and Jo needed her strength and love to take with her.

Kitty stood and watched her closest friend walk away. She listened for the car leaving Fell Hall before she burst into tears. Once she had composed herself she walked back inside and went to her room. She needed to absorb what had happened and give Jo's words some thought. She was not surprised to hear that Michael had done what he'd done because he wanted to protect her in case he relapsed before sharing his good news. It made sense. But why hadn't he explained that when she had become so upset? She snatched up her pen.

Dear Michael,

You will see by my address I am now back at Fell Hall. It has brought back fond memories of when you paid me a surprise visit here.

Stanley wrote to me when he was discharged from the RAF under medical terms. He struggles with his disability nowadays, but wanted to set up the home again – in Jenny's memory – and so I am no longer part of the Red Cross as a nurse, but I work alongside the association as matron of a receiving home for orphans.

Although I sent you a blunt letter asking you to stop writing, I have now reflected upon the last time we met, and want to acknowledge that it was a highly charged, emotional moment in our lives (to say the least) and your letters afterwards have not given me time to recover. As such, I would like to rescind my request that you stop writing to me, and instead ask that you feel free to write, but only about your work and life in Canada, I cannot deal with the appeals for forgiveness.

Jo has just visited and fed us doughnuts. She has to return to France to keep the American troops fed and watered and I know I will worry about her until she's back on British shores.

I am no longer the owner of The Stargazy Inn; Meryn has that role. I am fulfilling my calling, which is not one of pulling pints from behind a bar, and as soon as I realised, I knew I could set Meryn and Kedrick up for life.

I am due to visit the Gaskin brothers soon. That should be a wild visit.

Keep enjoying your life out there,

Take care.

Kitty

Chapter Thirty

C hildren came and went from the home, and though Kitty noted that each time the new arrivals stepped off the Red Cross bus there was always one child like Aggie who needed extra attention, by the time they left the home all were ready to start again and face a new adventure. Aggie's aunt took her in, and Aggie gave Kitty a promise to always be brave and to never forget Jo and her doughnuts.

Stanley put a lot of effort into the children, and she sensed the distraction helped take his mind off the fact he was no longer able to attend to his work within the air force.

The weekend of Rosey's christening was a child-free one at the home, and Kitty left on the Friday evening to visit her dear friends. Both parents were content and happy, Trixie thrived as a mother and Kitty made a teasing guess there would be another baby in the family very soon.

Smithy spoke to her about Michael, and she reassured him she had written and opened the door for future correspondence as pen pals, but that Michael was to stop begging for forgiveness. Both Trixie and Smithy gave her their thoughts on what she should do for the best in their opinion. They said more or less the same as Jo had, and she politely listened, telling them she was dedicating her life to Fell Hall for as long as it was open and any distractions over her broken engagement were no longer welcome.

Returning to Fell Hall on the Monday morning was a relief. Stanley left her alone when it came to Michael, and all Kitty had to focus on were the children when they arrived. That week they were due to receive twelve orphans and Kitty had brought in two women from the village to help. By Wednesday the noise inside the house was more than Stanley could bear and he took himself into Durham for the day to meet old colleagues from his flying days.

By Friday Stanley had still not returned and Kitty was anxious about his well-being. Daphne nagged Jack to drive into the city to see if he could find him. Jack protested that Stanley was a grown man and could do what he liked, but Kitty guessed he was also concerned.

That evening a car pulled into the driveway and both Daphne and Kitty, who were settling the children down to sleep, heaved a sigh of relief. Jack had tracked Stanley down and brought him home.

Once all chores were done, Daphne went to the kitchen and Kitty to her room. Kitty had letters to relatives and potential foster parents to write to, and bed allocations to make for the following week. She asked Daphne to relay the message to Stanley that she would catch up with him in the morning.

Guiding the children into the dining room for breakfast always took time and patience. Some were eager to eat, others were reluctant to wash and a few struggled to get out of bed. It was always a constant trip up and down the stairs for Kitty before her ladies arrived to take over.

'Morning!' Stanley called out to her from the bottom of the stairs as she reached the top for the fourth time.

'The wanderer returns!' she called out with a laugh. 'I have a few things to check with you later, so when I am done getting the children organised, I'll come and find you,' Kitty said and waved her hand over the balcony.

With Stanley back in the home she felt at peace again and Kitty allowed the contentment to flow through her as she finished encouraging a ten-year-old boy to make his way to the bathroom by threatening to tell Daphne to feed his breakfast to the other children. Once he went downstairs she gathered the discarded towels, made the beds in each room and threw open the windows. Remembering her own, she entered her bedroom, collected her paperwork and pushed open the top window. As she did so a movement at the bottom end of the garden caught her attention and she saw a man dressed in civilian clothes and a trilby hat facing away from the house. Stanley had brought home a guest or guests and she guessed they had escaped the noise of the children and settled for a walk enjoying a cigarette.

'So, you came home. Had a good time?' Kitty said, laughing at Stanley as she walked into the kitchen where he was sitting polishing his shoes by the back door.

'I have indeed,' Stanley said, in good spirits despite looking tired. He lifted his shoe polish covered hand in greeting.

Kitty walked to the back door, peered out and noticed the man still standing at the end of the garden. This time he was hatless and talking to Daphne who held the chicken scraps bowl to her hip.

'Do we – you – have a guest? The children are a bit lively today, but I will organise their lessons for out in the barn. It will give you more privacy and quiet,' she said.

'Feel free to keep to the barn idea but my guest has nothing against noisy children, although he might need rescuing from Daphne, she thinks he is an underfed bachelor,' Stanley said and grinned.

'Leave her be she loves an underdog. Look how she fussed around me when we first met,' Kitty said, wagging her finger at him. 'By the way, we will have another weekend free soon. Every child has a new placement – every one of them,' she said proudly.

Stanley raised his eyebrows in surprise. 'That is quite some achievement. Well done,' he said.

'Not me, the Red Cross, their local team is determined to help the Fell Hall children in any way they can,' Kitty said.

Stanley returned his attention to his shoes, bringing them to a shine with vigorous brushing. 'But not you,' he joked. 'You have no interest in ensuring they find a loving family.'

Laughing, Kitty headed for the room filled with the sound of laughter and asked for all the children to form an orderly queue. At the entrance of the doorway, she clapped her hands to gain attention.

'Children. Stanley has a visitor staying with him, so can you please remember to call him Mister Walker-Fell when you see them together, and please, please keep your voices down inside the house. Today, you will be having lessons in the barn, which has been transformed into a classroom. There are books and a blackboard, and best of all, no more sitting on rugs – you have tables and chairs!' she said and smiled at the children. The younger ones squirmed in the arms of the two support workers. 'Whilst the little ones under five have their time in this room, we will be learning about springtime and Easter, so as asked, please form an orderly queue and follow me outside.'

By the time Daphne announced it was time for milk at eleven, the children had learned about rabbits, snowdrops and where in the world the story of Easter had started. Kitty's teachings were basic but until they could formally find a teacher willing to take on a mix of children in vulnerable stages of grief, she kept them entertained.

Stanley's favourite part of the day was when the children joined him for their milk session, and he always arrived to take them back to the dining area where he read a story whilst they drank. Kitty often thought he should have trained as a teacher, but he said his patience only came about since they set up the home.

During milk time, Kitty set out paper scraps and scissors. In the period before dinner time, Kitty always tried to introduce art classes. It saddened her to think of the items she could have purchased for the children before the war, but the supplies were limited in most towns and Kitty made do with getting the children to use newspaper and whatever other scraps she could find. Across the blackboard, she wrote in large letters the word 'rabbit'.

'Rabbit. Brown or white?' a voice at the door asked, and Kitty swung around as the man in the civilian suit and trilby hat stepped inside.

'Michael?' she asked, her words choked and her heart pounding. 'Michael?' she said again, knowing it was him, but not sure she had taken in that he was standing in front of her in the flesh.

'At your service,' Michael said and pointed to the blackboard. 'Brown or white rabbit?'

Kitty turned the stump of chalk around in her fingers, unsure of what to say or do. Her insides churned with emotion. This time it was a thrill to see him, but she refrained from sharing her excitement, confusing herself with her thoughts. He looked different, his hair a little longer around the ears, his eyes wide and alert, his skin tanned, and Kitty realised this is what he had looked like before he had prepared himself to join up when they were at the Birmingham hospital together. She had missed this version of him. He removed his hat, ran his fingers through his hair and looked so handsome that Kitty's stomach flipped with the memories of being in his arms, of him whispering in her ear causing her skin to tingle all over.

'You are not in uniform,' she said, stating the obvious.

'I no longer need one,' Michael replied and leaned against the door jamb. 'Lessons finished?' he asked.

Kitty placed the chalk on its ledge. 'No, the children will be back soon. Stanley reads to them during milk break. I take it you are his mystery guest?' she said.

'I am. We were in the same pub. He came in with friends

and I recognised him. He told me you were living back at Fell Hall, and I should pay a visit. I refused at first as I have a train to catch tomorrow, but…'

'Why are you in England?' Kitty asked.

Michael stepped inside the barn and looked about. 'Nice classroom set up,' he said.

With a sinking feeling in her stomach, Kitty prepared to hear him hint he was part of the Canadian Secret Service. She did not know if the Canadians had one, but with him in civvies and avoiding telling her why he was back on British soil, she could only surmise that might be the case.

The sound of the children walking across the garden back to their lessons distracted her from asking any more questions.

One of the local women helped her settle them into their seats and Kitty stood in front of the blackboard.

'Welcome back, children, I hope you enjoyed your milk and story. This is Doctor Michael McCarthy, and he is from Canada. We will study Canada one day. It is a country hundreds of miles away across the water. Doctor McCarthy is Mr Walker-Fell's guest, so best behaviour at all times please. I am going to have my milk now and will leave you creating rabbits for me to see when I return,' Kitty said, and smiled at the beaming faces in front of her. She gave her two helpers a nod and ushered Michael outside.

'How long are you at Fell Hall for?' she asked.

Michael turned away from the direction of the house.

'Let's talk down there. In private,' he said, pointing to the bottom of the garden.

Unsure as to whether she wanted – or could handle – a deep discussion or standing so close to Michael, Kitty hesitated.

'There is something you should know,' Michael said, and Kitty heard the tension in his voice and guessed her fears about a special mission were true. She cursed Stanley for bringing Michael back into her life. Out of sight, out of mind had worked well for her. Now, faced with the challenge of knowing the final onslaught of battles to win the war meant urgent and secretive missions, and with her best friend already embarked upon one, Kitty was not so sure she could hold it together if her ex-fiancé was about to reveal a discreet message to warn her he was about to put himself in the firing line.

'I wrote to you about all we have to discuss, Michael. We both made choices,' she said. The initial excitement of seeing him had faded when he asked for a private conversation. Covering old ground and putting one another through upsetting conversations was not something she could face anymore. She had found a new life path to follow and did not need her past to creep in and bring turmoil where it was not wanted.

Michael walked back to where she had paused and faced her. 'I have returned to England, permanently.'

His blunt statement shook Kitty's resolve to stay calm, but she did and said nothing.

Permanently probably meant because of the new posting he was about to embark upon, and she gave a loud and frustrated puff of a sigh.

'I have a new life here,' Michael said, but Kitty remained silent. Michael fidgeted with his hat and Kitty looked around the garden desperate for a distraction.

'The war isn't over for either of us, and as I said, we both made choices. I hope you are happy in your new life, as I am in mine, but please, these surprise visits are unfair,' she eventually said.

'There was a time you used to enjoy my surprise visits,' Michael said quietly, offering up a sheepish grin.

Kitty pushed her hands into her pinafore pocket and gave him a frown.

'You find this amusing?' she challenged him and cocked her head to one side in question.

'On the contrary, I find it hard work. I appear to say the wrong things time and time again. I am in England and took the opportunity to come and see you when invited by the owner of the house. Is that so very strange, Kitty?'

Kitty heard the hint of annoyance in Michael's voice and not wanting the tension between them to increase to the point of a verbal falling out, she pulled her hands from her pocket, untied her pinafore and hooked it over her arm.

'In any tough situation, a cup of tea always takes the edge off, so I suggest we go and see if Daphne has a pot mashed and ready as she usually does for my break. We can sit in the dining room and talk undisturbed,' she said and turned heel towards the house.

After asking Daphne to relay that she was not to be disturbed and that Michael was with her should Stanley come looking, Kitty carried a laden tea tray into the dining room.

'We have an hour,' she said as she poured a cup of tea and placed corned beef sandwiches onto a plate for Michael.

'In that case, can I ask that you hear me out, please, Kitty? I only have a short time before I have to return to Durham,'

Michael said, accepting his food and waiting for her to finish preparing her own plate.

Biting into her sandwich, Kitty gave him a nod. She thought if she was eating it would stop her from interrupting and she had to accept that, until he had told what he wanted her to hear, he would not stop trying.

'I am back in England because I have chosen to live here. During my time in Canada, I had the opportunity to write about my ordeal and the effect it had on my life. I wrote a paper on the mental state of those returning from war and how hospitals would need to face the volume of traumatised patients. I then went on to write a paper on what General Practitioners should look out for and sent it to Smithy for a critique and to ask whether it would be a paper worthy of submitting to the medical board in Great Britain. During our time together at Christmas,' Michael said and gave an apologetic grimace, 'Smithy suggested I consider becoming a GP myself and return to England after the war, where I could also continue writing papers on my findings. He knows how much I loved living here during our training and I told him it was something I might consider. As it worked out, fate decided for me and soon after Smithy sent news of the retirement of an elderly village doctor and the death of another. I packed my things and applied for the position which interested me the most. I am officially on medical discharge from both armies, Kitty.'

Kitty tried hard to understand Michael's words. She had convinced herself he was going to talk in code about secret missions and not being able to write to her, but to hear he was now a civilian had confused her.

She placed the cup she clutched onto its saucer. 'So … if

you are unfit for the forces in two countries, how are you able to practice as a GP in Great Britain? Do you have to retrain?' she asked.

'No. I retain my certificate. I am not unfit to practice, just not able to fulfil the fitness standards required for the military. Plus, I am tired of being pulled from one medical conference to another and presented like a showpiece. My consultant realised I had become unsettled so sent me to Britain to assist the patient at the home earlier this year, but with all that happened between us, my melancholy moods added to my dissatisfaction and when I mentioned Smithy's idea and the opportunity to apply for a post, he agreed to sign me off on mild medical grounds. So, here I am, ready to meet a board of elderly villagers and show them my papers,' Michael said, taking a bite from his sandwich.

A noise from outside told Kitty their hour of quiet time was up.

'We need to talk somewhere else. I need to hear more about this, Michael. Go into the garden and I will organise my afternoon to give me time out to join you. It is lovely weather, and we won't be disturbed,' she said.

Seeing Michael walk across the garden and chatting with Jack on his way to the benches at the end of the lawn, Kitty had a feeling her life was about to go through yet another change.

Chapter Thirty-One

S ettling down in her seat, Kitty tried hard not to keep looking at Michael. Each time she did her heart fluttered. She knew the love she felt for him was reignited, but her concern was more about how he was prepared to treat her in the future.

She wanted no secrets to fester between them and a fresh start would bring with it the past. A past which could not be ignored.

She also wondered how much of herself had drawn him back to England, or was it his career, with her merely as someone familiar to visit until their friendship faded away? Despite the bright weather, her happy state dwindled with the awkward nature of their conversation.

'If I get the position, Kitty, it will mean so much to me. If I get the job you will understand but for the moment, I will not tell you where I am headed as it is bound to bring me disappointment. A lot already has, and this seems too good to be true...' Michael said, offering her a cigarette.

His action slightly irked Kitty as he knew she never smoked them, then she stopped herself from making a remark in case this was something he had forgotten due to his injuries. He did tell her he had some lapses when it came to small details because of his accident.

Kitty shook her head. 'I still don't smoke,' she said. 'And I think I do understand. Your career outside of the forces is important to you. It is your future and at one point you never knew if you would have a life to look forward to; we all worried about you. I will wait to hear your news. They would be foolish not to take you on though as you will make a good community doctor.' She watched him inhale and then exhale the smoke.

A siren struck up a whine from the castle nearby and Michael jumped. Kitty realised his nerves were still tender and although recovered from the physical injury, the mental side of his recovery was not one hundred per cent complete.

'It's the army base test. There, it's stopped. It makes me jump every time too,' she said and automatically laid her hand over his, pulling back quickly when she realised. The warmth of his hand and touching him triggered emotions she was not prepared to deal with so soon after seeing him again.

'I must go. I told Stanley I would get the bus back to my hotel. I'll be in touch, Kitty,' Michael said, jumping to his feet and walking away before Kitty could say goodbye.

'Michael wait!' she called out, but he continued walking without turning around.

'Bye. Mind how you go,' Kitty called out again, and this time Michael acknowledged her by giving a wave in the air, but still he never turned around.

His actions upset her, but Kitty wondered if he had had a

moment of embarrassment over his forgetfulness and nerves and just needed to get away and think. Or if, like her, he felt the atmosphere change between them when they touched, and it became unbearable. Did she approach him about trying to reignite their romance or let him go? For now, Kitty chose to watch him leave. She was in no mood to be rejected and needed to think long and hard about what she did want from Michael.

Not wanting to go to the children and disturb their lesson, Kitty took a slow walk around the grounds reflecting upon the feelings Michael's visit had brought back to the surface. The war had so much to answer for but now was not the time to dwell on what had happened in the past, Kitty had to stop the bitterness creeping in and think about what she wanted going forward.

'Get a grip, Kitty. Don't let your heart rule your head,' she warned herself.

She pleaded a headache once the children had been settled and went to her room where she spent a few hours before sleep going over the good times in her life, remembering the dangerous moments and how, with Michael at her side, she had not feared for her life, just focused upon rescuing others. She silently thanked Stanley for not asking about her meeting with Michael at the evening meal because she knew she was not capable of holding back the upset about Michael's injury and what it had cost them emotionally.

'I wonder if my friend Sarah will find her missing family amongst those poor people in Belsen. What awful, dreadful news,' Kitty said one morning over the breakfast table to Stanley. She craned her neck to read the front page, which was full of heart-wrenching headlines. The one that had caught her eye was about hundreds of Jews being incarcerated by the Germans and the harrowing stories their rescuers had relayed.

Stanley gave a flick of his newspaper, folded it and laid it down on the table and looked at her.

'I do not envy those helping the victims. It is beyond me how people treat their fellow man even in wartime. We must keep these newspapers away from the children,' he replied, tapping his.

With a shudder, Kitty cleared away her breakfast things. 'We cannot keep hiding things from them as they have to be the generation who keeps the peace, but I agree, this is not something they should have to read about and those images … well, I am not sure they should have been printed, but I am quite sensitive to such things,' she said.

'The world needs to know, Kitty. I understand the Red Cross are shipping out support. Am I going to lose you?' Stanley asked, his question holding an unspoken request.

Kitty stood still and looked at him. 'It's fine, don't worry; I'm not going, Stanley. The orphans in our care need me just as much. The bombs might not fall so frequently nowadays, but one hint of an explosion causes distress to those little ones. For as long as I am needed here, I will stay.'

'Any news of Michael?' Stanley asked, suddenly changing the subject and catching her off-guard. They had skirted around the topic of her broken engagement and Michael's visit for several days and Kitty had fallen into a more peaceful pattern of thinking once again, but now Stanley had brought it up she realised she could not avoid it forever.

'Nothing yet,' she replied.

Picking up his newspaper and walking stick, Stanley walked towards the door.

'Any fresh romance between you two?' he asked, flippantly.

'Rebuilding a friendship, *that* is what was between us, Stanley. Nothing more. He is following his dreams and I mine.'

Stanley gave a cough and threw her a grin.

'Of course. But no romance. I understand.'

He left the room laughing but Kitty didn't join him in his jovial state. 'Sarcasm doesn't become you, Stanley Walker-Fell!' she shouted out after him. She wanted no pressure on her and Michael to rekindle their engagement. They had to find a new way of coping with the situation.

The post brought with it positive news. Kitty looked at the postal date: April 23rd, 1945. Michael's interview had been four days previous and he had not wasted time telling her of his news and his new address. He had also issued an invitation for her and Stanley to visit.

He wrote that his lodgings were owned by the retired GP who was no longer interested in living there and had moved to a family property in the county of Norfolk. He had agreed on a peppercorn rent with Michael, plus the paid services of his housekeeper for two months until Michael could afford to pay for her or one of his own choice.

Kitty read the short letter several times, taking in the fact that her ex-fiancé now lived a few miles away in a village named Quebec, which, according to Michael, was also a place in Canada. It was one of the reasons why Smithy was so keen on pushing the vacant position notice his way. Being a great believer in fate, Smithy and Trixie had urged Michael that it was meant to be.

Michael wrote he would explain more about his new role if she took up his invitation. She smiled at his words. He knew Kitty well enough to know he had captured her attention and her natural curiosity would ensure a visit.

Upon agreeing on a day and time with Stanley, Kitty wrote back with a polite message of congratulations and acceptance of his invitation. According to Stanley, Michael now lived under an hour's bicycle trip away. Given that he could no longer ride a cycle, he said they would take a drive so she could get used to the route. His petrol ration was still allocated for the collection of the orphans, but in Stanley's eyes this was a mission to heal hearts, which was just as worthy a cause. Kitty laughed when he said as much but she knew there was truth in his words, and was glad she and Michael could retain their friendship at a closer distance, after which only time would tell what came their way.

Chapter Thirty-Two

April 1945

'I am absolutely certain you look perfect, Kitty. If we don't leave soon there will be no point in going,' Stanley shouted upstairs to a nervous Kitty who had spent the morning trying to convince herself each outfit she tried on was not suitable for visiting Michael.

Her final choice was decided upon by Daphne who reassured her she was not overdressed but looked a bonny lass as fresh as the spring day they enjoyed.

'At last,' Stanley declared as she descended the stairs. 'And can I be so bold as to say the gentleman will be turned,' he quipped and earned himself a withering look from both Kitty and Daphne.

'The bairn is nervous enough without the teasing. Go and enjoy yourselves and give my regards and this basket of scones to Michael. I doubt his housekeeper will make them as I do,' Daphne said with an air of authority, which Kitty always envied. Daphne managed Fell Hall as if a team of women, and guided Stanley through life as if a kindly aunt. Kitty adored her and bent to kiss the woman goodbye. 'Thank you, Daphne. He will be thrilled as scones are his favourites – especially yours,' she said.

The drive to Quebec was shorter than Kitty expected. On the way, Stanley took her to Stanley Crook, the village his mother's family had once lived – hence his name – and before she knew it they were pulling up outside a pretty red brick house surrounded by trees and green fields. Kitty caught her breath; the views were stunning and for a split second she forgot why she was there.

Stanley lifted the wicker basket with the coveted scones inside and stood beside her. 'It is a beautiful area to live. Michael is fortunate Smithy heard about the position. Let's go knock on the door. Ready?' Stanley asked, opening the small wooden gate, strolling up the central pathway to the front door and knocking. Kitty stood admiring the property, it reminded her of an old vicarage she had seen on her travels.

They waited for a short while and a young woman answered the door. She wore the in-vogue postbox red lipstick, and her bold auburn curls were large and fashionable. She was trim and neat with a clean white apron over her emerald, green dress. It dawned on Kitty this was the housekeeper, and her age was around Kitty's, which surprised her.

'Captain Walker-Fell? Miss Pattison? Welcome, Mich ... Doctor McCarthy is waiting for you in the garden. Come in and I will bring you refreshments,' the woman said, looking Kitty up and down.

Stanley stepped inside and promptly handed over the basket. 'It's plain Mister Walker-Fell nowadays. A gift from my own housekeeper for Doctor McCarthy. They are his favourite scones, and she would not hear of us visiting without making a batch for him. Through here?' he said and strode through to what appeared to be a parlour with large doors leading onto the garden. Kitty enjoyed hearing him use his authoritative voice and wondered if he had also noticed the inspection she'd received.

'Thank you,' Kitty said as the woman closed the door behind her.

Once outside she saw Michael sitting under the shade of an apple tree. Stanley reached him first holding out his hand.

'How are you, old man?' Stanley asked.

'In good spirits, Stanley, and happy to see you both,' Michael replied and shook his hand. He then turned his attention to Kitty.

'Kitty, you are looking well. What do you think of the place?' Michael asked and gave her a beaming grin.

'Hello, Michael,' Kitty said and for some reason felt shy. 'From what I have seen of it, it looks wonderful. Quiet and calm.'

Michael indicated for them to sit and returned to his own seat.

'Mrs Cummings will bring refreshments out in a while. I find it strange having a housekeeper, but she knows the place and keeps it clean. I'm fed and watered regularly, so am content enough.'

They sat chatting for around thirty minutes until Mrs

Cummings walked out with a laden tray. She laid it onto the table and turned to Michael keeping her back to Kitty. 'Is that everything, doctor? The scones were a gift from Mr Walker-Fell,' she said.

'Yes, thank you, Margaret. In fact, head off home. We will see to ourselves. Take time out with Arthur,' he said.

To Kitty's relief, it appeared the glamourous woman had a husband at home, and she relaxed back in her chair.

'Oh, I can stay. Arthur is with his grandparents for the day and will not be home until after six,' Mrs Cummings replied.

His housekeeper fluttered her eyes at Michael and Kitty felt a nip of jealousy. Then she challenged herself as to why it mattered to her so much. Was the woman a threat to her friendship with Michael? She watched his face as he listened to the response. Was it pleasure Kitty noted?

'Then I insist you join us, get to know my friends. Stanley and Kitty, this is Margaret and Margaret enjoys fussing over me,' Michael said, patting a seat nearby.

Kitty felt the disappointment and annoyance swirl around her insides. Was Michael deliberately flirting with the woman, and why on earth did he want his housekeeper mixing with his friends?

'Yes, do join us, Margaret,' Stanley said.

Traitor!

Kitty glanced his way and she saw the slight twitch of amusement flit across his lips. Stanley was playing with her. Drawing all her good manners into one sentence, Kitty managed to speak. 'Just don't take what these two talk about seriously,' she said, trying hard to add a lightness to her voice.

For an hour Kitty listened to the banter between the three, barely joining in with the conversation herself. The visit had not turned out as she had hoped. One brief moment alone with Michael was all she had wanted, a few seconds to see if her feelings for him were sympathy or her clinging onto the past. Each time she acknowledged what she felt might be love, she found a way of suppressing the thoughts. Envy was her enemy for the afternoon, and she had to take care not to allow it to cloud her deep-seated feelings. Could she let Michael go? Could she see him take up with another woman? Right there, facing him ragging Stanley for comments about the army over the air force, she was not sure she could bear it, and seeing him play up to Margaret's attention upset her more than she had anticipated.

'If you'll excuse me,' she said, rising to her feet.

'I'll show you the way,' Margaret said with a friendly smile, which took Kitty by surprise.

'Thank you,' Kitty replied, returning the smile.

'Were you the housekeeper for the other doctor for very long?' she asked for something to say as they walked.

'Since I was sixteen – ten years now. My son is five and Doctor Thomas was good enough to keep me on, allowing me to bring Arthur to work. I am a widow. It has been five years and the doctor took care of us both,' Margaret said.

Kitty retracted all thoughts of jealousy.

'I am so sorry. Did your husband meet his son?' she asked.

Margaret shook her head. 'He has his daddy's name and looks, and I have my memories. We tick along. Here we are, second door on the left,' Margaret said, pointing to the downstairs facilities. 'He is my world, and I am not looking for a replacement for his father – mind you, Stanley would be a great catch. Michael said he is a widower and he has been trying to match me with the milkman and any male patients he thinks will brighten up my days. But is my world, and we get by without anyone else and have found happiness in one another. Someone else in the mix might spoil what we have, and besides, I suspect life will have new plans for us in the near future.' She gave Kitty a smile.

Kitty smiled back. So Michael was not who she was flirting with, it was Stanley.

'Stanley could do with a good woman in his life again – if your plans fall through, let me know,' she said with a wink and giggle.

'I'll remember that, Kitty.' Margaret gave her a beaming smile. 'I'll be in the kitchen, don't wait for me. You go and enjoy the sunshine and the company,' she said. 'Goodness knows I doubt you get many adult days in peace with the children at the home running around. One is lively enough!'

Chapter Thirty-Three

Kitty joined Michael and Stanley again and sat back listening to them chit-chat about battle tactics.

The sun rose above the treetops, and she looked at the birds flitting from one tree to another in search of food. She left the men talking and took a small piece of scone with her, crumbling it in her hands as she walked. She sprinkled it beneath a tree and stepped away, watching to see if it was a tempting treat for a feathered friend.

'You have found my favourite spot,' Michael's voice cut into the silence.

'Shhh,' Kitty said, putting her forefinger to her lips. 'Look, over there. A little robin is curious about the crumbs I've left – oh, we've frightened him away.'

'Sorry,' Michael said.

Kitty lifted her shoulders and arched her back, rolling her neck from side to side to ease the tension.

'He'll be back. I'm with you about this spot, it is beautiful and the view is incredible. You have a lovely home. Have you opened your doors to patients yet?' she asked.

Michael tugged at the sleeve of his jacket and eased his arm out, removing the rest of his jacket as he spoke. 'The sun is stronger than I thought. I opened for an afternoon surgery on Friday, but it turned out to be more of a meet the villagers in one-day situation,' he said, laughing. 'There are a few minor injuries out there, but no major ailments. I cover a wide area, and am now the proud owner of the black Ford you see on the driveway. I am not cycling hills in the wind and rain!'

'I am pleased for you, Michael, getting your life back to a pleasurable place. Margaret is nice. She told me about her husband and son,' Kitty said.

Michael swung his jacket across his shoulder.

'It's a sad situation, isn't it? It's also sad that she will be leaving in a month. She told me today. Her sister-in-law has a large house in Sunderland and has asked Margaret to live with her. They are close and it will mean Margaret will be back with her family as she only moved here to be with her husband when he worked on the farm. It will be my loss but her child's gain,' Michael said and pointed to Stanley who was stretching his legs. 'Stanley said you're not happy, Kitty. I admit, I am surprised. I thought you were happy at the hall, with the orphans.'

Giving Michael a sideways glance, Kitty then moved to face him full-on.

'Stanley said that? Strange of him to say I am not happy, given how much I love my work,' Kitty said and frowned.

'I have noticed a sadness about you though. Is it us? Me being back in England and interrupting the opportunity for you to move on with your life? Because if it is I will stay away.

I only want you to be happy, Kitty. I have my work and am convinced it will be the best move I have ever made, and if need be, I am content to be alone in life, but you need someone to love you. You have so much love to give, not just to the children but to the people around you. And you deserve to feel loved in return,' Michael said, not giving Kitty the chance to respond. He gave a sudden sigh, dropping his jacket to the floor as he reached out and held her forearms. His movements startled Kitty, but she remained still, enjoying the warm touch of his hands and waited to see what would happen next.

'I will work here and live here alone. I can do that, it's in my nature, but sweetheart, I want you back in my life and for us to try again. It is tough knowing you live so close and seeing you again has fired me up inside. I was a fool to do what I did, but everything rampaged through my brain and whenever I tried to tidy things up, I created wider problems I couldn't deal with and withdrew from thinking about my life outside of Canada. Of you. Don't get me wrong, I thought about you endlessly, longed to hold you again, but I could not deal with the thought you might have maintained our relationship out of sympathy for me. Stanley pointed out that the damage I did to us as a couple might not be repairable, but I will do whatever it takes to convince you that I will always put you first from now on. And I will, if you will allow me to prove my love for you has not wavered – not at all,' Michael said, and Kitty was shaken up by the emotion in his voice and the intense way he spoke; he was almost pleading with her.

'I will confess you have stirred up a few feelings, Michael. What we had was a love I thought could withstand our times apart, but when you chose – and it *was* a choice – not to get in touch and tell me of your recovery, it caused me pain. Some might say I overreacted when you told me, and others that I did the right thing. Seeing your reaction to noise and how you've forgotten things from the past, I realise now that you thought you were doing right by me and protecting me from upset. I appreciate it, Michael, I do, but if we both want to try again, it has to be a fresh start. We have to find one another again. We've both changed since your accident,' Kitty said quietly and calmly. From the corner of her eye, she saw the robin peck at her crumbs and she smiled inwardly.

'We need courage and friendship to rebuild us as a couple,' she said. 'I am willing to try again, if you are, and if you can be honest with me.'

Michael looked at her and she saw his eyes were moist with tears.

'I was not dishonest, Kitty. I was a fool, and it broke me to think I might never see you again. Thank you for giving us another chance. You will have my love forever, I promise. As much as I want to kiss you, I will wait until you are ready. You guide me, Kitty. Help me get this right because I never want to go through this again. Now, shall we head back? Stanley looks a little awkward sitting with Margaret,' Michael said, and his laugh broke the serious atmosphere between them.

Kitty turned to look at Stanley.

'Poor Stanley, he does look a little awkward. He is not one for chit-chat, we can't leave him for too long. I will come back to speak with you one afternoon in the week when we can be alone. I still cannot believe you are living so close. Just a bus or cycle ride away,' she said.

Michael released her arms as she went to move away.

'You look beautiful by the way. The sweetheart I remember,' he said softly.

Kitty dared not speak. The moment was perfect and she gave him a sweet smile before walking back to speak with Stanley and Margaret.

Michael had worn his heart on his sleeve, and it was up to her to find a way to face what she had held onto deep inside. It was time for her to release the love she had for Michael and work past the pain.

Chapter Thirty-Four

Dearest Meryn,

Thank you so much for the invitation to your wedding. I have sent a formal acceptance card but wanted to write to you of my news.

Michael is back and living in England. He is but a stone's throw away from Fell Hall and I am going to make the most of this glorious weather and cycle to see him tomorrow. We are working on rebuilding our friendship and seeing if it could ever become something else again. Time, they say, heals. Seeing him again brought about a lot of emotional thinking on my part and he declares he still loves me. The place he lives is a village named after a Canadian city, and I think it reminds him of Canada while also offering the satisfaction of living back in Great Britain once more. Smithy found him the job as a village doctor.

I am delighted Kedrick is happy in Cornwall, and the inn is still running smoothly. How are the plans going for Lewis to return to live there when the war is over? There are a lot of rumours rumbling around about it being sooner rather than later, and that fills me with joy as I think we're all battle weary nowadays.

The Gaskin brothers are taller than me now and both are hardworking lads. Eric is the studious one and is looking into attending agricultural college when it is time for him to leave school. Their little sister is a darling child, and they clearly adore her. I thank God for their adoptive parents giving the boys a home. Some of the children I am caring for will be leaving for new homes soon, and there is one little girl I am concerned about as we cannot trace any of her family, not even distant relatives. Sending her to an orphanage is not on the agenda and will be a last resort as she is extremely frightened of large groups of people to the point of not being able to breathe. From what I gather, they were in a crowd when the bomb was on its descent, and little Ruth was caught in the panic. Fortunately for her, she was moved away before the explosion, but the horrible experience was followed with the news her family were all lost to her, all seven of them, both parents, an aunt, grandparents, a sibling and cousin. No wonder the child is fearful. Stanley is wonderful with her, and I secretly adore her. She is a little Shirley Temple with blonde curls.

My friend Sarah wrote to me, and she has had notification her family were victims in the Jewish camps. My heart cries for them all.

Give my love and best wishes to Pots and Wenna, and like you, I think it is time those two admitted they are fond of one another. Wenna mentions him a lot in her letters.

You asked after Jo; she is abroad doing her duty. I do hope she makes it home for your wedding and my uncle's, which is first, in June.

For once I can report my life is good and my spirits are greatly improved. I loved my time as a nurse with the Red Cross, but working alongside them in finding good homes for the orphans is definitely as fulfilling as helping a wound heal.

Well, my friend, I must sign off for now and plan lessons for tomorrow.

I send my love as always,

Kitty x

'K itty, are you there?' Stanley's voice drifted through the hallway into the kitchen where Kitty was peeling potatoes for Daphne. The fewer rations getting through, the more potatoes came into play, which meant a larger potful to be boiled. Daphne scraped carrots, refusing Kitty's help on those by declaring her hands were already orange and there was no point in Kitty spoiling hers.

'In the kitchen,' Kitty called back.

Stanley puffed as he rushed into the room.

'Slow down, you will make your stump sore if it chafes on the leg,' Kitty told him. 'What's the hurry?'

'My friend from the Air Force base has hinted Hitler is in trouble and we are pushing back the enemy units. There is talk that some of their troops have surrendered. We are close to the end, ladies. Peace is around the corner,' Stanley said with a flourish and sat on a chair.

'Every day there is more news getting through which gives us hope. We have a country to rebuild after the horrors, but we will get it done, that's for sure,' Kitty said.

'Thor'll still be tatties to peel, so don't get too excited,' Daphne said, emphasising her accent, and finishing off with an infectious belly laugh.

Jack poked his head through the back door. 'Need any

parsnips pulled, Daphne?' he asked and looked bemused when they all burst out laughing again.

'And parsnips, Daphne. There will still be parsnips, too,' Stanley said, rising to his feet and laughing his way out of the room.

'Something I said?' Jack asked.

'Just good timing on a conversation, Jack. Tea's mashed if you're stopping for a brew,' Kitty said.

Daphne chuckled. 'Listen to the southern girl with her mash and brew chatter, we've turned her northern, Jack,' she said.

'Aye, we've done just that, and the north is lucky to have her,' Jack said with a twinkle in his eye as he looked over at Kitty.

Finishing off the last potato, Kitty dropped it into the pot of water. 'You only like me for my potato peeling skills,' she said and waggled her fingers in the air. 'Now, I am off to talk about how carrots help you see in the dark, so be careful, Daphne, the children will be wanting double portions.'

Kitty left the room in high spirits. Stanley had found an elderly teacher willing to visit twice a week, which freed Kitty from the teaching role she had taken on and meant she had time for darning and sewing clothes for the children. Her recent achievement was reducing a men's coat down to a jacket for a sixteen-year-old boy embarking on an office runner's job who was distressed about his limited wardrobe. Everyone rallied around finding him suitable shirts and trousers, and when the pile and his new jacket were presented to him he burst into tears with no shame in sharing his joy and sadness that his parents were no longer around to see him step out into the world.

Before embarking on creating new spring and summer outfits, Kitty tidied the children's bedrooms and wrote replies to her recent letters from Trixie and Vera Craven.

Dear Trixie,

I hope this finds you all well and Rosey is no longer in pain with her teeth. Sleepless nights are draining. We have a little girl of four named Ruth staying with us and she cries out some nights and needs a lot of comfort to settle. Daphne is going to watch over her when we come to you for Rosey's christening. This will mean she will sleep in a different wing of the house in Daphne's room and I do hope the change in routine doesn't distress her.

I am looking forward to seeing you, and Michael will be good company on the train. We are taking things slowly, and I must give Smithy a big hug for helping find him such a wonderful job. I am going to see him tomorrow and I am nervous as we will be alone with no distractions and have a lot to talk about. We both need to work out what we want from our friendship. I know I still love him but am wondering how we can work after such a dramatic breakup. He has openly said he loves me but is showing me respect and giving me time to come to terms with his return and news.

We will see you in a week and I'm sure I will have further updates for you then.

Much love,

Kitty x

Dear Sister Craven (Vera),

Thank you for your letter asking after me and my life at Fell Hall.

All is well here, and I am thriving on the energy of the children, although their pain of loss brings sadness at times. Stanley Walker-Fell is a good employer and friend.

My ex-fiancé is fully recovered and is now a GP in a village nearby. We had a falling out at Christmas and are working out where we want our relationship to go from here.

Good luck with your interview as matron. You will be a kind and fair one. I will always be grateful for your support and advice.

My best wishes,

Kitty Pattison

———

'Give us a twirl, Ruth,' Kitty said, encouraging the little girl to show off her new dress to Daphne.

Obliging but not enthusiastic, Ruth turned around, swirling the full skirt of the bright red dress.

'It's bonny, Ruth. You are a lucky girl and Kitty is a clever one. Use your manners your mammy would want you to use, remember?' Daphne said with a kind, encouraging voice.

Ruth turned sideways to face Kitty and flung her arms around Kitty's neck when she bent down to receive her thanks.

'Now there's a thank you and a half,' Kitty said. Knowing Ruth was still shy of speaking, she was taken aback when Ruth responded with a shy 'thank you'.

At four years old, Ruth was small for her age and the moment she hugged Kitty and breathed her soft words, Kitty had a flash of wanting to protect this one child forever. A maternal instinct overcame her, and a choking sensation caught in her throat, threatening to bring on an emotional outburst, so she pulled back and stroked the child's cheek.

'You are welcome, dear. You can wear it for the party the soldiers are putting on for you all this afternoon. The one at the castle. You will be a princess at a banquet. Let's take it off and hang it up until later,' Kitty said and refocused upon the task of encouraging Ruth to join in with the other children.

'The party will only be us from the house, but obviously there will be soldiers too. I need you to be brave and show the soldiers they are doing a good job of protecting you by giving them one of your big smiles. Can you do that for me?'

Looking down at her dress, then back up at Kitty, Ruth nodded. Kitty smiled.

'Good girl, now, arms up…'

Chapter Thirty-Five

After the success of the party the day before, Kitty pegged out an array of clothes to blow in the breeze before finding Jack, who had given Jenny's old bicycle an overhaul and added a basket front and back for Kitty to use.

Arriving at the shed and seeing what looked like a brand-new bicycle propped up against it, Kitty called out for Jack. He came from the vegetable garden and greeted her with a wide smile.

'Oh, Jack, it is wonderful, beautiful. Blue with baskets. I can't wait to ride it over to Michael's,' she said.

'There's rain predicted for late afternoon. April showers are good for the garden but not for the cyclist. Take your mac,' he said, 'and do not ride in the dark. There are no lights on the bike yet.' Jack fussed about checking the chain as he spoke.

'It is perfect Jack, and I will take my coat. Thank you.'

With her basket filled with fresh bakes from Daphne, reading material about battle tactics from Stanley, which apparently would prove his point, and a small bag of new potatoes from Jack, Kitty rode away. The fresh breeze pinched her cheeks and the faster she peddled the more alive she felt. All worries about the children left her and a renewed feeling of excitement fluttered in her stomach. She anticipated two or three hours with Michael and sensed it was a day for her to let her guard down and for them to concentrate on themselves as individuals and as a couple.

Parking her bicycle at the side of the house, she paused to take in the sky filled with white cotton clouds and the intermittent rays of sunshine. Kitty pulled on her white cardigan and took a moment to calm her breathing. She unloaded the baskets and ventured around the back of the property to the kitchen door where Michael greeted her, his sleeves rolled up and a spade in his hands.

'Let me help you,' he said, taking two of the packages. 'I bet I can guess what is wrapped in the tea towel, dear Daphne's scones,' he said, and Kitty heard the happiness in his voice, which made her relax even more.

'You guess correctly, and Jack sent vegetables, but looking at the patch you are digging I will suggest he sends you seed potatoes next time. I take it you are digging out a vegetable garden,' she replied.

Michael opened the back door and stepped to one side to allow her through. She placed her packages on the table.

'I took a walk around the village and saw the victory gardens thriving, and with so much time on my hands when not on duty, I decided to start a project. It has proved my physical fitness is not what it once was, but in time I know it will increase because I have found I truly enjoy gardening,' Michael said, washing his hands at the sink.

'An elderly lady had little money to pay for a simple treatment, so I agreed on a bottle of elderflower cordial and sixpence. Let's enjoy a glass, then I will clear my tools away and show you around the house.'

Kitty perched on a stool and sipped the drink he pushed her way across the table.

'You do seem at home, Michael. I know it is early days, but do you think you will settle here?' Kitty asked.

'It feels like home, and I am convinced it is the combination of a traditional English property set in a place with a Canadian name,' Michael replied. 'I'll be back in just a moment, feel free to take a look around the kitchen while I'm gone. It's Margaret's pride and joy, and I have made a promise to keep it tidy,' Michael said, laughing as he went outside to his shed.

Kitty remained seated. The kitchen was pristine, and she imagined standing at the window looking outside to enjoy the natural world not destroyed by bomb destruction, hearing a robin sing and not a child scream out for its parent, and for herself a calming of the turmoil that raged inside whenever she thought of the past. Something about this brick building brought about a desire to embrace the present.

Kitty walked over to the largest window, overlooking the back garden, and watched Michael tidy away his gardening tools, noticing the robin hopping around the base of the tree where she had fed him. The whole scene was picture-perfect and Michael moved around in an easy manner, much as he had when they'd first met in Birmingham. It made her recall him helping her when she had twisted her ankle in the snow. She thought back to how he'd organised the piper to play a special tune on the bagpipes just for her in Peebles. Those tender moments had been lost in the dramatic changes to their lives and a sadness washed over her when she thought of how one person holding a gun had stripped away so much of their romance. A rogue tear dripped onto the back of her hand as she leaned on the worksurface and she stood upright and wiped her hands on a nearby towel. Seeing his body sway and hearing him whistle, Kitty yearned to love Michael as she had in the past, to give romance another chance. She stepped outside to join him.

'Our robin friend has returned,' she said.

Michael looked across at her approaching him.

'I have a surprise for him, but it is still wet with paint,' he said, and pointed to inside the shed.

Standing in the centre was a flat wooden bird bath on a plinth.

'Did you make it?' Kitty asked.

'I did, from scraps of old wood from a rotten bench and a few nails. Impressed?' Michael said.

'I am, let's hope Robin will be too,' Kitty replied.

'Ready for the tour?' Michael asked and pushed shut the shed door.

'More than ready,' Kitty said, holding out her hand for him to take.

Michael wiped the dirt from his own hand down his trousers and grasped Kitty's with the reassuring firmness she had missed, and together they walked back inside.

'And this is the last room, the master bedroom,' Michael said as he pushed open a door on the upstairs landing. They had seen four bedrooms and a modern bathroom, and Kitty was surprised to find Michael had chosen a small room as his own.

'Why aren't you sleeping in here?' Kitty exclaimed when she saw the view from the window. The rolling hills went on for miles.

'I go to bed late and rise early so don't have the opportunity to admire the view, and Margaret doesn't need to clean such a large room when only one person uses it. Besides, I am not sure I want to get too comfortable here – it's a family home and I am a one-man band. The surgery can be held from a cottage just the same, so I will consider my options when I am financially stable, and one becomes available. I might even invest in a home, rather than renting one,' he said.

Kitty turned back to look outside. 'But who will look after Robin?' she said. 'You must stay here; it suits you. When you have dug over the garden, maybe decorate this room to suit your needs – turn it into a reading room, or a place to write your papers,' she said, but as she spoke the words she knew she was just speaking for the sake of it, and Michael had to make up his own mind.

The clouds hinted at grey, and she gave a sigh. 'I think it is time for me to cycle home. It has been a lovely visit, and I cannot believe how fast the time has flown,' she said.

'Don't go yet, Kitty. Stay, eat with me,' Michael said, his voice soft and low as he moved towards her.

Kitty's breath hitched in her throat as she saw the love in his eyes.

The cycle home was harder than the one going to see Michael. The drizzling rain and the fact she had left him after eating a light meal, and endless moments of cuddling into one another again, made it a tough journey. Michael had offered to telephone Stanley to tell him Kitty would be staying – in her own room – at the surgery, but she refused to hear of it, saying it was best for her to return for the evening duties. Inside she knew she wasn't sure she could sleep under the same roof alone with him in another room and it was too early in their new relationship to take things further outside of marriage.

'Please do not tell me romance is *not* in the air once again,' Stanley said as Kitty walked into the lounge.

'We had a visit together, he showed me around the place, and we ate a light tea together and I cycled home. Hardly romance, Stanley,' she replied, but sensed a slight tingle of a blush on her cheeks.

'If you say so,' Stanley teased.

Kitty sat down on the sofa and picked up a magazine. 'I say so,' she said, and flicked open the magazine, hoping the fanning of the pages would cool down her face, which now burned. She knew she was giving the game away about her and Michael. Stanley was no fool.

Chapter Thirty-Six

After three more visits to see Michael, she asked Margaret if she could bring Ruth to play with Arthur. When she met him, he was a calm, placid child and Kitty wanted Ruth to enjoy the company of a child outside of Fell Hall.

With Ruth's situation of not mixing with the other children and her heightened fear of public spaces, Kitty wanted to spend one to one time with her and find a way to ease her into the idea of living in a permanent orphanage. Since the party and mixing with the soldiers, Ruth had spent her days watching the sky, convinced living so close to an army base was going to encourage Hitler's pilots to send more bombs. Some of the older children ridiculed her to the point where she had once hidden in bushes at the bottom of the garden, creating a frantic manhunt.

When asked if the visit was one Michael was happy with, he reassured Kitty the little girl would be made welcome, and even offered to pick them up, but Kitty insisted they caught the bus, saying Ruth needed to step outside into the world once again. She did accept his offer of a ride home though, cognisant of the fact that the little girl might be tired after a full day out.

April was coming to an end and the war news filtered through with more horrific findings. Orphans arrived and left for new homes, their distress often affecting Kitty. She wanted to shut out the horrors for at least one day in the week, so spending time with Michael at his home became her chance to unwind. She and Margaret got on well and once she learned of Kitty and Michael's past, she was more than happy to encourage Kitty's visits, often hinting the place might become Kitty's home in the future. Neither Kitty nor Michael ever denied it, but it was never a topic of conversation either cared to dwell upon.

The bus ride was an uneventful one, with Ruth looking skywards out of the window, only flicking her head low for a brief glimpse at whatever Kitty was pointing out at the time. Once they left the bus, Kitty encouraged Ruth to look at the pretty wildflowers growing in the ditches, but the minute a shadow of a bird flashed across the lane, Ruth's head would settle back into her habitual bobbing up and down. Kitty worried the child would never be able to walk alone as on many an occasion she walked into things or slipped near the ditch.

Once at the house, Ruth clung onto Kitty not letting go even to enjoy a drink offered to her by Margaret. Arthur and Michael were in the garden and with the child attached to her skirt, Kitty made her way towards them.

'Hello, you two, meet my friend, Ruth. She's a little shy, but I know she is happy to be here,' Kitty said, stroking Ruth's head as she spoke.

Both Michael and Arthur glanced their way in greeting then carried on digging and planting seeds.

'Nice to meet you, Ruth. My buddy Arthur's a little shy too,' Michael said and slowly rose to his feet, leaning in to give Kitty a kiss on the cheek. 'I am glad you brought Kitty to see me today, thank you.'

Ruth continued to scan the sky.

'No change then?' Michael whispered to Kitty.

'None. I hope she can relax under the trees, where she can't see the sky,' Kitty replied.

'Arthur, let's show Ruth where the robin eats his meals, but we need to do so quietly. I think he has a wife now and there are babies in a nest nearby,' Michael said, encouraging Arthur to his side. Kitty walked with Ruth still clinging onto her skirt, but the closer they got to the denser area of trees, the less sky there was to see, and Ruth finally lowered her head, looking over at Michael.

The robin did not disappoint and for a brief while they watched him flit back and forth towards a tree at the far corner of the garden. Margaret joined them and announced there was a slice of carrot cake for each of them in the kitchen. Arthur, with no encouragement, turned to Ruth and took her hand. 'I'll show you where we wash our hands. Mammy's cake is delicious, come and have some,' he said.

Ruth looked up at Kitty in question.

'Go with Arthur, I will be right behind, Ruth,' she said, but Ruth refused to budge from her safe space.

'How about we all go indoors? We can have a game of snap,' Michael suggested. 'Arthur is good at snap, do you play, Ruth?' Michael held out his hand for Ruth to take.

Ruth gave a short nod, looked to Kitty for permission, then reached out and slipped her hand into his.

'Off you go, I am coming too,' Kitty said to Ruth as the little girl turned around to check she was following. Kitty took in the scene in front of her and marvelled at the man with the tiny child trotting alongside him looking at everything he pointed to. Not once did she look up at the sky.

By the end of the visit, Arthur and Ruth were firm friends, and although neither child said much, they communicated through play.

'Is she coming with us to the christening?' Michael asked. 'She is so attached to you it will be hard for her not to have you close by.'

'Daphne is going to watch over her,' Kitty replied.

'She has taken to you,' Margaret said and looked over at the children now flicking through a book of animals.

'And I to her, but she must learn to live without me around. Neither of us can get too close to one another. It isn't easy saying goodbye under normal circumstances, but if I let her in here' – Kitty patted over her heart – 'it will be hard to let her go. I was surprised she went to Michael, but that gives me hope she is trusting others, and she sits in the kitchen with Daphne and is fond of Stanley, so my couple of days away will not affect her too much. The other children won't be around as it is a changeover day, so she will get a lot of attention.'

'I cannot imagine how she feels losing both parents and her sibling like that, poor thing,' Margaret said with feeling.

Kitty pulled a face.

'Sadly, I can. I have been through the loss of parents through tragic circumstances. Fortunately, I never witnessed it like Ruth did, and that she had to endure such a thing is heartbreaking. Michael is an orphan, too,' Kitty said, glancing over at Michael and giving him a smile.

'Ruth is lucky to have you watching over her,' Michael said, reaching out for Kitty's hand and patting the back of it. 'I know I was.'

———

Back at Fell Hall, a different Ruth entered to the one that had left that morning. She thanked Michael for inviting her, without any encouragement from Kitty.

'Your manners would make your parents proud,' Michael said.

'Mammy always told me if someone is kind, you must be kind back and always say thank you. Sometimes she would tell Daddy off for forgetting his manners,' Ruth said shyly and giggled at the memory.

Kitty's heart swelled listening to the conversation.

'Go and find Daphne and tell her about your visit and your new friend, Arthur,' Kitty said.

'Bye-bye, Michael,' Ruth said and skipped towards the kitchen.

Both Kitty and Michael took a moment to watch her before stepping back outside to Michael's car.

'Michael the hero. Thank you for taking the time with her,' Kitty said.

'It's not hard. She is a cute child and we both understand her loss. I saw a little of you in her, that scared child facing the world. But instead of the sky, you tend to look to the sea. I'm confident she will win someone's heart and find a kind home. You of all people should know never to give up hope.'

'That's true. Thank you for a lovely day, Michael. I will see you at the station. It will be good to see Trixie again,' she said and leaned forward, kissing him on the cheek before walking back to the house.

Chapter Thirty-Seven

May 1945

'I cannot believe it is May already,' Daphne said and knocked on the kitchen wall 'White rabbits for the first of the month.'

Kitty laughed. 'My aunt used to do that, and it drove my uncle mad, he can never be doing with old wives' sayings,' she said.

Both women jumped when Stanley and Jack burst into the kitchen.

'He's dead!' Stanley shouted. 'Hitler's dead. I've just had confirmation from my friends on the base. Yesterday. He shot himself.'

Kitty stared at him. 'Breathe, Stanley, breathe. What does this mean for the war?' she asked.

'Without their leader and with the recent unrest, I suspect surrender will be on the cards.'

Kitty stood with her hands over her mouth in shock.

Daphne sat down in a seat and Jack went to her. 'Alright, lass?' he asked as Daphne lowered her head into her hands.

'Aye. Just thinking of my boys. Never coming home. Shot because one man had power and then no courage to face the consequences. My boys died for what?'

Stanley gave an embarrassed cough.

'I am sorry, Daphne; I did not think. We will count the cost, but those boys of yours will always be remembered as heroes, not Hitler. Your boys fought for peace and my goodness I think they have won. With Kitty going to Yorkshire, take yourself off to rest for a day or so. Jack and I can rustle up a meal between us. Go and see your sister. Be with family, the other ladies will help with Ruth,' he said.

Kitty still couldn't speak. She thought back to the days of crawling about in the rubble after the heavy bombings, of the dead bodies she had pulled from the wreckage. She recalled the screams of the injured on the beach in France when she and Michael took a rescue team, and of the soldiers she had nursed, like Stanley, who gave up their personal lives to fight for the right for freedom.

'Kitty?' Stanley's anxious voice filtered through her thoughts. 'Ready to go to the station?' he asked, and Kitty nodded.

'Do you think it is nearly over, Stanley?' she whispered.

'Time will tell, but I think there will be a lot of talk amongst the politicians on all sides. Germany is now at its weakest and there are some in Hitler's army who are ready to put an end to it all. The news is fresh; we will know more in a day or so,' he said.

The train journey was a noisy one with what sounded like every person chattering at louder levels than normal. Everyone seemed animated and upbeat as the word of Hitler's death was shared around the carriages.

Once she and Michael arrived at Trixie's, Kitty tried to ignore the conversations relating to possible peace, not wanting to live once again on hope and what might be; she needed something more concrete before she could celebrate. Instead, she focused on Rosey.

'You look well, Trixie, motherhood suits you,' she said when they sat alone watching Rosey sleep in her crib.

'She's a good baby. Sleeps, eats and smiles. I have a good life, which helps. I must say you and Michael look happier than at Christmas. I take it you have decided to try again?' Trixie said.

'We are taking it slowly. At a pace as if we have only just met. I won't rush into anything yet, but I do still love him. He needs to establish himself as a GP first, and then think about whether he wants that life or one back in Canada,' Kitty said.

Trixie gave a tch sound. 'Kitty, he came back for you. The job was an added bonus for him. He had already returned to England. He is back to win your heart again, he knows he did things the wrong way, but he did it for what he thought were the right reasons. Give yourselves both a chance.' She gave Kitty a sympathetic smile. 'If this war is near its end it is time to rebuild the country and for some, their lives. You two have a chance to be happy again, stop finding reasons not to love him properly.'

'But he didn't think about me, only himself. Surely that's reason enough for me to let him go?' Kitty said, gulping down the pain of her words before the tears flowed.

Trixie tutted again. 'Lose the stubborn thoughts of why you shouldn't marry him, and realise that if he is willing, then you can have a life together,' Trixie said and pointed at her daughter as she stirred in her crib. 'You could have this kind of contentment. You have given everything to the Red Cross, you still work hard alongside them supporting others, so when are you going to support yourself?'

Kitty lowered her head and shook it slowly from side to side. 'I'm not sure how to do as you suggest. I've always put others and their feelings first.'

Trixie reached over and clasped Kitty's hand.

'I am your friend; I will be here for you until the end of time. The war brought us together and we have held onto our friendship. Do the same for the love in *your* life. Be kind to yourself, Kitty.'

Kitty smiled at her. 'You are good for me, Trix and if you and I can keep being honest with one another, then maybe Michael and I stand a chance too. Time heals, or so they say, and I think the process has begun. I just worry with the war over he might want to return to his homeland…' she said.

Trixie clicked her tongue with an impatience she rarely showed. 'When will you get it into your head? He lived here for eight years before the war, and he was taken to Canada – he did not choose to go there for his recuperation – and when he did have a choice, he returned to you – in a roundabout way, I agree, but he turned up, he never avoided the visit. It's you who has to accept him back as the man he is now, not the one you once knew. As I see it, he has not changed that much, he has just forgotten a few simple things, nothing major. He has no health problems anymore and seeing him with Rosey, I know he will make a wonderful father.'

Kitty looked at her and put her lips together in a sad grimace. Trixie was right, Michael would make a wonderful father and she had always hoped it would be their luck to become parents together. She went to speak but Trixie held up her hand to stop her.

'Tomorrow you will be godparents to our daughter, and Smithy and I have no reservations in choosing you both. Be the couple we see, don't keep looking backwards for the one you once were.'

Kitty felt her friend squeeze her hand and again bit back any sadness, taking in Trixie's words. She was right, Kitty had to find a way to move out of the static state she had placed herself into and either walk away from Michael fully or open her eyes to what her future could be like, if only she could break down the barrier of protection she had put in place around her heart when he returned. Without her mother in her life, she had always turned to her aunt for emotional advice, but now she was no longer alive, Kitty struggled without a mother figure to confide in, and realised Trixie had just stepped into the role even if it was only for a brief moment.

'I promise I will try, Trixie,' she said just as Smithy and Michael entered the room, both men extremely upbeat.

'It's true, the British radio news has just announced Hitler's suicide!' Smithy said with loud excitement and swung Trixie an apologetic glance when Rosey stirred in her crib. They all waited for the baby to settle back down.

'Our vicar said this week was a good one as rather than funerals he is overrun with weddings in his parish, especially next weekend, hence us having Rosey's christening on a Wednesday. Let's hope it remains that way and there are more celebrations to add to them!' Trixie said with great excitement.

'It will be wonderful for the country to be able to celebrate something together at last. I think the last time was the coronation. Keep listening to the radio, boys, we need good news not just hints of maybe,' Kitty said.

'Kitty, I am going to stretch my legs before dusk, do you fancy a walk with me?' Michael asked.

From the corner of her eye, Kitty spotted Smithy nudge Trixie, and both smiled at one another.

'I think I might, I'll just fetch my coat,' she said.

Once outside, Michael crooked his arm and held it out for Kitty to take and without hesitation she looped hers through.

'The air's fresh. I cannot wait for the warmer evenings,' she said as they walked towards the end of the village. Michael stopped walking beside a small green area free from houses and turned her to face him.

'Small talk won't get us moving forward, Kitty,' Michael said. 'I have spoken to Smithy about us, and he said I should be bold and upfront with you to regain your trust. So, I am going to ask you formally to be my girl again. Not a friend who visits, but a woman who can see a future together with me. One whom I do not have to think about whether I should kiss her or not, one who is not afraid of me letting her down again. Kitty, please can we declare ourselves a courting couple once again?'

Kitty lowered her head and looked to the ground, knowing now was not the time for her to hesitate with her answer. Michael had spoken from the heart.

She lifted her head and looked him in the eye. 'I think it is time for me to stop living in the past, so yes. Yes, I will be your girl again, and please don't think about kissing me, just do it!' she said.

Michael did as she asked, and pulled her close. Kitty relaxed her body and melded into his. His warm lips pressed firm against her own and fed her a passion she had thought was never going to be hers again. She felt the depth of his love as he clung to her and in return, she silently showed him this kiss had been worth the wait.

It was a kiss which healed all pain, told a tale of impatience and want – it was a kiss so intense a wildness set into them both and eventually Michael stepped back from her, breathless and his eyes wet with emotion.

'There are some things I will never forget, and kissing you is one of them. But I think we need to stop for decency's sake,' Michael said, his voice husky as he slowed his breathing.

Kitty's heart pounded and for a short while did not want to consider decency's sake, but she knew Michael was right and gave a regretful nod.

Kitty shook with pleasure and registered the small beads of sweat across Michael's brow. Her insides fluttered with excitement as he traced a finger across her lips and stroked her cheek. His hand trembled as she leaned her cheek into its palm. Their passion had roared and raged like a furnace out of control and if not contained would take a path neither wanted until their wedding day. A day Kitty knew would happen if luck was on their side once again.

Rosey's simple christening ceremony led to a happy afternoon of relaxation. Both Kitty and Michael agreed the focus should be on Rosey and not them, so they kept their romantic feelings to themselves, only snatching the odd kiss when no one else was around. By early evening the kitchen chores were finished, and Rosey was settled down for the night. With eager anticipation all four adults sat around the radio waiting for the latest news report.

The moment they heard the Germans had surrendered in Italy, they shared a quiet cheer and Trixie opened a bottle of sherry and poured a glass for her and Kitty while the men enjoyed a rum.

'Here's to a glimmer of hope,' Smithy said, and they all chinked glasses to cheer on his toast.

Travelling back home with Michael the next day made Kitty happier than she had been in a long time. His humour and easy manner were back in full flow and the love between them grew by the minute. By the time they arrived at the station, they no longer hid their feelings for one another and when they saw Stanley waiting to collect them, they were openly holding hands.

'Now there's a sight which makes me smile,' he said to them both and kissed Kitty on the cheek. 'Welcome home and I am delighted to see that you have both come to your senses. Well done, old man, you have won the heart of the best girl around these parts again. And what about the news…'

The chatter and banter on the journey back to the surgery and then Fell Hall filled Kitty with so much joy she doubted the day could get any better. The days spent talking with Trixie had helped her anxiety disappear. Seeing Michael waving her off from his house was hard, but Kitty knew it was a place they could turn into a home together if given the opportunity.

Chapter Thirty-Eight

Kitty raced down the stairs and then composed herself at the front door before walking swiftly down the garden path to greet Michael as he climbed out of his car the following day. His visit to Fell Hall was not unexpected.

'What a start to the week! I won't rest until it is official tomorrow. It's over. Over five years of hell and back is at an end!' she said, her words rushed and excited as she flung herself into his arms.

Michael lifted her off her feet and twirled her around as if she had no weight. His lips found hers and their kiss was unashamedly long. Eventually, they pulled apart for decency's sake. Kitty pushed her foot back into one of her pumps, which had slipped off during their embrace, and straightened her hair.

'Sadly, I can't stay as I have to get to a home visit, but I wanted to see you after hearing the news. Sweetheart, we are about to start afresh. Churchill must be bursting to shout it out from the rooftops. What are your plans for the week?' Michael stopped talking to kiss her again. 'I will come tomorrow, and leave Fell Hall's telephone number on the front door of my cottage. Anyone who needs me can call here. I want to be with you when history is made in my adopted country,' Michael said.

Kitty smiled at him. She loved how Michael felt Great Britain had adopted him, enough that he had returned to help the country heal and grow with her at his side.

'We have no children at the hall apart from Ruth, and none arriving this week. Stanley insists Daphne needs an assistant even though I said I am more than willing to continue extra chores, which means I am interviewing a girl to help us this afternoon. I aim to clean the orphans' bedrooms and wait for the Red Cross to alert us of more arrivals. With the war ending I suspect we will find more than ever. By the end of the week though, I will be free to visit when you are not holding surgery … but I will have to bring Ruth along as it is not fair on Daphne to train the new girl and watch over a little one at the same time,' she said.

'Honey, you can visit me anytime, you know that, and how can I refuse a visit from Arthur's little buddy? Margaret is leaving with him next week, so it will be good for the children to play together for a few hours. I'll miss him. When you come Margaret can introduce you to the new housekeeper. I met her this morning, a Mrs Temple. She's a bit of a grump in my opinion but if she keeps a good house I am not going to complain too much. She even managed to grumble about Churchill and people in Quebec planning a victory party. And you should have heard her when I said I intended to be here with you to celebrate. Apparently, I am not the sort of village doctor she expected. Young and foreign was not what she had in mind,' Michael said with a loud laugh.

'Someone is in good spirits and rightly so,' Stanley called out to them.

Michael waved to him. 'Ah, Stanley, how are you doing? I've just come to get myself a victory hug from my girl. Can you believe we're at the end of a very dark tunnel?'

Kitty listened to the two men exchange opinions about some areas in the world where battles were still ongoing, before Michael made his apologies, saying that he really had to set off to visit his patient.

'I will leave you two to say your goodbyes and hunt out the celebratory wines I have saved for special occasions. I look forward to celebrating with you tomorrow, old chap,' Stanley said, patting Michael on the shoulder.

Kitty and Michael walked to his car hand in hand, and with each step Kitty felt the past drop away. When he pulled her in for another kiss, she closed her eyes and allowed her happiness to suffocate the unwanted memories as she made new ones.

After refreshing the upstairs rooms where the orphans slept. Kitty went to check on Ruth and Daphne, who shooed her away as they were busy baking for the following day. Daphne had stored away ingredients that would not spoil for special days and had decided to use them all for a Victory Day feast.

Kitty pottered about the house until the interview, which was a success. The young girl of sixteen was the daughter of a woman who had worked at Fell Hall in the past. Kitty decided she was suitable, offered her the job and sent her to introduce herself to Daphne.

Taking advantage of more alone time, Kitty took a bath and back in her bedroom she selected a well-worn dress to wear for the rest of the day, then chose one to air for the following day – a green floral party dress as it was going to be a day which deserved such an outfit. As she pulled it out, her eyes went to the wedding outfit she had made for her uncle's wedding in June, and she stroked it smooth on its hanger. The thought her uncle would marry during peacetime made her smile. Sadly, the letter sitting on her dressing table, which she had received from Meryn that morning, did not.

Dear Kitty,

My news is not happy news. I am struggling with being told that Lewis is a cheat and that he has put me in a difficult position. Instead of being his fiancé I have been used as a mistress. He is married! Can you believe he has a wife and three children back in America? He also had two others like myself and promised them marriage as well – what a fool I am!

As the men were moving out a soldier approached me with a note, not from Lewis but from himself. It appears several of Lewis's unit know about my deafness and he wanted to approach me alone to tell me the news that Lewis has now been shipped back to America. The soldier learned that Lewis had not confessed to the truth with me. I have also had a visit from Kedrick's father, Bobby. He had learned that Lewis was not my son's father and he asked me if he was, and I told him the truth. I allowed him to meet Kedrick, and he now visits every day. Pots is so angry about Lewis and of course, he was never fond of Kedrick's father, but Bobby has been supportive of me since Lewis left, and he has given me money to put in the bank

for Kedrick. I know Wenna worries, but it is not right of me to keep
father and son apart now the truth is out. My own feelings for Bobby
are not romantic anymore, but I am certain we can be good friends
for Kedrick's sake. Bobby is staying in Britain for an extra six
months, so Pots will have to calm down or Kedrick will lose his
daddy, and I am convinced he misses Lewis, so Bobby fills a gap
for him.

I truly hope you are happy and well, and I cannot wait to see you
again. I am sad but not silly, I have my son and need to keep going.

Stay well and safe my dear friend,

Much love,

Meryn (and Kedrick) x

Kitty read the letter several times and was shocked to the core. Lewis had not only let Meryn down but several of their friendship group too. How could he have lied to and deceived such a vulnerable young woman? After she had inwardly raged, Kitty settled down and tried to pen a letter offering support. After three attempts she was finally satisfied with her words.

Dear Meryn,

My darling girl, I am so sorry to hear about Lewis.

It breaks my heart to think he was not honest with you – with
any of us. How dare he give you hope and promises of a new life out
there? I rue the day I introduced you. I thought he was more of an
honest man than he turned out to be, and I am sorry it was you he let
down. I would like to shake the hand of the man who found the
courage to come and tell you the truth about Lewis, and am thankful
Lewis has returned to his own country away from the wrath of Pots.
I truly hope Bobby can keep in contact and Pots does not frighten

him away. What happened between you and Bobby in the past was wrong, and you learned a hard lesson, but Kedrick is the child of both of you and it is a brave man to come back to the inn after being sent away by Pots.

Thank goodness for Wenna and her motherly help. She will guide you through this and I thank goodness you have the inn to bring you an income. As soon as I am able I will come to visit.

Be brave my dear and know that I am thinking of you as we wait to hear news of peace.

Your friend,

Kitty.

Walking to the post box, Kitty was torn. She wanted to rush to Cornwall to comfort Meryn, but she also wanted to celebrate with Michael and Stanley. Meryn's news was shocking to Kitty and the thought that she had let Lewis into her friendship circle made her feel dreadful and taken advantage of. He had lied and cheated, led them all on with his generous gifts. They had been blinded by tasty treats and he had slid into their homes as comfortable as a relative, all the time knowing he had a wife and children worrying about him in another country.

The one silver lining was that Kitty knew her young friend was in good hands and the motherly Wenna would guide her through the distress. As an innocent brought up in the small Cornish village, unable to hear the banter and teasing shared in the public house, having two men take advantage probably made the girl feel worthless. She was a sensitive soul, and it would take her some time to recover from the shock of cancelling her wedding day, but Kitty hoped Meryn would not give up on finding love. Thank goodness Bobby had found it in himself to not make a song and dance about not being informed of Meryn's pregnancy when he was sent on his way after being caught taking advantage. His friendship was clearly an important boon for Meryn and it would be good for her to see that, although he had flattered her into submission, he had not shied away from his responsibility as a father once he learned about his son.

Despite her initial upbeat mood about the end of the war, Kitty felt the tap of melancholy on her shoulder and did her best to shrug it off.

She had to stop fretting and learn not to take on everyone else's problems. She had a life of her own to rebuild and, although it felt selfish, it was her relationship she needed to focus upon. She told herself to trust that Wenna would give the comfort Meryn would seek under such circumstances and planned to visit just as soon as her own life was on track once more.

Back at the hall, she played shops and built a house under the dining table for Ruth, by draping a sheet over the table and finding items for her to sell. Memories of her childhood with her aunt doing the same came flooding back and Kitty thanked her stars she had a loving family to scoop her up after her parents' death.

The news that Ruth would remain at Fell Hall for another month saddened Kitty as the child deserved a settled home before she became too comfortable at the hall.

By the evening Kitty and Stanley sat alone reflecting upon their first meeting and the days prior, when the first stages of war had begun and they were caught up in the Roker Beach bombing. Stanley spoke gently of his wedding day with Jenny before the war, and of his struggles after her death. Kitty told him of her confidential escorting of Hitler's man, Hess. She also confided about the woman she originally knew as Annabelle, trusting him with the news of Jo accidently seeing her in France, both of them working for the good of Great Britain. However, Kitty ensured she did not break her promise not to reveal the meeting with Lizzie and the Secret Service agents.

Stanley told her of operations where he had predicted German flights and how the outcome was not always a positive one and many times they slipped through the net. He admitted he had cried for the civilians lost in the bombings.

It was an evening of open, honest friendship and Kitty felt their relationship moved from that of employee/employer, and into one of brother and sister. Neither had siblings but she imagined this scenario was happening all over the country with family members, and she knew Stanley was to be part of her life forever. He would be her support alongside Michael if anything happened to her uncle. War might have altered a lot for the negative, but it had also brought about positives. Because if war had not broken out, she would never have met the most important people in her life.

Chapter Thirty-Nine

The following day Michael arrived just before eleven o'clock and Stanley, Michael, Jack, Daphne, Ruth and Kitty all dressed in their Sunday best, stood listening to the church bells ring out the official end of the war in Europe.

There was not a dry eye in the house. Even Ruth understood the importance of the day and Kitty suspected the child had questions she did not know how to ask, about her future. There was one thing living through a war, and another dealing with peacetime and the changes that came with it. Everything would be different and for a child with no family to celebrate victory or be reunited with, it must have been overwhelming and confusing.

Kitty held her close, thoughts going through her head of how she could persuade Stanley to keep Ruth at Fell Hall. It would need to be a topic of conversation for a later date, for now she reassured Ruth they were going to help her, and it was all right to smile, skip and play for the whole day. Ruth was given permission to be a child, and the look in her eyes as she peered up at Kitty was that of trust and adoration. Nothing would stop her until Ruth had the nurturing home she deserved.

Later in the afternoon they tuned into the radio station and waited for the official announcements and the declaration that it was Victory in Europe Day.

Daphne dabbed her eyes at regular intervals and Kitty noticed Jack comfort her each time. It was a touching scene and she hoped they would find comfort in their companionship at Fell Hall. Stanley tapped his walking stick impatiently against the fireplace, and Michael gripped her hand, with Ruth on his shoulders as they stood staring at the large dome framed machine, which was about to share words altering their lives, this time for the positive. This time to announce peace.

When the deep voice of Winston Churchill boomed across the room, they listened with intense concentration. When he mentioned a bird that chirped in the heart, Kitty thought of the brave robin in Michael's garden. The world had hundreds of heroic robins, some dead, some wounded, some alive and bereft of energy, others finding a new path to follow either through choice or necessity, and some still fighting in countries outside of Europe; every one of them beyond brave.

When the Prime Minister had finished talking there was a moment of silence before they all cheered and called out 'God Save the King'.

Outside they could hear the soldiers from the castle cheering and the villagers shouting out their joy.

Nearly six years of fear had come to an end. Now was the time to release the pent-up tension. Kitty and Michael embraced and clung to each other tighter than ever before.

This was a new start. A precious moment. There was no need to speak; their shared kisses spoke volumes.

Walking through Brancepeth with Ruth gripping her hand tightly, Kitty was overwhelmed with the atmosphere around them. The mass outpouring of joy was everywhere and shone in every face she looked at. Ruth trotted alongside her and giggled when they were hugged and kissed by strangers, handed beers, cider, sandwiches and cakes, and on more than one occasion persuaded to join in with the dancing. Each street celebrated in style. After two hours of partying, Stanley declared his leg sore, Daphne complained her bunions ached, and Kitty her jaws hurt from smiling too much. Michael carried an exhausted Ruth in his arms, and Jack three bottles of light ale, a gift from a friend who suggested he didn't ask where it had come from, just enjoy them as a reward for helping out the village in times of trouble. By the time they had walked the length and breadth of the village, all of them had hoarse voices from singing and eventually they agreed it was time to return home. Kitty made up a bed for Michael in the guest room, and they spent the evening sitting under the stars before reluctantly parting in the early hours.

The household moved into a slow state of greeting the following morning. Michael went home after breakfast, and the residents of Fell Hall settled into the usual daily pattern, with Jack a little slower than normal and Daphne soaking her feet to ease their ache. Ruth went to feed the resident pet rabbit, a chore she happily took upon herself and Kitty encouraged.

A sluggish postboy rode his bike along the driveway and handed Kitty a telegram. She tore it open.

Back in Blighty. Jo.

As always Jo was economical with the words, but the meaning brought so much joy and relief to Kitty that she allowed the tears of joy to roll down her face, only stopping to cuff them away when Ruth appeared to join her for breakfast.

'Are you sad, Kitty?' Ruth asked in a soft, concerned voice as they walked inside.

Kitty kissed the top of the child's head taking in the aroma of her freshly washed hair. She lifted her onto a seat at the dining table and poured her a glass of milk.

'Far from it, darling. I am very happy. My best friend has returned safely back to England, the war has ended and I have good company to celebrate it with. It is the happiest day I have known for a long time.'

Ruth gave a slight sigh and Kitty gave her a quizzical look. 'Ruth, you are too young to sigh like an old man. What is the matter, my lovely?'

Without saying a word, Ruth popped her thumb in her mouth and climbed onto Kitty's lap. Kitty understood and moved into a more comfortable seat. Kitty understood that Ruth might worry that if she confessed she was happy it meant she had to stop being sad about losing her family. A child could only deal with so many emotions, and she herself had been in the same position once.

'We will make it right for you, Ruth. Let the sadness go. You are still so little, and your mummy and daddy would want to see you smile. We'll have a little cuddle, shall we? It will help both of us,' she said as she pulled Ruth closer.

The soft sounds of Ruth's breathing and the small movements of her rosebud lips as she fell asleep in Kitty's embrace gave Kitty goosebumps. She remembered doing the same in her aunt's lap, a safe place of comfort.

'You sleep little one. I will fight your demons away,' Kitty whispered as she stroked Ruth's soft fair hair.

It was over an hour later when Stanley entered the room and Ruth woke. She looked up at Kitty and leaned into her chest again.

'Hello, girls, did I catch you napping?' Stanley asked.

'Ruth is about to have milk and biscuits, Stanley. Stay here, we need to talk,' Kitty said quietly.

Chapter Forty

Cycling to Michael's took a little longer than normal with her precious cargo. Jack had adapted the bike with a small seat attached to the back and Ruth was securely in place, with her arms wrapped around Kitty's waist.

Once they arrived, Ruth ran to find Arthur in the garden and give him the picture she had drawn of them both. Kitty had explained about him leaving that afternoon, and said that she should give him her address so they could share pictures when he was gone.

Stanley had agreed Ruth should stay at Fell Hall and not be transferred to an orphanage. He wrote to the Red Cross and local authorities declaring he and Kitty were prepared to be her guardians until a more suitable home was found for her. They both had little doubt the answer would be 'yes'. With the amount of children needing temporary accommodation, it would mean one less for the authorities to have to deal with.

'All packed?' Kitty asked Margaret.

'Yes, my brother-in-law came to fetch most of it a few days

ago. Michael kindly allowed us to stay here so I could close up our cottage. Arthur has taken it well, thankfully. It's nice to see he and Ruth look so happy and carefree out there. I wish they could stay like this; I don't want him to grow up and carry the burdens of adulthood,' Margaret replied.

Kitty patted Margaret's arm. 'You have been through a tough time, let yourself relax a little when you get to your new home. Write to us at Fell Hall, I would love to keep in touch,' she said.

Margaret laid a hand over Kitty's. 'Michael is a lucky man. I wish you only happiness, Kitty,' she said.

'Good luck,' Kitty said and the women embraced.

Michael entered the kitchen and went to the sink to wash his hands.

'I see, Margaret gets to hug you first,' he said with a grin as he wiped his hands dry.

'Silly. You will get a hug from Ruth if you ask,' Kitty replied, ducking the tea towel thrown her way.

'Don't forget to send me an invitation to the wedding,' Margaret said as she picked up her belongings. Her words were left hanging in the air as she walked to the door and called for Arthur.

'Ruth is going to be upset to see him go,' Michael said and Kitty was thankful for the change in conversation.

'I have explained it to her, but she is still so excited by Stanley telling her she might be able to live with us a while longer, I think if we make a fuss of her when they go, we can keep her upbeat.'

Kitty was pleased to find that waving Margaret and Arthur goodbye was not as upsetting for Ruth as they had expected. Michael scooped the child into his arms and carried her into the garden with the promise of a surprise.

Intrigued, Kitty followed them and watched as Michael set Ruth down and told her to cover her eyes. He went behind the garden shed and reappeared with a large wooden object.

Kitty's eyes widened. Michael had made a swing.

'Open,' Michael instructed Ruth and she did as asked.

Both Kitty and Michael burst into laughter as Ruth jumped and bounced around in excitement. Michael put the swing on the ground on one side of the garden and then lifted Ruth onto the seat. She held tightly to the rope on either side of her as Michael pushed her higher and higher. She squealed out in delight, her smile filling her face and Kitty clapped in delight to see the little girl so happy.

'Your woodworking skills are impressive,' she said.

Michael grinned.

A shrill sound came from the house and Michael frowned.

'I'll answer it,' Kitty said, but before she turned around a voice from the kitchen doorway boomed out across the garden.

'Urgent call for you, doctor. I've taken down the information and put the address on your desk. It's Mrs Andrews. Last breath, I expect.'

Michael put his hand up and waved to the buxom middle-aged woman in a floral pinafore apron who had called out to him.

'On my way, Mrs Temple,' he said.

'Where on earth did she come from?' Kitty asked. The woman hadn't been in the house when they arrived or when Margaret left.

'She has a door key and lets herself in, but I wasn't expecting her today. I'm sorry, but I have a house call today when you've come to visit. I'm afraid you will be left with her roaming around muttering to herself, so just make yourself comfortable and try not to be intimidated by her – I was the first time I met her. She voices her opinions loudly,' Michael said with a grin as they both walked to the house.

'I think I'll manage; I have worked with hospital matrons don't forget,' Kitty said, laughing.

With one eye on Ruth happily swinging, Kitty stood by the large kitchen window waiting for Michael to collect his medical bag from his office.

Mrs Temple hovered in the background and as soon as Michael had left the room, gave a huff sound and said in a blunt manner, 'I suppose you are his fancy piece from Fell Hall. If you and the child want feeding I will need rations from you. His food won't feed an army.'

Kitty turned away from the window and stared at the cold face. She tried to justify that the woman may have lost family and her personality was a protective front, but Kitty doubted it. No, she would bet money on the fact that Mrs Temple was a sour, spiteful woman whose family trembled each time she entered a room.

'I am Kitty Patterson, Doctor McCarthy's girlfriend, yes. Ruth is the name of the child and she is in my care. As for food, we always bring a good supply from the gardener of Fell Hall,' Kitty replied, using a firm voice of authority. The woman was Michael's housekeeper, not his mother, and Kitty deserved more respect.

'He did say he wasn't expecting you today, so as I am here

and have brought him plenty of supplies, might I suggest you enjoy a rest day and come back tomorrow.'

Michael entered the room just as she spoke.

'Good idea, sweetheart. Mrs Temple, I will see you tomorrow. Kitty, I will be back soon,' he said and rushed out of the door.

'Well, I think I will leave you to it and head home,' Mrs Temple said, poking a hatpin into her hat with such force Kitty thought she might have a patient of her own to attend to. She marvelled at the way the woman had turned the dismissal around to a decision she had made for herself. Kitty was done with battles and war so merely smiled sweetly.

'I hope we meet again soon, Mrs Temple. Next time I will ask Jack our gardener to pack a few items for yourself. Maybe even a rabbit for you and Michael to enjoy one day,' she said and returned her attention to Ruth on the swing.

She flinched when the front door slammed and made a mental note for Michael to give the woman a key for the backdoor. The front door was to welcome friends through, not women who wanted to rule others. Dictators had no place in what Kitty now hoped would be her future home, though she dared not approach the subject in case Michael was not quite ready to take their relationship into marriage. Deep inside she knew he would be willing, but until he approached the subject, Kitty was not going to, wary of coming across as being pushy or too eager. She couldn't deny, however, that watching Ruth and standing inside this beautiful home brought about a longing, and Kitty knew only Michael could ease that want.

Chapter Forty-One

Days ticked along with Kitty visiting Michael on a more regular basis. Stanley received official notification that Ruth could stay at Fell Hall, and Mrs Temple grumbled her way through life at the surgery.

The German Army continued to surrender in countries throughout Europe, and the newspapers filled their pages with the successes of Great Britain and the Allied forces.

Food was still hard to come by, but the upbeat spirit of the fortunate helped ease the pain of those going through the traumatic losses caused by the war in Europe, and those awaiting news of family still fighting further away in the continuing world war.

Fresh faces arrived at Fell Hall, with all sixteen beds soon filled by children. For some, it put them in a better place mentally than their previous lives, but for others, it made things worse. Kitty spent nights reassuring unsettled children to the point of exhaustion and Stanley, after announcing his concern for her, had employed two resident support staff to help. This change and extra support was welcome but it also meant Ruth would no longer have a room of her own. After giving it a lot of thought, Kitty made a corner of her room free to accommodate her. She knew the little girl's nightmare screams would disturb the majority of the children and, until they were less frequent, it was better for all if she did not sleep in the dormitory rooms.

Stanley expressed disapproval over Ruth disrupting Kitty's privacy, but Kitty knew it was not going to be long before Ruth would be able to cope, so stood her ground. A week later she was proved right when Ruth slept through the night, and during the following days of late May, she even made a new friend and no longer clung to Kitty, but simply ran back and forth to tell of exciting new discoveries in the garden.

Waving to Michael as her train left the station, Kitty felt a wave of sadness he was not joining her on a trip to Durham to meet with Jo, but he had insisted it was important she had time with her dearest friend. They were like sisters who needed to unwind and express themselves freely together, and he was busy setting up new clinics with the district nurse.

As the train pulled in, she could see Jo pacing the platform in her usual impatient way. Alighting from the train, Kitty called out to her and Jo's smile warmed her heart. Her dearest friend had survived.

'Hello, you,' Jo said as they embraced.

'You're safe,' Kitty said in an emotionally choked whisper.

Jo linked her arm through Kitty's. 'You had doubts?' she quipped. 'How unlike you, Kitty Pattison.'

'You are horrible,' Kitty replied, laughing. Being able to banter freely without the weight of the world upon their shoulders kept Kitty and Jo buoyant as they walked. They chatted and pointed out things of interest until they arrived at the bed and breakfast run by her landlady friend, Nelly.

'Kitty!' Nelly welcomed her with a squeezing hug. 'How's that doctor fiancé of yours?' she asked.

'Not my fiancé anymore, but he is back in England. A village doctor in Quebec, so he will probably visit sometime,' Kitty said. 'I'll explain more later.'

'That's a shame, you were made for each other,' Nelly said. 'Jo's already got the key for the room, I'm sorry I haven't got two rooms spare. Since peace was declared the city has been busy, not that I'm complaining.'

Once in the room, Kitty freshened up and unpacked her small case.

'Don't get too comfortable, I've made arrangements for us,' Jo said. 'A friend is staying nearby, so I thought we could meet in the tearoom around the corner.'

'A friend?' Kitty asked. 'A male friend?'

Jo picked up her jacket. 'You'll see,' she replied.

Inside the tearoom, Jo manoeuvred Kitty into a quiet area with a table set back from view. She noticed a tall, slim redhead sitting there already and as Jo touched the woman's shoulder the stranger faced Kitty, her smile wide and grey-green eyes shining. She stood up to greet Jo with a brief embrace and then held her hand out to Kitty.

'Howdy. You sure are the honey Jo described. A true Brit

beauty,' she said in an accent Kitty had never heard before but guessed to be American. Michael's Canadian accent was softer.

'Nice to meet you, but I am afraid I'm at a disadvantage as she has never mentioned you ... um, I'm sorry, I don't think I caught your name,' Kitty said, taking the woman's hand and receiving a tight gripped handshake.

'Gina – Virginia if you want the longwinded version. And you truly are a quaint English girl with your manners. Just like your Princess Elizabeth,' Gina said, sitting back in her seat. Jo sat opposite and Kitty joined her.

'You've met the princess?' Kitty asked in awe.

'I had the pleasure briefly. Good to see her get her hands dirty like the rest of us,' Gina said.

'How wonderful,' Kitty said and looked at Jo. 'I know you haven't met her because you would have told me; wouldn't you?'

An expression flashed across Jo's face.

Kitty looked at Jo with suspicion, her friend was holding something back.

'You did? You met the princess!' she exclaimed as the realisation hit.

Jo gave a dismissive huff. 'Don't be ridiculous. As you said, I would have told you. I was just about to say our other guest has arrived.'

Kitty leaned sideways and looked around Gina to get a better view of the tearoom, and to her surprise, she saw Lizzie walking their way. Giving a frantic glance to Jo, then at Gina, Kitty pushed back her seat.

'It's um, Lizzie,' she said not really sure what to say or do in front of Jo's American friend.

'It is, and she is joining us for tea. Don't worry, she and

Gina know one another. We three worked together for a while, a small job after the doughnut vans. I didn't get the chance to let you know,' Jo said, her voice loaded with an implied *say nothing to give away you know I went to France.*

Kitty looked at Gina then Jo and, as she watched Lizzie approach the table, she guessed that they were part of a team. To Kitty's horror, Lizzie's face had more scars and she wore a large bandage on her left arm. She no longer looked anything like the proud Annabelle Farnsworth Kitty once knew but like someone who had either been beaten or caught in a bomb blast. Lizzie's hair was cut to just beneath her ears with fewer curls than before and her eyes were dark beneath her fringe, with tell-tale circles indicating a lack of sleep. Kitty gave her a shy smile trying hard not to look at her with pity. She guessed Lizzie had endured quite a trauma and decided to be civil and not distant with her. Now was not the time to hold onto the past.

'Hello, all,' Lizzie said as she arrived at the table. 'Gina, Kitty, this is a nice surprise.'

'There's a few surprises going on here today,' muttered Kitty with light joviality swinging Jo a glance.

Jo patted Lizzie's back. 'Welcome back. You had us worried for a while,' she said.

'Now, there's a first, Joanne Norfolk worrying about me,' Lizzie said with a light-hearted laugh.

Something in their banter suggested a stronger friendship between Jo and Lizzie, which surprised Kitty having seen them at loggerheads when they were Jo and Belle in the past.

'Good to see you back, my friend. Glad to see you in one piece,' Gina said but made no move to approach Lizzie nor Lizzie to her, the two women simply sharing a knowing look.

Jo and Gina's words made Kitty realise Lizzie must be fresh back from a mission – and possibly interrogation – and a profound sense of admiration rumbled through her.

'It's good to see you again.' Kitty rose to her feet to shake hands with Lizzie, but Lizzie stepped forward and gave her a one-arm embrace.

'It's good to see you again too, Kitty. You look well,' she said, and Kitty felt a tremor of guilt for ever doubting the woman who was probably a heroine of the Secret Service given the bruises and scars she wore.

'I'm parched,' Lizzie said as she sat and poured tea from their pot into a cup produced by the waitress.

'Did you get your ticket out?' Gina asked and Kitty noticed Jo swing her a strange look.

'I did. Three days to go. Did you collect yours, Jo?' Lizzie asked, replacing her cup in its saucer.

Kitty listened to the flow of the conversation. Something strange was going on and she felt on edge. Here were two women who had obviously worked for the Secret Service, two knew she knew, but the other, Gina, she wasn't sure about.

'Did you two work together in the entertainment unit?' she asked, addressing Gina and Jo. 'I know Lizzie worked for the Red Cross.'

There was an awkward silence amongst the three and it frustrated Kitty when she saw them share yet another loaded glance.

'I am feeling a tad uncomfortable sitting here with you all sharing secretive looks between yourselves. I will go and powder my nose and when I return I hope you will have spoken about whatever it is that is making me feel out of place sitting here,' she said and pushed her chair back.

Jo tugged at her arm. 'Sit down Kitty. I will explain,' she said.

'I'm all ears,' said Kitty, her mood dampened. She had been looking forward to sharing time with Jo alone and was frustrated to find herself in this awkward situation instead, with Lizzie appearing so unexpectedly.

'I was going to tell you later, but now seems the right time. I am going to work in America and I leave soon,' Jo said.

No longer surprised by Jo's ability to move from post to post, Kitty shrugged her shoulders. 'That will be interesting, how long for?' she asked.

Jo drank the remainder of her tea.

'For however long I want to live there for,' Jo said looking at Kitty. 'It is a permanent position within the American government.'

Giving her friend a hard stare, Kitty tried not to react to what she had just heard. She gripped her hands together in her lap and felt all eyes were upon her, waiting in anticipation.

'Honey, don't worry about Jo. She'll be in good hands,' Gina said and Kitty saw Lizzie nod in agreement.

'You knew?' she said, addressing Lizzie.

Lizzie bit her lip making her look more like the Belle of the past.

'I did. I'm going too. All three of us have accepted work out there,' Lizzie replied and Kitty saw a flush of red cross her cheeks.

'That's not what I expected to hear,' Kitty said to Jo. 'But I guess I shouldn't be surprised. You have worked with the American girls on the doughnut run long enough; they must have really sold their country to you.'

Jo nodded and Kitty noticed she also blushed.

'Oh, we Yanks, as you call us, just love a Brit. Jo is ready to explore. She's good at her job,' Gina chipped in before Jo could speak. Kitty ignored Gina and addressed Jo again.

'I know Bristol isn't a place you would want to return to, so realistically it is a great adventure to try out. Will you all live in the same place, like an army base or something like that?' she asked, fishing for more information.

Jo shook her head. 'No, it is a civilian position, and I will … well, Gina has a place of her own and I am moving in with her,' she said, and Kitty noticed a slight flush across Jo's cheeks.

'I'm going to be living with my husband's family until we get a place of our own,' Lizzie chipped in, forcing Kitty to lean back in her seat with shock.

'You're married? To an American. Jo is moving to America, living with an American woman…' Then the realisation of what she said about Jo struck her, and she looked to her friend for further confirmation. She recalled the time Jo had arrived wearing lipstick for the first time and noted Gina wore what looked to be the same shade. Knowing she could not ask the question for fear of getting them both into serious trouble with the police, Kitty said nothing and simply turned to Lizzie.

'Congratulations on your marriage. What is your name nowadays?' she said with a slight cut of sarcasm.

Gina gave a loud burst of laughter and heads turned their way.

'You sure ask a lot of questions. You would fit right in, come and join us,' she said, and Kitty noticed Jo look to the floor.

Was she embarrassed? Feeling awkward?

Kitty couldn't quite put her finger on it, but something was not registering as right with her – Gina was too loud for Jo. Female or male, if Jo was to choose a partner their personality would not be so large. She knew Jo well, and suddenly she wasn't convinced of the supposed relationship. Was it a front for something?

An anger rumbled inside Kitty. The whole affair was too much for her to comprehend and she was annoyed at Jo for putting her in the position of shock and upset.

'I think I ask enough to warrant an answer,' Kitty said in a harsh whisper, leaning into Gina, sharing the hostile sensation brewing inside. The woman was far too overfamiliar and it irritated Kitty.

'If you are here to recruit me for something in America, I am not, I repeat *not* interested in leaving Britain. Is that understood?' Kitty said, giving a sweeping glance around the table. Their blank faces and silence gave her an answer – that *had* been their intention. Furious that Jo had put her in such an awkward position, Kitty turned to her friend.

'So, as you have failed to draft me into working for the American government, or whatever unit you work for, I think it's best I leave. I am happy for you if you are happy, Jo, but I do not appreciate being ambushed in this way.'

Gina gave a cough; it sounded a fake one and Kitty chose to ignore it before she said something she might regret saying in public.

'Write to me via Fell Hall if you are able,' Kitty said softly to Jo and stood up to leave.

'Don't leave, Kitty,' Jo said, rising to her feet as well.

'I have to, Jo. Our worlds are completely different – always have been – but we will always be friends. I am pleased to know you are not going to be alone when you leave Britain but it is best I return to Brancepeth. Now, let me give you a hug for the journey,' she said and grabbed hold of Jo giving her a tight squeeze. She then turned to Gina. 'Take care of her,' she said. Moving towards Lizzie, she hesitated.

'Tell Belle I forgive her for being such a beast, Lizzie. Good luck in America – all of you, safe journey,' she said and walked away from the table.

She knew Jo would leave her to walk away, and hoped the other two women would do the same as she was only just holding on to her tears of letting go.

Kitty walked back to the bed and breakfast at great speed, sad to the core that she and Jo would become nothing more than pen pals, and she was jealous to think that Lizzie-dash-Belle, a woman they had both once despised, would have the bulk of Jo's friendship in America. The war had shaken up Kitty's world once again, creating a void that would never be filled by another friend in the future. She had a love for Jo that only the best of friends could ever understand.

Once back, she wrote Jo a farewell note expressing her shock, sadness and love. She also left some money as her share of the room. She packed away her things and made her way downstairs, avoiding Nelly and feeling guilty for not saying goodbye. She knew Jo would make up a story as to why she had left early, so there was no need to put herself through the upset of making one up herself.

Chapter Forty-Two

Kitty rushed to the train station and checked with the clerk about a return ticket home. The woman told her there was no return train for several hours, but a bus left from outside the station and would arrive within the half hour.

In just over two hours, Kitty was back at Fell Hall. Making use of the telephone in the hallway, Kitty spoke to Michael, asking him to visit whenever he was free, saying she would explain in person why she was back home the same day she'd left and reassuring him all was well. As she replaced the handset, Stanley appeared from the kitchen and threw her a puzzled look.

'Missed your train?' he asked.

Kitty picked up her bag. 'No, but in a way I wish I had. I've been and had no need to stay,' she said.

'Didn't Jo turn up? No wonder you look worried,' Stanley said.

'She turned up, and to be honest, Stanley, I am worried about her but can do nothing about it. Jo has a new life ahead of her in America, which means we couldn't stay together long,' Kitty said, adjusting the truth so no further explanation was necessary.

'Good for her. Give her my regards when you write to her next. By the way, I caught a couple of the boys tramping through the vegetable garden. Jack tore them off a strip but it appears they have been sleeping rough since losing their mother. They are fifteen but look much older' – Stanley pointed to the kitchen – 'and they are in the kitchen with Daphne. You can tell it's been a few days since they've eaten. After chatting with them I have offered them food and board in exchange for labouring work here. I have something in the pipeline that will keep them busy for several months, after which I will help them find jobs to suit,' he said.

Thankful Stanley was too distracted to ask any more questions about Jo's journey to America, Kitty stepped onto the bottom stair. 'I turn my back for a few hours, and you fill the house with waifs and strays. You have a big heart, Stanley, I hope they don't let you down,' she said.

Stanley laughed. 'Daphne's fallen in love with them already. I think James and Patrick will fit in nicely,' he said.

Michael arrived just after five o'clock. He was ushered in by Daphne and invited to stay for a meal just as Kitty returned from congratulating Ruth on moving into a room with her friend, and two other children.

'Michael, I didn't hear you arrive,' she said and gave him a kiss on the cheek. 'The boys have lovely manners, Daphne, but if you want food left for our meal you had better set them about a different task than eating.'

Daphne rushed to the kitchen with a laugh. 'They remind me of my own,' she said.

A silent Kitty and Michael watched her open and then close the door.

'Poor thing, she misses her sons so much. Stanley has taken on two lads in need of mothering, and I have a feeling they will all help each other,' Kitty said, giving Michael another kiss.

'Let's go and sit so you can tell me why you are home early.' Michael looked around, listening. 'And it appears … without Jo? You look worried, sweetheart, talk to me,' he said.

Kitty guided him into the small room off the hall she now used as a sewing room and storage space for paperwork relating to the children.

'Jo is going to America to work,' Kitty said. 'And she is going soon. Plus, an old acquaintance of ours is going too.'

Michael put his head to one side. 'So they have jobs out there?' he asked.

'Lizzie is married and moving out there to live with her in-laws. And Jo … well, Jo has a friend and is moving in with her – Virginia is a *very* good friend,' Kitty said and watched while Michael absorbed her news.

He flicked his head in a nod of understanding. 'I see, and how do you feel about this, Kitty? It must be a shock for you.'

'Jo having a close female companion? No, not as much of a shock as I would have expected. I'm also not entirely surprised to hear she is moving to America, but it is a shame it is happening so soon. But Jo and Lizzie being friends and working together?

Now, that *is* a shock. When Lizzie was Belle and we were all in training, she and Jo were sworn enemies – you know that from personal experience,' Kitty said and waited to see if Michael heard where she had slipped Belle's name into the conversation.

He had.

'Belle? As in Annabelle Farnsworth – the dead spy? You have lost me now, Kitty. Who is Lizzie?' he asked.

'Lizzie and Belle are the same person. Her war work was for Great Britain and not for Germany as we thought. It is – or was – top secret, so please keep it that way.' Kitty turned and looked to make sure no one had overheard. She trusted Michael and needed to share the burden of what she had learned. 'That's all I know for now. She and Jo found themselves on the same, um, training course, let's say. They tried to recruit me and get me to join them in America. Obviously, I said no,' Kitty said.

Michael gave a low whistle. He swung his head slowly from side to side, looking at the floor. Eventually, he looked up at her and burst out laughing.

'Only you could make friends with a lesbian and a spy, then get asked to join the American government, Kitty Pattison. Your secret is safe with me because I don't think a soul would believe me if I told them anyway.'

Michael's laugh perked Kitty up and helped her to see the funny side of what she had just described.

'I think we had best leave it here, in this room. Stanley knew a little about Jo's work, but not her private life, and as for Belle – I mean Lizzie – that's a door best kept shut. I am just sad I felt the need to leave instead of staying and spending time with Jo. But I realised we have both changed and have to take the next path offered to us in life, and there was no use putting it off any longer,' she said.

Their conversation ended when Stanley joined them, and Daphne announced her two new waiters were ready to serve a meal.

When she said goodbye to Michael, Kitty knew the best thing she had done that day was to walk away from the strange situation in Durham. Being back at Brancepeth gave her comfort and it amused her to think she now thought of remote villages far north of her birthplace as home.

Chapter Forty-Three

B efore she settled down for the night, Kitty wrote to her uncle and Wenna. As she did so it made her wonder how many letters she had written and received from the time she left Parkeston until VE Day.

The letters she had received were all carefully stored away, tied with twine and ribbon in a small suitcase. She rarely read them over, but when she did the memories they brought made her realise how far she had travelled, how many people had touched her life and how many she had helped.

As the horrifying news of the Nazi war camps became public, the more she thought of Sarah looking for her family, and tried to keep a steady flow of encouraging letters, which she sent via the Red Cross. Unsure they would ever meet again, Kitty hoped they would at least remain pen pals during peacetime.

She had created a letter-writing session to teach the children to write to one another when they no longer lived at Fell Hall and was always touched when she received the odd one or two. The telephone was a handy gadget, but letters were tangible, something to cling to when the recipient needed comfort.

She drafted out a special letter for her uncle and his bride for their wedding day, and one in preparation for Ruth's leaving Fell Hall. She wanted the little girl to have memories to look back upon and to know she had brought joy to so many when she stayed with them.

Dear Uncle Jack,

Thank you for your letter with regards to the sleeping arrangements when I arrive home for your wedding. Michael has accepted your kind invitation and has asked you book him a room at the hotel as suggested. We are finding our way together again, and for him to be part of your happy day makes me happy. Not long to go now!

Jo sends her regards, and she should have arrived in America by now. She has an important job out there, so we probably won't see each other again, but will remain pen pals. Stanley gave me Jenny's old Box Brownie camera as he had one of his own, so I will be able to take photographs of your wedding and send her a few.

Michael has settled well as the village doctor, and I am still enjoying life at Fell Hall. We have a regular flow of orphans and Stanley has employed more staff to cope. This gives me free time to sew for the children and enjoy time reading. I have agreed to run a small clinic for Michael's practice once a fortnight, where I treat minor things such as splinters and blisters. This means he is free to run a clinic in a nearby village where he is also the visiting doctor due to the sad death of their practitioner. The district nurse gave me her blessing as it gives her an afternoon to put her feet up. I lead a varied life and when I am not doing all of that I am writing letters to people I hold dear.

Little Ruth is still with us, but there is talk of her going into the orphanage with one of the children she has attached herself to, and although it will be sad to see her go, I can't say it might be for the best. At one point I was tempted to suggest I adopt her because I thought she would never find her place in the world but, now she is ready, those thoughts are long gone.

Take care of yourselves. My love to Doreen.

Your loving niece, Kitty x

Dear Wenna,

I hope this finds you all well. Thank you for watching over Meryn and I am pleased to hear she is in better spirits. I am still shocked by Lewis's behaviour, and it just shows we do not always know the people we befriend. I thank goodness for wonderful ones such as yourself and remember the day you dragged me into your Anderson shelter from the street. I laugh about it now, but I was so scared and will be eternally grateful to fate for introducing us in such a way.

What a scare for Meryn – for you all, when Kedrick was so poorly, but I am pleased to hear he is over the measles now. I am pleased to hear your own children are in good health and that you are coping without your mother. I remember her with fondness and, as you know, you have my condolences for your loss.

It does not surprise me you and Pots are walking out together! You make one another happy, and that is a precious thing nowadays, to be happy. I did giggle when you wrote to me with his response to

you when you asked him to give up the pipe. Pots without his pipe is
– well, like Winston Churchill without his cigar!

I bet Cornwall looks beautiful and I cannot wait to visit you all
again. First I must attend to my uncle and ensure he is presentable
on his wedding day. Michael is coming with me, and we will enjoy a
few days by the sea in the east of the country.

Jo has taken herself off to America to live, she has gone with two
friends so will not be alone.

I will write again soon, but I really must get some sleep.
Much affection,
Kitty x

By the time the bedrooms were cleaned after a long night of
intermittent sleep due to a stomach bug rampaging through a
group of children, Kitty was exhausted. She had not disturbed
the staff knowing they would be busy the next day and wanted
them fresh to take on her duties. She told Stanley she would be
taking a few hours for herself in the afternoon, but he insisted
she had a rest day. As he had an appointment for a hospital
check-up, he offered her a lift to pay a surprise visit to Michael,
saying that if he wasn't home she could escort him to his
appointment and then visit a few shops in the town.

'I still cannot get over your ability to drive your car again,
Stanley. Yours has been an incredible journey and Jack's
adaptation of the pedals is clever,' she said as they wove their
way around the country lanes.

'I am one of the fortunate ones and my family money helps
me lead a comfortable life. Which is why I have decided to
fund one of the unused wings in Fell Hall for two disabled

children. My new project I spoke about. What do you think, Kitty? I know you won't be working here forever when you and Michael marry, but I bet a pound you will want some input in how it is designed,' Stanley said as he pulled up outside of Michael's house.

'Stanley, I live and work at Fell Hall. You cannot go around saying I am going to marry Michael when it is not true,' Kitty said indignantly.

'*Yet*. You are not marrying him, *yet*. The man's a fool if he lets you fester away with the orphans at mine. You both need to get your act together before you turn grey like me,' Stanley said, teasing her.

'Fester? Your choice of words is beyond me, and I love my work,' Kitty replied.

Stanley went to open his door.

'Stay where you are, I am capable of getting out of a car myself. Besides, you are too old to be jumping around,' Kitty teased back and laughed. 'I'll give Michael your regards and tell him about the idea of the new wing. He might have a few ideas and contacts that could help with the planning application. Drive carefully, and I will see you when I see you.'

Kitty waved him away and turned towards the house. Michael stood in the doorway and ushered her into his office.

'I cannot believe we are alone at last,' he said as they pulled back from one of several kisses.

Kitty smiled at him, the sunlight highlighting the dark chestnut of his hair and glowing about his shoulders.

'Where is Mrs Temple?' she asked, looking around just in case the woman lurked in a corner somewhere.

'Gone. She is a sanctimonious gossip. I could not trust her with patient confidentiality, nor was I prepared to be told by the minister that my housekeeper thought you unworthy of my company and an unwed mother. When he came to me to share what he thought was fact, I soon put him and that mad woman in her place. I think it is safe to say the sermon on Sunday will be about asking for forgiveness and the gossip will be about the loudest mouth in the village,' Michael said, finishing off with a slap of his hand on his desk.

Kitty burst out laughing. 'Gracious, I can't leave you alone with another woman for five minutes. Two housekeepers gone in a month,' she joked.

'Let's go into the back room, it is comfortable in there,' Michael said.

Once seated on the sofa, they took a moment to enjoy the view out into the garden.

'Kitty, what do you think about being the housekeeper here?' Michael suddenly blurted out and Kitty stared at him in surprise.

'I beg your pardon?' she asked.

Michael got up from the sofa and looked down at her.

'What I mean is, how do you feel about looking after this house for me?'

Kitty stood up and walked to the French doors then faced him.

'Do you need me to look after the garden too?' she asked sarcastically. 'And the answer is no. No because I have a job that takes up all of my time. With Ruth crying out in the night, I barely have time to myself and when I do, I get offered a job to clean a large house.'

Michael slapped his knee and grinned at her.

'*With me.* I want you to look after this house *with me*. Sorry for my poor choice of words, sweetheart. What I meant to say was, will you marry me and become the wife of the idiotic local doctor?' he said, and Kitty watched as he lowered himself to one knee. 'It won't be easy as I have to build the surgery into one that makes a profit – the old doctor gave his services away for free, from what I have gathered, and the war has depleted funds – but please, please say you will be my wife and come live here, building a home and life in England's Quebec.'

Kitty had had an inkling this was what he was trying to ask but had chosen to tease, and seeing him kneeling on the floor with panic on his face, she decided it was time to put him out of his misery.

'Michael, please stand up,' she said and held out her hand to assist him to his feet. 'To become your fiancé again will be wonderful, as to becoming your wife, it is something I dearly wish for. So, yes. Yes, Doctor Michael McCarthy, I would love to marry you,' Kitty said and allowed Michael to hold her tighter than he had ever done in the past.

'You have made me the happiest man alive, Kitty Pattison, and I will never let you down again. I love and adore you,' Michael said.

'As I do you,' Kitty said, embracing him. Michael was the hero of her romantic journey during the war and now she looked forward to their future together in peacetime.

Acknowledgments

Dear Reader,

My mother passed away during the writing of this book. I had the privilege of nursing her at home for a month until the end. Mum was born on the 23rd November which makes the UK paperback launch day even more special.

Happy Birthday Mum

x

Although she was too weak to read, Mum did beg me to read my draft of book three to her and insisted I complete the series and to never give up writing. A promise I will keep going until the words no longer flow.

Within the series, readers learn about Kitty Pattison and of her home in Hamilton Street, Parkeston, Essex. I write about walking Dovercourt Bay promenade, and mention other places where my mother and I grew up. The street and house is where my family lived for many years, and I grew up there until I was eight years old. There was a real community spirit where everyone looked out for the children and each other. I remember it well and tried to bring a few of the memories into each book featuring my Red Cross nurse, Kitty.

Kitty was loosely based on my mother who always wanted to be a nurse, but her parents could not afford to send her for training. Had she and I been adults during WWII we both said we would have probably joined the Red Cross. Mum did become an auxiliary midwife at the local maternity home, and I qualified as a nurse during the seventies. The second world war brought many different nursing challenges and all those who served during those years have my utmost admiration and gratitude.

In the books I used names from my family who had also lived in Parkeston. Trixie mum's sister and Jo(e) (the preferred name of her brother), Robin, and their parents Tom and Maude, a couple who supported people during WWII by growing food for residents of Parkeston, and offering shelter to those displaced from their homes. They were also caretakers of the Methodist church, a role I gave my fictional characters Kitty's aunt and uncle.

My thanks goes to Eden Camp in Malton, Yorkshire for allowing me to mention the original POW camp in my story. The museum is dedicated to WWII and is well worth a visit. It inspired my first novel *The Secret Orphan* and I draw on memories of the visit for each book I write. They have had a revamp and I intend to return and enjoy their hard work at ensuring life during the war is not forgotten.

As always I am thankful for the support of my editor and publisher Charlotte Ledger and the One More Chapter team at HarperCollins UK, for getting this book out into the world. Also, my thanks to my writing pals Deborah Carr and Christie Barlow for being there whenever I need them to keep me focused.

Thanks to you the reader for your continued support of my work.

I will sign off now as I must return to the desk and plan book 4 of the Red Cross Orphans Series!

Glynis

x

ONE MORE CHAPTER

The author and One More Chapter would like to thank everyone who contributed to the publication of this story...

Analytics
Emma Harvey
Maria Osa

Audio
Fionnuala Barrett
Ciara Briggs

Contracts
Georgina Hoffman
Florence Shepherd

Design
Lucy Bennett
Fiona Greenway
Holly Macdonald
Liane Payne
Dean Russell

Digital Sales
Laura Daley
Michael Davies
Georgina Ugen

Editorial
Arsalan Isa
Sarah Khan
Charlotte Ledger
Jennie Rothwell
Caroline Scott-Bowden
Kimberley Young

International Sales
Bethan Moore

Marketing & Publicity
Chloe Cummings
Emma Petfield

Operations
Melissa Okusanya
Hannah Stamp

Production
Emily Chan
Denis Manson
Francesca Tuzzeo

Rights
Lana Beckwith
Rachel McCarron
Agnes Rigou
Hany Sheikh
Mohamed
Zoe Shine
Aisling Smyth

The HarperCollins Distribution Team

The HarperCollins Finance & Royalties Team

The HarperCollins Legal Team

The HarperCollins Technology Team

Trade Marketing
Ben Hurd

UK Sales
Yazmeen Akhtar
Laura Carpenter
Isabel Coburn
Jay Cochrane
Tom Dunstan
Gemma Rayner
Erin White
Harriet Williams
Leah Woods

And every other essential link in the chain from delivery drivers to booksellers to librarians and beyond!

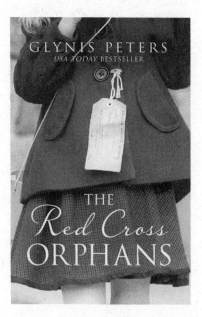

A journey into war, but not one she'll take alone...

Orphan Kitty Pattison is young, naïve and ready to do her bit for the war effort when she volunteers with the Red Cross and pledges to help those most in need. It's one of the most nerve-wracking moments of her life, but then she meets fellow volunteers Joan Norfolk and Trixie Dunn, and a bond of friendship is forged in the fire of life on the wards during the Blitz.

Days are spent nursing injured soldiers back to life and nights are spent anticipating bombs falling from the sky and then trawling through the wreckage to save who she can, but the light and laughter she finds with Jo and Trix see Kitty through the darkest hours.

Available in eBook, audio, and paperback now

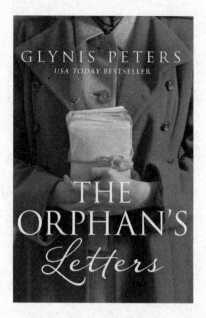

Absence makes the heart grow fonder, but does nothing to heal the pain of spending every minute waiting to hear the worst...

As the Second World War rages on, nurse Kitty Pattison's life takes a nomadic turn as her work with the Red Cross sees her traversing the country, moving from post to post.

With her best friends Jo and Trixie also scattered across the UK, and her soldier sweetheart Michael off on the continent undertaking medical missions he can't discuss, the war takes its toll and long days are followed by sleepless nights interrupted only by nightmares of what she's seen on the wards.

Available in eBook, audio, and paperback now